VAMPIRE AWOKEN

MORETTI
BLOOD BROTHERS

BOOK SEVEN

By Juliette N. Banks

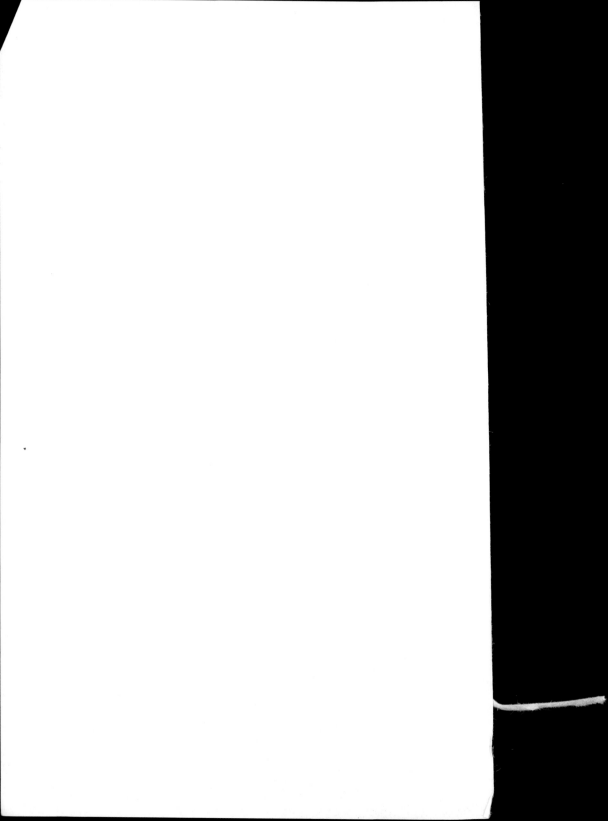

COPYRIGHT

Author: Juliette N. Banks
Editor: Jen Katemi
Cover design by: Elizabeth Cartwright, EC Editorial

ABOUT THE AUTHOR

Juliette is an indie romance author who has taken the genre by storm with her popular vampire series The Moretti Blood Brothers. Juliette has a vast background in consumer marketing and is previously published with Random House. She lives in Auckland, New Zealand, with Tilly, her Mainecoon kitty, and all her book boyfriends.

Official Juliette N. Banks website:
www.juliettebanks.com

INSTAGRAM:
https://www.instagram.com/juliettebanksauthor

FACEBOOK:
https://www.facebook.com/juliettenbanks

https://www.facebook.com/groups/authorjuliettebanksreaders

DEDICATION

To my mum, Lynette, who passed away in April 1982 - forty years ago to the day of writing this dedication.

Ari's depth of loneliness in this story speaks to the loss only a little girl with no mother could understand. So this book felt like the right one to dedicate to you and say thank you for all your support from 'over there'.

I look forward to seeing you again when it's my time.

Juliette xx

ALSO BY JULIETTE N. BANKS

The Moretti Blood Brothers
The Vampire's Origin (Exclusive BookClub)
The Vampire King (FREE)
The Vampire Prince
The Vampire Protector
The Vampire Spy
The Vampire's Christmas
The Vampire Assassin
The Vampire Awoken
The Vampire Lover

Realm of the Immortals
The Archangels Battle
The Archangel's Heart
The Archangel's Star

The Dufort Dynasty
Sinful Duty
Forbidden Touch
Total Possession

FREE GIFT:
Download <u>The Vampires Origin</u> to read the short story about the beginning of Ari and Gio Moretti's life which you may want to read before starting **The Vampire Awoken.**
It's recommended but not essential.

CHAPTER ONE

Ari Moretti lifted his tumbler of whisky to his lips and took a drink of the liquid gold. Or otherwise known as Macallan.

"Relax, Oliver, I don't blame you. Ben put you in a tricky situation," he said, referring to his former head assassin who had recently left Seattle to return to Italy with his new mate, Anna.

Oliver shook his head. "When he called for the code of silence, I should never have agreed. He was always such a boy scout, you know."

Ari shrugged. "It's what mating males do: they're insane."

Oliver laughed and tilted his empty glass back and forth. "Another one?"

Ari looked around the dark, moody wine bar and nodded. It wasn't packed, but it was a steady evening for the establishment. On the weekends, it pumped. Not that he frequented it as often as the other vampires that worked for him at The Institute.

While Oliver turned and ordered them another round, Ari found the familiar faces of the regulars and a few new ones. He was enjoying a night out; he didn't do it enough.

After playing host to Ben and Anna in Italy, and then a few times while they were in the United States, Ari had found himself breaking out of his usual routine.

When you were as old as he was—fifteen hundred and twenty-two years—you had a high level of self-awareness. Part of that meant being really honest with yourself.

He had become a bit of a hermit in recent years. Happy with the life he'd created, Ari had gotten into a routine of training his assassins, sending them out on jobs, and being the guy behind the laptop. With a big group of researchers and tech, but still.

Sure, he occasionally went out and fucked, but he could take it or leave it.

What he wanted more than anything was to meet his mate. The bachelor lifestyle had long ago lost its glamour. He'd also lost all hope of finding him or her. He was the oldest vampire alive. He knew that as fact because he and his brother, Giorgio Moretti, had been the first two vampires.

They were the originals.

He was the sole remaining original vampire.

The first Moretti.

Well, technically, the second.

Giorgio had been born minutes before him, and Ari often wondered if that was why Gio had been able to procreate and meet his mate, while Ari never had.

If he could get an answer to that big fucking question, he would. He'd been asking a long damn time, and never found one.

So, yeah, he was keen to stay for a bit longer and throw a few more back. Plus, he had a reason for getting the young vampire out for a drink.

2

"There we go, sir," the bartender interrupted his thoughts, sliding a new glass in front of him.

"Put them on my tab, please," he instructed, and the guy nodded and left them.

"Anna is awesome," Oliver said, turning to lean his elbow on the bar and watch the room. An assassin never turned his back completely. "It's seriously fucked up what happened to her, but at least we know she's safe now with Ben."

Ari let out a small laugh. "Ah, yes. That poor girl is likely to be bubble-wrapped the rest of her life."

Ben had proven to be quite the protective mate, and in Anna's case, it was warranted. She had been one of the vampires kidnapped by humans and experimented on.

"So, with Ben gone, I wanted to speak to you about stepping into his role," Ari said, turning to face the vampire.

Oliver's glass lowered to the bar, and he cleared his throat. "Are you joking?"

Ari smiled.

"No."

"I mean, yes. It would be an honor, sir," he said, nodding.

"Good. You start on Monday. In the meantime, don't fucking mate anyone." Ari laughed.

"God, no. Seeing that shit up close scared the daylights out of me," Oliver joked, feigning a shiver, and they grinned at each other.

Ari knew Oliver was only half joking. While mated males were crazy in love with their mates and their protective predator nature heightened, everyone aspired to be in their shoes one day. The unconditional love they experienced was unlike anything, except perhaps parenthood. But even then, Ari had to wonder.

3

His eyes flicked to a table in the corner where a woman sat with a small notebook and pen scribbling and tapping her pen on her teeth. Her hair was pulled on top of her head in what he'd heard females call a *messy bun,* which was highly accurate, and it exposed her neck beautifully.

Ari watched as the expression on her face changed from second to second as she appeared to be trying to work out a problem. She then dropped her pen in a frustrated fashion and lifted her glass of wine to her lips, taking a very long sip.

Rich mahogany eyes suddenly met his, and he felt his body heat.

Interesting.

He didn't look away and nor did she.

"Hey, guys," Jason, one of his other assassins, greeted as he sidled up beside Oliver. Three other agents joined them.

"'Sup, guys?" Oliver said. "Oh, by the way, I'll be kicking your asses on Monday. Guess who's the new head assa—"

His voice trailed off, realizing where they were.

"Ass?" Jason asked, slapping Oli on the shoulder. "Head ass is totally accurate. But congrats, dude. Well deserved."

A round of congratulations filled the air, and drinks were ordered.

Ari stood. "I'll be back."

Oli glanced at the female Ari had been staring at and grinned. "She's gorgeous."

Ari nodded. "Yes, she is."

He held back his smile as he walked across the room. Her nervousness was obvious… and warranted. Having a powerful original vampire stalk toward you was not for the fainthearted.

And he was in hunter mode.

4

She would be his tonight.

And by the look on Oliver's face, he might be sharing her. Yeah, he was totally up for that, and had a feeling the two of them would persuade her.

"Good evening," Ari said, smirking as a blush covered her olive cheeks and she swallowed.

Oh yes, she would do for an evening.

CHAPTER TWO

Two hours earlier

"Sage!" Teresa called.

Sage pulled off her reading glasses and groaned. Dropping them on the desk beside her laptop, she rubbed her eyes. She'd selected her roommate very carefully. Tony was an awkward geeky IT guy who wouldn't hit on her—*check*—would pay his rent on time—*check*—and was highly unlikely to find a girlfriend.

Fail.

Complete major fail.

Tony and Teresa had been dating for a few months and were the most nauseating couple on planet earth. Well, as far as she was concerned. When they weren't snuggled up on the couch having little kissy make-out sessions, they were giggling at something private or cooking up a mess in *her* kitchen. Still, she'd put up with all of those things if she didn't have to listen to their awkward vanilla sex through her bedroom wall.

Not that she was in any position to judge. Her sex life consisted of one rabbit vibrator and that suited her just fine.

Mostly.

The erotic novels she read on her Kindle had created all kinds of thigh-clenching fantasies in her mind, and recently she'd been wondering what it would truly be like to experience them. Not that she ever would. Fantasies were exactly that—something you imagined as you were getting off, and once that delicious orgasm struck you popped the rabbit away and carried on with your carefully planned out life.

Right?

Because Sage had big life plans and they didn't include *ménage à trois* or being tied up by silk ropes and tortured deliciously by a man layered in muscles. Or finding out what it felt like in the... you know... the back end.

Heck, she didn't know if she'd even enjoy any of those things.

No, her plans were a lot more sensible, and it was better if she got her head out of the smutty books and got on with what she had named her *Life List*. Sage had created it when she was thirteen, and was on track when her sister, Piper, had messed things up.

"Sage."

Oh crap, she hadn't answered Teresa.

"Come in," she called out.

"Do we have any icing sugar? It's just we were going to make cupcakes and you have to have icing, otherwise they're muffins, right?" Teresa said, with a grin.

Sage just stared at her.

Firstly, *we* didn't have anything. This was her house. Her kitchen and her ingredients they were cooking with. Secondly, she didn't have time for this. She had to finish her application for the promotion going at work.

Sage was a laboratory assistant for a pharmaceutical company and when the opportunity had come up, she'd leapt at it. Number three on her *Life List* was becoming a

7

principal scientist. That dream was years away, but this new position was the next step in getting there. She'd already had two interviews and had been asked to complete a submission by Monday. Then she'd hear back by the end of the week.

"Honestly, I'm not sure. Why don't you head to the store and grab some?" Sage walked past Teresa and caught sight of the domestic bomb which had exploded in her living room.

Her nicely folded throws were haphazardly spread across the sofa where the loved-up couple had been—ugh, whatever they'd been doing— and the kitchen was covered in, she assumed, the cupcake ingredients.

Sage was tempted to say something to Tony on the spot, but it was cruel to call him out in front of his girlfriend. Plus, she needed his rent money.

Item two on Sage's *Life List* had been buying a home, or more accurately, getting a mortgage. She was so proud of herself for saving her deposit and finding a home she loved, but she had stretched herself a lot and now money was tight.

Tony's rent money eased that, but if she got the promotion, she'd be able to reassess things. Who was she kidding? She'd be giving Tony (and Teresa) notice.

Sage was serious about this promotion and had been told she had a very good shot at it. While she was confident she'd done well in her interviews, she didn't want to get complacent. She had to focus on her report and finish it to hand in on Monday.

Sure, she had the weekend, but Sage wasn't one to sit on things. Plus, it wasn't like the two lovers would disappear. They were around constantly.

Ugh.

"I'll go to the store," Teresa said, bouncing over to kiss Tony on the lips, who looked at her as if he'd won the lottery.

Sage was pretty confident she was his first proper girlfriend and felt a sliver of guilt.

"You know what? Try the top shelf on the right." Sage waved her hand toward the kitchen. "Just clean up when you're done, okay?"

"Sure, no problem," Tony replied and scooped Teresa up in a hug.

Sage rolled her eyes. She'd given up trying to decipher their excitement and reason for embracing about *everything*.

"I'm going to head out for a few hours," she said. There was a local bar she enjoyed, and it wouldn't get busy for a few hours. If she hurried, she could have a few wines and get her report done before it filled up.

Okay fine, there was also a cute guy from work, Carl, who sometimes went there so she might run into him.

Not that he noticed her.

But he matched the next item on her *Life List*. Marriage. Sage had specific criteria for the type of man she wanted to marry, and Carl ticked them all. He was tall, handsome, healthy—because, babies—and had a good job. He played baseball—not that she'd been listening in on his conversations, okay fine she had—and was family focused.

He worked in the finance department, and they often saw each other in the cafeteria.

Correction: Sage often saw him.

Carl knew who she was. He'd been in a few meetings with her, but he rarely said more than hello, and asked how her day was going in that way people did but didn't care.

Regardless, she was still optimistic the opportunity for sparks between them had yet to happen. He'd winked at her once when a few of them were in the cafeteria and Louise, the receptionist, had spilled her soup. Carl had attempted to make the older woman feel less silly and made a little joke. Sage had helped with the clean-up and lifted her head at the right time, grinning.

His wink had made her blush, and he'd smiled at her.

So, she was hopeful, and wondered if it was that he had a girlfriend right now and couldn't ask her out.

She sighed.

Her life could have been so different. Sage thought she had met 'the one' years ago. Colin. Instead, he'd cheated on her with Piper while they were in college, and the event had changed her life.

Sage had been steadily dating Colin since high school and even lost her virginity to him. She'd always romanticized about marrying her high school sweetheart— which had now been crossed off the *Life List*—and becoming a mom. Her career would come later, they'd decided. She was okay with that, knowing Colin supported her dreams of being a principal scientist.

Instead, the two people closest to her had betrayed her.

Sage had been devasted.

Piper was a year younger than Sage and the two couldn't be more different. However, they had been close. Like chalk and cheese and yet they fit. Her sister was bold and confident with a curvy body and large breasts. Sage was the same five foot six inches in height but barely had an ass and her chest was a token effort from God.

The most noticeable difference between them was their hair; Piper had long dark curls and Sage had an unmanageable mop of auburn curls.

Growing up, their overbearing mother had dressed them similarly, even though Piper climbed trees and played in the mud, while Sage had elaborate weddings for Ken and Barbie.

The good news, if one could call it that, was she hadn't found Piper and Colin in bed together. Instead, she'd overheard Piper speaking to him on the phone and there had been no second-guessing what had happened.

Sage used to wonder if she might have ended up marrying Colin if she'd never heard them that day. It would be nice to think Piper would confess, but when she confronted her about it her response had been horrible. She'd said it was just a one-time thing and Colin didn't love her anyway, so Sage should forgive her.

Piper was wrong.

The next week Sage had moved into another room to finish college and had barely spoken to her sister for two years.

Their father had eventually called a family meeting and forced them to make up. Her parents were good Christian people who went to church every Sunday and were appalled at the breakdown of their friendship over a boy. Never once had she heard them tell Piper what she had done was wrong, only that the two of them needed to make up.

Sage suspected it was a case of not wanting to deal with the messy stuff, but it still irked her to this day.

While marrying her childhood sweetheart was off the *Life List*, Sage was determined she would meet the perfect man and create her own family.

Five years later, Sage hadn't dated anyone seriously. She was hoping things with Carl might progress, but in the meantime, Mr. Rabbit and her erotic novels were a good distraction from her single status, financial stress, and impatience as she waited to hear about the promotion.

Sage opened her wardrobe, selecting a navy dress which flared at the hips and finished just above her knee. She pulled on long brown boots and twisted her auburn hair into a bun.

With little thought, she brushed on a cream foundation, coated her lashes in thick mascara, and finished it off with a peach blusher. She froze when she glanced at her lipstick options.

Last night she'd read about a heroine who had her bright red lips wrapped around…

Stop.

She had to stop fantasizing. Maybe she needed to read some sweet romances.

Fuck it.

She ran the red over her lips and rubbed them together. "If I can't have the fantasy in real life, I can pretend for one night."

Puckering once more in the mirror, she ran her hands over her hips and tidied her skirt, then let her fingers run up over her average-sized breasts.

Her nipples hardened.

"God, I need to get laid." She groaned. "And not by Mr. Rabbit."

Going by the heat between her legs, Sage realized it had been months. She wished she was more confident, like her sister, who seemed to have a new boyfriend every month. Instead, Sage focused on work and kept one eye on Carl.

Perhaps she was wasting her time?

One glance out the window told her it was a clear night. Small miracles given she lived in Seattle, Washington.

"I'll see you both tomorrow." She pulled on her coat and grabbed her bag and laptop. One glance at the flour flying through the air as the two lovers waved farewell and she grit her teeth and left.

Ten minutes later, she was sipping on a Sauvignon Blanc and taking in the patrons at Tuesday's Bar. As she'd expected, it wasn't busy, but it would soon be, so she had to focus. She pulled out her laptop and began tapping.

A while later, she glanced up and took a large sip of her now warm wine. Her eyes roamed the bar until they landed on two men at the bar. Both were tall and muscular, with a dangerous aura about them. Perhaps it was the black clothing or their size, but their good looks did nothing to change that.

The taller of the two drank a golden liquid—whisky, she assumed—and had a square jaw with that sexy scruff. His leather jacket fit perfectly over what she imagined to be a sculptured set of shoulders. His dark jeans hugged a really great looking ass, and his boots looked expensive even though they were plain.

There was something else keeping her attention on him. The way he held himself gave away a sense of strong personal power. His chin never dipped, and his back was strong and straight.

Even from her seat she could see the large watch poking out from his sleeve and Sage knew from working with wealthy pharmaceutical executives this man had money.

The second man was interesting, and hot. While they both looked around the same age—early to mid-thirties—he seemed younger. Or was it that the other man seemed older?

The younger one laughed, and Sage smiled. His dark blonde hair and what looked like blue eyes made him hard to miss. Her eyes roamed past his black shirt to a pair of solid thighs.

God, yes, he works out a lot.

Later, when it was just her and the rabbit, she was going to choose one of these men as her fantasy. Lifting her drink to her lips, she watched them both and couldn't decide.

Must. Get. Laid.

She let out a sigh.

When she glanced back the dark-haired man was staring at her with a rich intensity. Her heart stuttered as his eyes locked onto hers. She swallowed and then froze. The room around her disappeared as he held her in place with just his gaze. Sage's body filled with a heat from the inside out.

Finally he blinked, and she looked away.

Sage studied her notes, not reading a thing.

Holy shit.

In those few seconds it was as if she knew what he was thinking. His eyes had promised things and her body was jumping up and down saying yes.

My God.

She had no idea a single glance could create such a chemical reaction in a body, but that man had near hypnotized her.

She couldn't look at him again.

She looked at him.

Dammit.

Dark eyes captured hers and this time there was a sparkle to them, and Sage desperately wanted to know what it meant. Her cheeks heated as her imagination soured.

Men like this never noticed her.

They looked at Piper, but not her.

And that was fine because this man did not match her *Life List.* He'd be a sexy distraction for a night at best. If he was even interested.

Sage knew she shouldn't have worn the red lipstick. It was giving off the wrong message. She wasn't that woman. God, she probably looked like she was sitting in the bar alone looking to pick up.

What was she thinking?

I should leave.

More ridiculously good-looking men showed up and joined the man's group. They were getting a lot of attention from the women around them, and the men, and Sage suspected his friends would distract him as she slipped out.

She finished one more paragraph and then shut her laptop. When she glanced up, he was walking toward her.

Ohgodohgodohgod.

She swallowed.

He stopped at her table. Sage waited for him to say something, but he didn't. Slowly, the edges of his lips curved.

"Invite me to join you." He... purred.

Swallowing, Sage tried to pry her eyes away and tell him she was leaving, but instead, she nodded. "Yes."

Yes?

God, she was a moron.

He grinned and pulled out a chair, then sat down with his legs spread in the most dominant and masculine manner she'd ever witnessed.

She tried to think of something to say, but she was too overwhelmed with the powerful and incredibly beautiful man sitting in front of her.

He placed his glass on the table and the hunger in his eyes told her everything he wanted from her. Sage was pretty sure she wouldn't be able to stop him.

Nor would she want to.

"My name is Ari."

CHAPTER THREE

Ari stared at the gorgeous young woman.

She was fertile as hell—the predator in him could sense it, which was ironic given he likely wasn't—and there was a fire in her eyes which was doing a pretty good job of masking her fear.

Unless you were an ancient predator.

Which he was.

An ancient predator.

One of the oldest on the planet—if not the eldest.

Ari had left the royal family after losing his identity as a Moretti. No, fuck it, he had been one of the original Moretti's. Eventually he'd created The Institute where he trained the best warriors on the planet.

Vampire warriors.

As vampires, they were already more powerful than humans, but the difference was, his males had him.

Ari had been born in 500AD and trained in the Roman army before becoming a vampire. He had fifteen hundred years of research in perfecting the art of war and every weapon known to man or vampire. He'd studied the vampire body and learned how to optimize its strength and performance.

It had been important he find a purpose when it became clear his role in the Moretti family was not what it should be. Looking back, Ari knew he should have disagreed with Geo's request he remain invisible as a Moretti to strengthen his role as king.

Hindsight was a wonderful thing. He'd believed he was supporting his brother and doing the right thing to create their race and strengthen their future.

The only thing he'd done was diminish his own.

Year after year, century after century, he'd lost himself.

For years, after he'd left, he had rebuilt himself and created an incredible world while keeping an eye on his relatives from a distance.

Now Ari was ready to make decisions.

That was why he'd revealed himself to his nephews, King Vincent, and Prince Brayden, in Italy last month.

The question on their mind, of course, now they knew he still existed, was the same their father and grandfather had had all those many years before. Would he, if he mated, create his own line of vampires?

The million-dollar question.

Actually it wasn't.

The question was *if* he would mate, and he'd been asking that one for over fifteen hundred years. Talk about having faith. Sure, he hadn't created any vision boards, lit candles on a full moon, or prayed to God, but now, Ari was done.

He'd lost hope.

Maybe it was a glitch in the matrix? Who the fuck knew?

But he was done. At some point, you had to let go of the insanity and accept there was no one for you.

No one could say he hadn't given it time.

He was tired.

Not physically—his energy never faded. He was tired of being alone, tired of hiding who he was, tired of putting others first.

It didn't matter now because Ari had decided he was ready to hang up his hat.

The timing depended on how long it took them to destroy the humans and their scientific labs—the same ones responsible for the experiments on his race. Xander Tomassi, the man at the top of this sordid food chain, had slipped through their fingers once again, so Ari and his team at The Institute were collaborating with the Moretti royal army to get the job done.

Ari was committed to leaving his family, which included the entire race because it was his Moretti blood that ran through every vampire's veins, in a solid good place before he left.

After that, he would choose a time and place, then step out into the sun. The sun he hadn't felt on his skin for over fifteen hundred long years.

Until then, Ari was going to enjoy the fruits of this world, including the gorgeous woman with all her wild hair if she would allow it. He had rather broad tastes when it came to sexual pleasures. Men, women, groups, hard, edgy, and occasionally he enjoyed something soft and innocent looking.

Like any predator.

And he was a predator—the most powerful on the planet. Not that he'd gone head-to-head with a lion or rhino, and it wasn't on his bucket list either, but for argument's sake, vampires were faster and more powerful than anything else on earth.

And this little sweet thing was about to be his latest snack.

"Sage," she replied, reaching across the table to shake his hand. Ari blinked at the shiver up his arm as they connected. Interesting. "Sage Roberts."

Ari felt the faint tremor through her palm.

"Do I make you nervous?" he asked, releasing her hand.

She wiped it on her dress and his eyes followed her every movement, including the moment she swallowed.

"Oh, um, yes, probably. I'm not good at this sort of thing," she replied.

He tilted his head, enjoying her discomfort. "This sort of thing?"

Her cheeks flushed pink, and his dick hardened.

"Oh God, see, I totally have no clue. Sorry, I read this all wrong."

No, sweetheart, you didn't. I just want you all soft and pliable.

He smiled darkly, his fingers eager to touch her again. Her dress revealed just a peek of blushing pink cleavage and her lips were plump and red. She was a small-framed human with slim arms but miles of wild auburn hair.

She chewed her lip and began to look down.

"You didn't read *anything* wrong, Sage," he said, placing his forearms on the table. "I'm not here to ask you to marry me. Today or any other day." Her lips parted at his brashness, but he continued. "But I would like to take you home."

Her eyes widened and eyebrows shot up. "Are you joking?"

"No." Ari smiled.

"You're very direct," she said. The bar had gotten busier, and she was clearly concerned about someone hearing their conversation if her darting eyes were anything to go by.

Ari couldn't give a fuck who overheard them. Sage was a gorgeous woman and he'd be a fool to walk out of here without her.

He wouldn't walk out of here without her.

"Yes. I've found in life, it's better to just ask for what you want." Ari smirked. "And Sage, I'd quite like you."

I will have you.

In his experience, which was a lot, he knew this was where a woman would either bolt or stay. Now unless she was a sex worker, a woman wouldn't just hand herself to a man, she would make him work for her. Usually, that started with a question. To show they weren't completely rolling over and spreading their legs.

What would Sage do?

When she began to chew her bottom lip, Ari's cock hardened. Fuck, he hoped she had a question or two for him. Those lips of hers would be perfect for so many damn things.

Her eyes roamed his face hungrily and his cock twitched again. He'd been drawn to her beauty but also the hunger in her eyes from across the room. Not just for him, but also for Oliver.

That had intrigued him.

"Why?" she asked, and he grinned at the question falling from her lips.

"Why not? You're a beautiful woman. I felt you watching me, and I think we want the same thing." Ari sipped his whisky. "Would I be right in assuming you want to touch me?"

Blush.

"It's okay to say yes. I want to touch you too. Somewhere private," he said.

Swallow.

Sage shook her head, and he could see she wasn't comfortable with this. Which is exactly why he was doing it. Comfort zones never produced excitement and he knew Sage was looking for some, even if she'd never admit it to herself.

"Does this usually work for you? Picking up women like this?"

Ari leaned back in his chair and smiled. "Yes."

She frowned, and he nearly laughed.

When she began to pack up, he did something he wouldn't normally do in a human environment; he used vamp speed to grab her wrist.

"Stay," he ordered and Sage's gaze flew to his. "Let me make you feel beautiful. Let me pleasure you." Ari's voice was a hungry whisper. "One night, and I promise you will never forget it."

If she resisted, he'd let her go.

There were a dozen other beautiful women in the bar who would be more willing, but for some reason Ari wanted this one.

More swallowing and lip biting.

No, he wasn't going to let Sage go. She needed dominance from him, and God knew he was the most qualified male on the planet to give it to her.

He stood.

"Come," Ari said, towering over her. "I will take you home and you can decide from there what you'd like to do."

Without asking permission, he pulled her to her feet and began to pack her things. Like a deer in the headlights, she did as she was told, accepted her bag and placed it on her shoulder.

"Fine, but just so you know, I don't usually do this." Sage picked up her coat. Placing one hand in the small of her back, he guided her across the room with a small grin. But first, they had one stop.

If Sage wanted to quench the thirst he saw in her eyes, Ari was happy to provide that for her. Which meant he needed a few things. Well, one more thing.

"I need to clear my tab. I'll be one minute." Ari led her over to his team. He knew they were an intimidating group of males, so partially shielded her view with his powerful body.

"Well, hello there." Oliver grinned as they approached.

"Oliver, Sage. Sage, this is Oliver." Ari gave the male a glance he knew would be easily translated. Sure, he could have used telepathy, but it was unnecessary. Oliver knew the drill. He had two minutes to gain her trust, or he was out.

Ari wasn't entirely confident Sage would be open to two men, even though he'd seen her watching them, but he was giving her the option. It was likely she was the type of woman to fantasize in the bedroom, but when offered all those naughty things in real life, she wouldn't have the courage to follow through.

Which was fine. Humans lived such brief lives and if they wanted to spend it having average sex, then it had nothing to do with him.

At some point—a really long time ago—sex had gotten boring for him. Finding those to play and experiment with had been challenging. Over the centuries—and to begin with in Europe—humans and vampires had become more open-minded, even if it was behind closed doors offering him more options. Things had yo-yoed from era to era, but now he found enough bodies to keep him fulfilled when he wanted it.

"Nice to meet you." Sage blushed, and Oliver's eyes sparkled with interest.

"Now, how did Ari find such a pretty wee thing in a bar like this?" Oliver drawled.

Ari shook his head as Oliver emphasized his southern accent. Unlike many of his males, Oli had been born and raised in the United States. At only two hundred years old, he was one of the younger vampires at The Institute. He'd been in Seattle for a long time but every now and then, out came the slow prolongation of his syllables sending the ladies weak in the knees.

Ari could nearly hear Sage's blush.

"You two are dangerous with all your charm and pick up lines," Sage said, crossing her arms.

"You have no idea, darlin'," Oliver replied, winking.

Ari suppressed a grin as he turned to Sage. "Do you live nearby?"

Sage nodded. "Just down the road. I walked down."

"Were you working tonight?" Ari asked, referring to her laptop. "Isn't it distracting with all the noise?"

"No. Well, yes." She laughed, then screwed up her face. "My roommate now has a girlfriend, and it's like living inside a Harlequin novel."

Ari stared at her blankly, then turned to Oliver. "Do we know what Harlequin is?"

"They're sexy novels," Sage replied quickly, embarrassed.

Ari studied her more closely. She was clearly a well-educated woman by the way she was dressed and spoke but was lacking in confidence. Not much, but he suspected someone had hurt her and she'd never really recovered. She was young and smart—Ari was confident she would eventually pick herself up and move on. Still, he wondered what her story was—everyone had one.

He also wondered why on earth he was thinking about her background. Usually he focused on the outside package, not the inside.

It wasn't like she was his mate.

None of them ever were.

"If you can't beat 'em, join 'em, I always say." Oliver winked.

"God no. He's not my type at all," Sage replied and then froze. Ari saw the moment she realized what she'd confessed to, inadvertently. Sage had considered a threesome, or at least it was something she desired.

Oliver stood away from the bar and plunged his hands into his pockets, glancing at him and grinning.

"But does it interest you?" Oliver asked. "If the opportunity arose?"

After fish-mouthing for thirty seconds, Sage shook her head. "No. I mean, who hasn't thought about it, right?"

"Right." They both answered as soberly as they could, and Ari nearly burst out laughing.

Oliver drank a long draw of his beer. "Are you leaving?"

She nodded, looking uncomfortable. "Ari was going to walk me home, but I think I should just go."

Sage hiked her bag on her shoulder.

"I'll walk you," Ari said, giving her a firm glance. She nodded.

"Do you mind if I walk with you both? I'm ready to head out," Oliver said, then added, "We could share an Uber home from Sage's."

"Sure." Ari knew very well they would teleport back to the mansion.

Sage watched them warily, then a buzzing in her bag distracted her. She stared at the screen and laughed.

"Yes!" Sage squealed. "I have the house to myself tonight. They've gone to stay at the girlfriends."

Oliver tossed back his beer and banged it on the bar. "That *is* good news. Let's get you home."

Ari smirked.

CHAPTER FOUR

Sage walked along the sidewalk between Ari and Oliver, feeling about as safe as a woman could feel. No one was getting near her with these two gorgeous creatures protecting her. And they *were* protecting her. A woman knew these things.

Yet her body trembled, but it wasn't from fear. Not that kind of fear.

The two of them were walking gods. Layers of muscle and ounces of confidence. Her panties were shot to hell.

Oliver coughed, and she glanced at him.

"Oli." Ari growled.

"Sorry, I just wanted a glance on the inside," he replied, and Sage turned her head from man to man, trying to decipher their odd conversation.

As they walked and talked, Sage asked the usual getting-to-know-someone questions. Ari, who had an unusual accent she couldn't place, owned a type of global private men's-only gym and Oliver worked for him, traveling around the world training people.

She told them she was a scientist. It was hard to get excited about your job when most people couldn't understand what you did, and describing it sounded boring as hell. If she got her promotion, she'd be able to talk even less about it. It was a top-secret division no one really knew anything about, which is probably why it appealed to her. And everyone.

The competition was really tough for this promotion, but her fingers were tightly crossed.

"Do you wear a lab coat?" Oli asked, grinning at her.

"Yes."

"With just sexy lingerie underneath it?" He turned around, walking backwards as he teased her.

Trying to ignore how good looking the big blonde man was, Sage rolled her eyes and laughed. Ari put his hand on the small of her back and the touch sent sparkles of desire through her body. She let out a trembling breath and glanced up at him.

"You didn't answer him." Ari leaned down and burned her skin with his heated gaze.

Sage turned to Oliver and saw his eyes were hooded in that sexual way, and when she glanced at his crotch, she knew she wasn't just imagining it. Her eyes darted back to his and while his playful expression had returned, the heat was still there.

She swallowed audibly.

What the fuck am I doing right now?

Unless she was completely out of her mind, she was pretty sure both of these incredibly good-looking men wanted to have sex with her. Or she was reading too many novels.

Surely, they were playing with her.

With her roommate gone for the night, it was as if the universe was lining everything up.

Nope. She had to be wrong.

"Yes, panties, a bra… and clothing."

"Such a tease." Oliver shook his head. "My fantasy of lifting you onto one of those steel counters and sliding my fingers underneath some pretty lace just died a sad little death."

Heat pooled in her panties and her heart began to pound as his words took shape in her mind. She was utterly flustered by the way he looked at her while Ari held his hand on the small of her back.

Oh God.

It was all so utterly erotic, like one of her novels, Sage could barely breathe.

Sexual tension spun like a web around the three of them as they got closer to her house. She was pretty sure they weren't teasing her now.

"I think you're overwhelming her, Oli," Ari said, his hand running up her back, setting off little sparks. "Am I right?"

Sage glanced up and found a darker, less playful fire in his eyes. He was in charge, and there was no question about it. Her pussy clenched. She didn't want these men to think she was innocent. The fact that she basically was—though not a virgin – was beside the point.

"I mean, what Oliver said was graphic, but no worse than the books I read."

"Harlequin?" Oli winked.

"No. Much steamier than that." She knew she was playing with fire, but it felt fun to let loose. Who else could she talk to like this? Sage doubted anything in those novels would surprise these two sexy men.

And yet, she didn't want to give them the wrong impression. She wasn't sure she could follow through on her bravado.

"Tell me more." Oliver said. "Like erotica?"

"Yes."

Stop talking.

"Nice. With men and women, or two men? Or more than two people?"

Sage laughed. "You are obsessed with having a threesome, aren't you?"

Someone tape my mouth.

Oliver stopped walking. "Yes. With you, gorgeous."

Sage slowed her walk and Ari's hand went firm on her lower back. "Me?"

"And Ari," Oliver said.

Sage noticed they'd reached her house. She looked at the two men.

"Are you joking?"

"Invite us inside, Sage," Ari instructed her.

Was this really happening? Two men. Her fantasy coming true. And not just two men, but two of the most gorgeous men she'd ever laid eyes on. Clearly, they worked out a lot. Unsurprising, given Ari owned a gym.

Could she really do this?

Was she crazy?

Oliver stepped forward and cupped her face gently. "Nothing happens you don't want. Your pleasure is our pleasure."

Sage let out a little noise as her body buzzed in excitement at his touch.

"It's…"

"Naughty?" Ari asked, turning her face to his. They were both standing so close it was intoxicating. "Bad?"

"Yes." She nodded.

"Do you want to be naughty with us?" Ari asked, his fingers slipping into her hair.

She wanted to nod, really wanted to nod, but she was frozen.

"Shall we show you how this can be intoxicating and wonderful?" Ari asked, and when her mouth parted, his thumb caressed her bottom lip. Automatically, her tongue found his and Ari slipped inside.

"That's it, good girl." He purred. "Oli is going to get your keys and let us inside. Say no at any point, do you understand?"

Her head nodded.

Technically, *she* nodded, but it felt like her body had taken over and decided this was going to happen with or without her brain agreeing.

CHAPTER FIVE

Ari shut the door behind them and made sure it was locked. Usually, he'd rent a hotel room, but with someone like Sage, it was best to go where she felt safe. There was no way she would trust them to take her to a hotel.

Not that she was any safer with them in her home if they'd been serial killers.

His fangs twitched at the thought of someone trying to hurt this young woman.

The hell? Why should he care?

Not that he wished harm on any innocent vampire or human, but the fang thing was a little extreme. He shook it off and focused on what he was doing so they could all enjoy their evening.

Go slow. I have a feeling she'll open up once she gets a feel for this, Ari said telepathically to Oliver.

A promotion and this morsel in one night. I have gone to fucking heaven.

Ari kept his eyes on Sage. He took her coat and bag, placing them on the kitchen counter. His own leather jacket followed, revealing the long-sleeved black t-shirt underneath.

"So how do we do this?" Sage asked, and he heard the tremble in her voice.

"First, let's dim these lights," Oliver said, turning on lamps and killing the bright ones.

Instant vibe change.

"Do you want a drink?" Sage asked.

"No," Ari said, taking a step, then another, then another, until her body was up against his. Her breath hitched as he cupped her face. "I'm going to drink you, Sage. Would you like that?"

Before she could finish her feminine gasp, he lowered his lips to hers and God, she was so fucking sweet. As he'd predicted, she reacted beautifully. Her mouth and tongue lapped and swirled in time with his, sending his cock sky high.

Next, she pressed her body into his and her nails dug through his shirt into his biceps.

Oli moved in behind her.

"Oh!" Sage squeaked, her mouth disconnecting from his when Oliver's hands landed on her hips.

"It's okay," Ari said, running his hand over her neck and feeling her tension began to subside. "Just let him touch you."

She closed her eyes, and he felt her muscles soften. Ari ran his gaze over her face, reveling in her natural beauty.

"Do you want a safe word, or you can just say stop?" Oliver said into her hair as his hands roamed around to her breasts.

Sage nodded, her eyes on Ari. "Stop is fine. Don't actually stop. Just stop is fine."

Oliver looked at him and grinned.

Yeah, she was gorgeous.

"Good girl," Ari said, then turned her face so Oliver could kiss her. He watched Oli's tongue meet hers just as his had, and he took his turn to discover her breasts. She arched into him as he tweaked her nipples.

She moaned, and it hit him straight in the cock. He was going to need all of this human tonight.

Oliver's hand slid under Sage's skirt and though he'd told the guy to go slow, Ari didn't know if he had the patience himself. He needed this fucking dress off her now.

He reached down and palmed his cock, and Ari knew he was going to want her more than once.

Jesus.

"Up," he ordered, and she lifted her arms as if she knew he was the dominant in the room. The dress fell away.

"Fucking gorgeous," Oliver said as they both took in her soft cream skin and black lace lingerie. Her bra, a half-cup type, lifted her smaller breasts as if serving them to him.

Ari pushed the straps off and nudged down the lace, while Oliver undressed to his briefs. Then, as his eyes stayed locked on hers, he lifted her onto the end of the dining room table.

"Oh, God." She moaned.

He wasn't God, but he could confirm there definitely *was* one. He was pretty much the only living being on earth that could. But it wasn't him, and it definitely wasn't Oliver.

"How are you doing?" Ari asked, his thumb rubbing over a nipple.

"Okay, yes. Oh, hell, this is terrifying and incredible," she moaned. Her gaze flew to where Oliver was slowly stroking his cock on the other side of her. "You are both so…"

Yeah, they got that a lot.

Ari slid his hand between her legs and nudged them apart. "You're burning up, Sage. Am I going to find you wet here?"

She nodded, not looking away from him.

"Can I kiss your pussy, Sage?" Ari asked. "Can I taste you?"

"Yes, please, yes, do all the things," she cried, as his fingers met lace.

Oh, yeah, she was good and ready.

Drenched.

Ari undressed while Oliver gripped her face, kissing her, and running his hands over her. His fingers slid under the lace just as Ari's had and he watched the two of them while stroking his large cock.

Oliver had taken her hand, and she was stroking him.

"Yes, darlin'. See, you are a naughty wet girl. I knew it. Keep going. Press harder." Oliver moaned. "God, you are soft and wet."

Watching her with Oliver's cock was hot, but when her eyes shot to his full of heat and desire, it sent pre-cum leaking right out of his own cock.

Jesus.

Ari stepped closer and Oliver moved to the side of the table. They had tag-teamed like this many times and as the dominant alpha, Ari took the lead.

He slipped Sage's panties down her legs, and she moaned loudly. He was done pandering to her nerves. If she wanted to be pleasured beyond her wildest dreams, he could do that, but it meant Ari was now the master of this act.

He was in charge.

Unless she stopped them, they would do as he said.

"Lay her down," Ari said, and Oliver palmed her stomach until she reclined. "Sage, I want you to suck Oliver's cock."

"I want…"

"Now," Ari said, and he spread her thighs. "And relax, gorgeous." Then his mouth was on her wet, hot pussy.

33

Mother fucker, she was sweet and tangy, and the type of dessert you knew you were going to want seconds and thirds.

"Oh, my, fuck," Sage cried as he flicked over her clit. She tried to arch.

"Open for me," Oliver said, and her cries became muted which Ari presumed was the result of Oli's cock entering her mouth. "Fuck me, you have a hot mouth."

This woman, she was insane.

Ari reached down and began to stoke his cock while his tongue lapped and circled around her pussy, then he pressed a finger inside her.

She was tight. Like, really damn tight.

Shit.

He clenched his cock tightly. Soon he'd be deep inside her, and he knew her pussy was going to massage him to heaven.

Another finger and Sage writhed against Oliver's palm, keeping her from arching. Ari could feel the trembles through her body as her arousal peaked. His strokes on his cock increased.

Finally, she shuddered, her mouth wide as she screamed around Oli's cock. Ari lapped all her creamy juice, still working his fingers while the little minx rode the pleasure.

Ari's eyes found hers and she was glowing. He couldn't take his eyes off her.

She was the most beautiful thing he'd ever seen.

She blinked at him until Oliver took her face and pressed back inside her mouth, pumping as she sucked the vampire off.

"Yes, fuckkkk, swallow baby, holy, yes." Oli grunted as he came.

Sage half sat, wiped her mouth, and looked at him, dazed.

The strangest feeling was beginning in his chest, and it was so foreign Ari had no idea what it meant. His gaze flew to Oliver who gave him a strange look. Ari gripped Sage's hips and pulled her closer to him, his cock banging against her wet core.

In moments, he'd be deep inside her.

Normally, from here they'd take turns. Oliver had just come, so Ari would go first. Then Oliver could take her how he wanted or go in the rear. It was unlikely Sage was prepared for that.

And yeah, no fucking way that was happening. Ari was done sharing this female.

He didn't understand it but right now he didn't give a fuck. He just needed Oliver to leave.

Right fucking now.

I need you to go. He telepathed to Oliver, his eyes remaining on Sage.

You okay?

Yes. Leave us now.

He never explained himself unless it was necessary, and while he knew Oliver deserved an explanation, he was feeling a little murderous and that was scaring the fuck out of him.

Now Oliver.

Got it.

"Thank you, beautiful," Oliver said, cupping her cheek as his eyes darted to Ari's. They both knew if he touched her again, Ari would have him up against the wall.

He had no idea why he was feeling so possessive of this female. Sure, at times he wanted a woman to himself. They all did. They didn't share all of them all the time.

This was different. Ari was feeling overwhelmed and a little out of control. He wasn't sure he liked it.

Or the way Sage was looking at Oliver.

"Are you leaving?" she asked.

"Yes," Oliver said. "I will see you again."

The fuck you will.

Ari took her chin. "Say goodbye, Sage."

He hated the confusion on her face, as she said her farewell, especially after what she'd shared with the vampire, but Ari needed to bury himself in her, and fast.

They both heard the door click.

Ari lifted her from the table and carried her to the sofa. He lowered his head and this time their kiss started softly as if getting to know one another. Quickly the kiss heated, and they were panting for their next breath.

"You are fucking beautiful."

Sage ran her fingers along his face. "So are you. Every inch of you is perfect."

If she knew why, or that she'd had sex with two vampires, she wouldn't think them so perfect.

But they were close to it. As vampires and warriors of The Institute they *were* honed to perfection. Being an original made him even more powerful, and Sage was about to reap the rewards.

"I'm going to fuck you, Sage," Ari said, pressing his cock at her entrance. "You know the word if you want me to stop."

Please don't.

"I need this," she said, arching into him and taking the tip of his head inside her. "Please."

Ari pressed into her inch by inch until he filled her completely and a sense of powerful ownership took him over.

"Fuck," he cried out as her pussy clenched around him.

She was a damn witch.

"MY GOD, you're big." Sage gasped, feeling completely impaled but in the most delicious way.

She felt like she was living a dream right now and never wanted to wake up. The most gorgeous, enormous man was deep inside her, looking at her like she was breakfast, lunch, and dinner. She'd analyze everything to the square inch tomorrow but right now Sage was flying high in her own delicious fantasy.

"Are you in pain?" Ari asked and when she shook her head, he lifted her and arranged her legs so she was straddling him.

"Oh, shit, that did not help." Sage moaned as she slid down his cock even deeper. Ari gripped her hips and held her steady until her body got used to him.

"Oops," he said, a glint of laughter in his eyes. It was the first time she'd seen him crack a joke. Sage smirked and dug her knees into the cushions, taking control of the depth issue going on, but Ari's thighs were so big it didn't help.

"Damn, you're big everywhere," she ground out as she tried to accommodate his size. It's not like it wasn't obvious from the moment she'd met him. He was tall and broad, and even his hands were large. But being on top of him like this, she felt petite.

She wasn't a big woman, but in contrast, Ari was really large for a man.

"There's no rush, just take it slowly," he said. "We have all night, and your body will soon adjust."

She nodded.

Everything had been a blur and Sage finally felt herself relax into the moment. She took in his gorgeous body. Heck, who could blame her? He was a masterpiece.

Men like Ari didn't walk around the streets every day. His dark brown eyes were stunning, his body honed to perfection, and he even had one of those infamous V's leading down to, well, the cock inside her.

She lay her hands on his glistening pecs and ran them up and over his shoulders and down his arms.

"How are you so perfect?"

Yet for all his physical beauty, there was something more. Perhaps she was romanticizing the moment, but there was something about the way he was holding her and touching her. She felt... adored.

Sage knew she wasn't—they'd only just met—but that's how she felt.

In any case, Ari wasn't husband material, nor was that what he wanted. So, for her first one-night-stand, this was a wild and incredible experience, especially when she considered moments before there had been another man here.

His thumb went to her clit and began to circle.

"Oh, God," she cried.

"This feels so fucking good, I want this to last."

"I can't last if you keep doing that." Sage gasped, her pussy clenching around him.

"Oh, yes," Ari cried, tightening his grip and thrusting up into her. "Baby, you can come as much as you want. I want to savor this so... hell, do that again."

Sage dug her fingers into his arm as she ground into him.

"I want all your juices. Come for me, Sage, come around my hard cock."

And she did. Twice more.

Ari flipped her, lifted her, pressed her against the wall and then eventually carried her into the bedroom where he lay over her and slowly, but torturously, finally came inside her.

It wasn't until a few hours later she realized they hadn't used a condom. And she wasn't on the pill.

Shit.

Ari must have felt her stiffen and lifted his head. "What is it?"

"Oh God, I'm sorry, I'm not on birth control."

His head flopped back down, and he let out a dry laugh.

"Trust me, it's not a problem." He pulled her down onto his chest again. "I cannot impregnate you. It's fine. Go to sleep."

Sage frowned. It wasn't fine. Not at all.

Ari, and Oliver, might have been the most exciting thing to have happened to Sage in, well, forever, but she was absolutely getting the morning-after pill tomorrow.

She had plans, and it didn't include being a single mom, or married to a gym owner who had threesomes with his staff. No matter how damn sexy he was.

Her body might have said *yes please* tonight, but tomorrow when she woke, Sage knew she wouldn't be proud of herself. Sure, she felt thoroughly ravished and pleasured, but this wasn't her life.

This wasn't the sort of thing she did.

She'd go back to living vicariously through her sexy books.

CHAPTER SIX

Ari lay dozing beside Sage, wondering what the hell he was still doing here. He should be on his way home, and yet he hadn't moved.

The truth was, he liked the feeling of her lying on his chest and the way her little fingers were gently, even in sleep, drawing little circles on his chest.

Light from the living area bled through into the bedroom. He *intended* they turn off and darkness replaced the light. Ari was the only vampire capable of telekinesis, and no one knew he could do it. At least, not since Giorgio had died a thousand years ago.

Ari lifted his arm and checked the time on his watch. It was two in the morning. He had work to do, and it was important he get back to The Institute even if Sage's warm soft body was where he wanted to stay.

He couldn't remember feeling like this before.

It'll pass. It always does.

As he slid out of bed, Sage wriggled and pulled a pillow to her chest as a replacement.

Ari retrieved his clothes from around the house and quickly dressed. He threw his jacket on the arm of the sofa and made his way back into Sage's bedroom. He stood on the side of the bed and stared down at the little human with her auburn hair splayed over the pillow.

She was deliciously naked under the covers, and while he'd already tasted every inch of her, he found himself wanting more.

He should just leave.

Instead, he nudged the covers and sat down, slipping his hand underneath until he found her legs. Sage mumbled and he leaned closer, gently touching his lips to hers. Then he nudged her legs apart.

"Amungishung," Sage muttered as he circled over her clit. Her eyes flickered open and then abruptly pressed closed as he slipped a thick finger inside her. "Ohgoddd."

Thumb and finger going, he took her mouth in his and greedily fucked her with his hand until she cried out.

Sliding out, he sat up slightly and licked her juice from his fingers. "Sage, you have a delicious pussy."

She tipped her head into the pillow and turned on her side, smiling, looking like a woman completely and utterly pleasured. His chest filled with what he could only assume was pride.

Weird.

"Are you leaving now?" she asked softly.

"Yes, I have to go," Ari said, and the vulnerability in her eyes touched a part of him he was rarely aware of. "You were simply beautiful."

He was waiting for the usual questions, the phone number swap, the anger when she realized this was it. And none of them came.

Instead, she smiled at him.

"Thank you. I never thought I could do that, not in a million years. You were both amazing. I will treasure the memory."

He stared at her as a chill brushed over his skin.

"And the orgasms." She grinned.

Ari frowned. Sage wasn't the kind of girl to sleep with a man and happily watch him walk away. He wasn't buying it.

Or was he the one having trouble leaving?

Jesus.

He ran a thumb over her cheekbone, then walked to the door. In a few steps, he would teleport back to the Institute and never see her again.

Never?

Never was a long time. If anyone knew that, he did.

"Goodbye, Sage," he said, and they both gazed at each other across the room for a long moment before he turned and left.

ARI strapped on his watch and then took another look in the mirror. Yep, he looked the same as he had for over fifteen hundred years.

Roughly.

He'd started his life as a human and had never been able to shake the unnatural sense of living so long and not aging.

For natural-born vampires, it was normal. They grew up watching those around them age until their thirtieth birthday, when they were classed as a mature vampire.

Aging did happen, but damn slowly.

Like really fucking slowly.

They called themselves immortal, but they weren't.

Vampires could die.

Step out into the sun and you were toast. Burned toast. Removing the head was quicker and less painful. A stab to the heart sat somewhere in between.

He'd never contemplated taking his life. Ever. Until recently.

Ari felt he had done his time, but life without a mate after fifteen hundred damn years was asking a lot. He didn't want to live another five hundred, let alone a thousand years alone.

There wasn't exactly anyone he could talk to about it. He'd found over the years that most vampires, mated or otherwise, got to around their millennium birthday and began to make exit plans.

Eternity was overrated.

He'd hoped to meet his mate and one day create his own line of Moretti's. Giorgio and Frances, he knew, had held a deep fear he would challenge them in their position of leadership. It was why his existence had been kept quiet and eventually so silent even the current king had not known who he was.

Now he did.

Ari had gone to Italy after his head assassin, Ben, had gone AWOL over his mate, and re-introduced himself.

They had known him as the commander of the royal army—a position he'd held for many centuries before they had been born. He'd trained his nephews, Vincent and Brayden Moretti, even when they only knew him as Ari.

Just Ari.

Not Ari Moretti.

It was only the power of the Moretti blood that had convinced them he was family.

King Vincent wanted to know if he was a threat—he'd seen it in his eyes—but Ari wasn't interested in discussing that with him. His focus was on ridding the world of any threats to vampires, and then he'd go on his merry way into the sun.

At least that's what he'd thought.

Ari wanted to see another sunrise and feel the heat on his skin. The last time he'd felt it had been 522AD. At best, he'd probably get twenty minutes before it painfully—he assumed—turned him to dust.

An image of sitting next to Sage on the beach as the sun rose flashed before his eyes.

The hell?

Okay fine, so he hadn't completely stopped thinking about her all morning. And yes, he had already jerked off. But hell, he could still taste her on his tongue.

It wasn't like she was the first female to capture his attention over the many years, so he wasn't going to fall into that old *she's my mate* myth. She was simply a sexy-as-hell little kitten who was unaware of her allure.

The mixture was intoxicating.

Ari had long ago accepted there was no mate for him. He yelled and begged at the God who had created him and promised him a mate, and who remained silent.

At times, he sounded like a childish brat. He'd screamed, asking why Gio had lived such a rich life full of love and family when he'd endured such loneliness.

Ben had asked him once why he had never resisted his brother's request to hide his identity. Hindsight was a great thing.

Ari had questioned himself over and over until he turned himself inside out.

It didn't make him wrong or right.

It didn't make his brother wrong—hell, Ari had often wondered if he would have done the same thing.

Every time he landed on the same answer: no.

At the heart of it, Gio had feared he was more powerful, and he was right. Ari had always been the alpha of the two, but he was also respectful of his brother. It was his bloodline. He had no interest in taking that away from Gio.

If only Gio had been secure in his own power and leadership and seen there was space enough for both of them in this world.

Fortunately, in some ways, he had never mated during those first one hundred years to populate his own bloodline. God only knows what would have happened if he had. Would the two of them have warred?

It was a strong possibility.

By then, it was clear. If he'd tried to stake a claim, it would've been seen as treason. With no mate or reason to reveal his true identity, Ari had remained silent.

Not that anyone would be able to actually kill him.

Gio could have tried and was likely the only vampire ever capable of succeeding due to their undiluted original Moretti blood. It was possible he would have overpowered him and then what? Kill the king? His brother?

No. That was never his desire or goal.

So, he had remained silent.

Over time, baby Frances had grown into a fine king, mated, and had his own sons, Brayden and Vincent. Gio had passed his fears down to Frances, who had all but eliminated Ari's existence as a Moretti.

He held the title of captain of the army, which allowed him to spend time with his family, even if they didn't know he was their uncle.

Right up until the day he had left.

Ari had roamed the earth aimlessly until he'd settled in the United States and created The Institute. It had been a gift giving him a purpose and place to be recognized for who he truly was, even if only by a trusted few.

To everyone else, he was known as Ari.

Their customers only knew him as the director. Many of them were leaders in top global positions and those contacts were coming in handy since vampires had been exposed to the world.

And wasn't that a huge fuck up?

It was something he and his brother had fought to protect since the moment they were turned vampire. They'd experienced firsthand how humans reacted to their existence, and it had been ugly.

As technology and science evolved, so did the atrocious opportunities for humans to literally pull a living thing to pieces to study it.

Fortunately, thanks to some fast thinking by Vincent Moretti, his social team had turned a media frenzy into a "fake news" campaign, almost shutting the whole thing down.

Almost.

In the shadows, small groups were still looking for proof. Fortunately, most people were calling them crazy conspiracy theorists. His team was keeping an eye on them. Sometimes they'd had to intervene.

That didn't mean flying in with guns and killing them all. This wasn't the movies. His team was made up of all kinds of skilled vampires. Assassins, yes, but also black ops, digital and technical guys, pilots, administration, engineers... it was a whole operation.

They got paid well for what they did by people who had all the money you could imagine at their disposal. And more.

Ari only worked for the good guys, but figuring out who the good guys were took a shit ton of research and access to stuff most people should never have access to.

But it was how his people did their job better than anyone else.

Ari had seen a lot of life over the past fifteen centuries and what he saw was a race of humans who had never learned from their mistakes and kept repeating them.

They posed a great risk to the vampire race.

Vampires had spent a long time living peacefully alongside humans, hidden, and Ari had watched as the age of communication developed, knowing their time was nearly up.

In Italy, he'd sat down with Vincent and shared what he knew about the situation. Yes, exposure was a big one, but in the shadows was a group of evil fuckers who needed to be stopped.

Ben had taken care of one of them: Diego Lombardo, the Italian president. He'd been a large investor and instigator responsible for experiments on over a dozen kidnapped vampires.

A few had been recovered; some hadn't made it. Anna, who was now Ben's mate, was one of the lucky ones.

Central to this group was a pharmaceutical company. No fucking surprise there—those assholes were mixed up in pretty much every bad thing going on around the planet, under the guise of healthcare.

Ari snorted.

Fuckers.

He was glad he wasn't human.

A big focus for them right now was finding the main laboratory where they knew, or believed, they still held a single vampire. He had been the first, according to the intel his team had recovered, and they had reason to believe he was still alive.

Poor damn guy—he'd be fucked up if he was.

Or they could have dumped him outside into the sun. The thing about vampire bodies is they were easy to get rid of.

Ash disappeared into the wind.

Ari was determined to find him before he departed this earth himself. No human, or vampire, should be subjected to experimentation.

It was utter fucking evil.

Trust was low still between Ari and the royal family, but he hoped they could overcome that and work together on this common goal.

Today they were meeting via video conference to discuss their next steps. Ben, his former head assassin, was now working for the Moretti family, after he and Anna had decided to stay in Italy, so when the screen lit up it was his mug grinning back at him. He was head to toe in the iconic black Moretti uniform vampires around the world recognized and respected.

"Hey boss."

"Not anymore. Where are the royals?"

"I'm here," Brayden said, adjusting the camera so the rest of the room was visible. "Vincent's on his way. Something about nappies and, yeah, I didn't want to ask."

Ari scrunched his nose. "No."

The king and queen had recently welcomed a baby boy, the new prince, into the world. A celebration for the entire race, but it had been extra special to meet Lucas Moretti.

Ari never thought he'd meet his newest nephew when his birth was announced on VampNet, the secure vampire web, and he'd be lying if he said it hadn't caused a big fucking lump in his chest.

Lucas was only the sixth pureblood Moretti to be born.

"You remember Craig," Brayden, the other Moretti prince, said.

"Commander," Ari said in greeting.

"Ari. Good to see you," Craig replied.

"Christ, did you have cornflakes for breakfast? That was so polite I nearly fell off my chair," Ben asked, mocking shock and surprise.

"I can knock you off if you like." Craig sneered.

Ari smirked.

"Jesus. It's not even midnight. At least give us a few hours before you two start," Brayden said, shaking his head. "You want him back?"

"No," Ari lied.

He'd take Ben back in a second. Not only was Ben the best assassin he'd ever had, but he was also extremely close to the young vampire.

But Ben had mated, and he would stay with his mate until his dying breath. Plus, the assassin life was no life for Anna or Ben now. They had a no-female policy at the mansion for that very reason.

"I'm here!" came the booming sound of the king. "Ari, sorry to keep you waiting."

"Your Majesty." He lifted his coffee to his lips. "How is the little prince?"

Vincent pulled up a chair and sat. Even though the male was no bigger, in fact marginally slighter than Brayden, Craig and Ben, he had a presence about him. He was a king, there was no question about it.

"Smelly," he replied, bunching his lips. "I was not prepared for that side of fatherhood. Nor my queen insisting I take part in the resolution of said smell."

Ari watched Brayden barely contain a grin.

"Anyway, where are we at?" Vincent said, giving the prince a sideways glance.

Ari placed his coffee on the desk and clicked the mouse to bring up a document on his second screen. His eyes flicked over the live data from his team. He'd been briefed, but things could change on a dime.

"Right now, we don't know where Xander is, but that won't last for long. We're following a strong lead and have boots ready to go when we do," he replied.

Craig then shared some of the data their team had begun to decipher after the raid on the pharma executive's house.

"We think we might have a location, but the details are shaky," Craig said.

"My team can follow it up if you send me the details," Ari said, taking notes.

"Anything you can find would be helpful," Brayden replied. "However, Craig and I are heading back to the United States with a crew, so we'll check in when we land."

Ari frowned.

"Back to Maine?" he asked. The Moretti's had built an enormous castle in the late nineteenth century where they had lived until last year.

"No. We'll be in your neck of the woods," Brayden replied. "Washington State. The location we have is in Seattle."

Shit.

"The labs are here?" he asked.

"Potentially," Craig replied, nodding.

"Right under our fucking noses." Ari scowled. "Well, that will save on fuel, I guess."

Craig snorted.

BioZen had offices and laboratories all over the world, so he'd known there was a Seattle location, but there had been nothing to indicate it should be on their radar. He'd thought they were simply offices. Admin shit.

"Do you need accommodation?" Ari asked, surprising himself. He'd hidden his existence from the Moretti family for over four hundred years and here he was inviting them for a sleepover.

Having the Moretti prince stay in The Institute's mansion might cause a stir, but his vampires were all highly trained and used to working in the highest levels of confidence.

"Thank you, but we have a property close to you. It would be great to check out your operation, though," Brayden said. "Ben still won't tell us a fucking thing."

Ben shrugged.

Ari expected nothing less.

"That's why he was the best." Ari smiled.

"Hey, I'm not dead. I'm still the best," Ben said, mocking offense.

"Debatable," Craig added, deadpan.

"Anyyyway... I'll be heading to DC," Vincent said. "To meet with POTUS and the other members of Operation Daylight."

The king had shared basic information about the project team, which had been set up to prepare for the inevitable exposure of vampires to humans. It was all the high-level paperwork and legal shit Ari couldn't stand.

Like Brayden, Ari was a hands-on soldier and left all that legislative stuff to the kings. He knew it was important; it just wasn't his thing.

He'd much rather be swinging a sword.

"I still think this is a bad time to travel," Craig said. "I'm not sure if it's safe, my lord."

"Then make it safe. That's your job, Craig." Vincent stood and slapped him on the shoulder. "I have complete faith in you."

Brayden and Craig shared a glance.

"I'll leave you with my team, and the prince, to nut out the details and perhaps I will swing by on my way back to Italy," Vincent said, as Craig ran a hand over his face.

"Nice to see you again, Your Majesty. It would be my honor to host you if you find yourself in Seattle," Ari said. "You are all welcome at The Institute."

Vincent disappeared from the screen, and he heard the door click.

Craig leaned forward and looked him dead in the eye through the screen. "Ari, can you send a team to spec out DC before he gets there? We have guys on the ground, but they're not our senior crew."

"No problem. Ben, link up with Jason and brief him to send a team. He'll run it past me, and I'll approve it," Ari said.

"Got it," Ben replied, tapping on his smartphone.

"Update me when it's done," Craig instructed the new senior lieutenant commander, or SLC.

"Yes, sir," Ben said.

While the two vampires wound each other up, Ari had no doubt Ben was very clear where those boundaries were and acted professionally when it came to the important stuff.

Ari missed working with the powerful vampire, but Oliver was an excellent replacement. He'd worked with Ben for many years and was a highly skilled assassin and respected teammate.

It was a reminder he owed Oliver an explanation for last night. Ari just wasn't sure he had one yet.

When the call ended, Ari leaned back in his large executive chair and spun away from his desk, looking out into the night sky full of stars. Soon the sun would rise, and Sage would start her day.

Would she be sore?

A smile began to form on his lips.

Would she feel regret or shame? He hoped not. She had been incredible. A desire to see that blush on her cheeks again rushed over him.

He let out a long breath.

A female invading his thoughts when he was working wasn't normal. He had to admit it. Sage had gotten under his skin.

He felt this nagging sense he'd opened her up and left her vulnerable. He wanted to know she was okay with what they had done. Watching her with Oliver had been sexy as fuck, but the moment she had come, a protectiveness triggered within him.

He'd never felt that way before.

No, it wasn't protectiveness, although that was there. It was possession.

The words on the tip of his tongue were foreign to him, but Sage was his, and he wasn't happy about sharing her.

Oliver had been wise to leave fast and not ask any more questions.

And yet Ari had also left her.

Sage would carry on with her life, and date, fuck and marry eventually. Some man would spread her legs and use his tongue on her wet sweet flesh that had felt like it belonged to him.

Ari gripped the arms of his chair and the metal bent.

Fuck.

Matteo, his assistant, would have to order him another one. Or he'd get Alice to do it. They had both worked for him for a long time and wouldn't blink an eye.

"Fuck!" Ari refused to go down the path of wondering if Sage was his mate. Not again. He just fucking wouldn't.

He'd done it dozens of times, only to be disappointed. Each one harder and more painful.

No.

He'd made his decision. He was departing this world when the current danger for his race was over.

In the meantime, perhaps he could spend some more delicious time with Sage, enjoying her body and sharing carnal pleasure.

The trouble was, she didn't seem interested beyond the one night.

CHAPTER SEVEN

Sage lay blinking at the ceiling as the morning light streamed through a gap in her curtains. Memories of the night before came rushing back, and even if she'd had amnesia, the aches in her body would have given her a clue about what she'd been up to.

She just wasn't sure how she felt about it.

"Holy shit." She whispered into the emptiness of the room.

She'd never had so many orgasms in her life. Who was she kidding? It wasn't the amount she'd had, but the quality of them. She'd felt like she was going to explode. They were like full body orgasms.

The kind that made you scream.

And she had.

But that wasn't the holy shit part. Sage hadn't just experienced a wild night of sex with a man. She'd had two men pleasuring her.

Two men.

Every time she moved, her body ached. Her nipples were sore, and her hips felt bruised. Inside felt… joyful.

Weird. But accurate.

Oh God, and she'd had unprotected sex. About twenty-five times.

And two men.

Sage closed her eyes and felt Oliver's hands on her body, his mouth taking hers and the way he'd guided his cock between her lips. There had been a playful assertiveness to him, which she liked, but it was Ari's touch that sent her to heaven.

Whether his mouth was on her pussy, he was inside her, or wrapped around her, Sage had not wanted it to end.

But it had.

Sage was clear about what last night had been. Just one night. One extremely sexy and crazy wild night with two incredibly handsome men.

She never dreamed one, let alone two, men would ever look her way. And they'd spent hours pleasuring her and fulfilling one of her greatest fantasies. Fucking two men had been way more intense and orgasmic than she ever dreamed it could be. She was strangely proud of her courage but slightly embarrassed she'd done it.

For a girl looking for a husband, last night was taking a slight detour, yet she couldn't find a regretful bone in her body, mostly because Ari had turned her completely to jelly.

Sage turned into the pillow and let out a little joyful scream.

God, he was amazing.

Oliver's sudden departure had been odd. Sage had no experience with these things, so she'd just accepted it, but she had thought he'd stay and, well, do more. She had quickly been distracted when Ari pressed inside her and the rest was one enormous blur of ecstasy.

She knew marriage wouldn't be filled with that much passion, but Sage hoped her future husband was a little adventurous. That wink Carl had given her might be a sneaky insight into something more.

Perhaps she should ask him out?

Sage had a shower and cleaned up the mess in the kitchen. Even that hadn't been able to wipe the smile off her face. She felt like she was floating on air.

Because it was Saturday, and she had the house to herself, she poured a bath and filled it with all her favorite girly stuff and soaked until it got cold.

By the time she got out, she had several missed calls on her phone.

Mom.

Piper.

Mom.

Piper.

Piper.

Piper.

Ugh, for God's sake. Sage phoned her mother first.

"Hi, Sagey," Maryanne Roberts said, using the pet name Sage hated. "Just checking in to see how you are."

"Hi Mom. I'm fine. Just enjoying a quiet Saturday at home by myself."

"That's not healthy. You should be out with friends," her mother replied, and Sage rolled her eyes.

"I am going out tonight," she lied.

"Oh lovely. With Carmen and Matti?" Maryanne asked, referring to her college friends. She had stayed in contact with them frequently, but they all had demanding jobs working in the science and medical fields, so catching up wasn't always easy. People like her mother, who worked as a receptionist, would never understand life outside the nine to five.

"Yes," Sage lied again. Having an overbearing mother meant she had learned to lie rather than get into long debates or listen to lectures. "How's Dad?" she asked, and got the usual sigh.

"You know, he's good. Spending a lot of time on his golf game when he's not working."

"Maybe you should go with him?" Sage said.

"No. Goodness no. You have to let a man have his sport, or man cave, or whatever thing they choose."

Sage considered this and decided her mother was right. Everyone needed the space to be who they were outside of being a sister, mother, wife, or whatever actual title they were given.

"What about you then, Mom, what are you doing?"

"Oh, darling, I have the church. Now stop distracting me. How is work going?"

"I'm waiting on news about the promotion next week. Stop pretending that's not what you want to ask about." Sage rolled her eyes.

"I was trying to be delicate."

Pfft.

Sage really wasn't in the mood to have this conversation, so she quickly made an excuse.

"Mom, sorry, Piper is calling. She's already left me four messages, so I better go before she just turns up here."

When they hung up, she sat staring at the phone.

It was like this every time she had to speak to or see her sister. Sage had to wind herself up and remind herself she had forgiven her. Because she did love Piper. A sister bond was never broken, but it could be splintered.

And that was where they were at.

Still.

She dialed.

"Hey," Piper answered.

"Hey."

"So, you *are* taking my calls?" Piper asked, annoyance lacing her voice.

Sage sighed. "It may surprise you, but I have a life and am not always on call for Piper Roberts."

"I haven't seen you in three weeks, Sage," Piper said. "Let's get a drink or I can come over and watch a movie."

Nooooo.

She'd already lied to her mother and said she was going out, so she had to follow through.

"I'm busy tonight," she replied. "Next weekend, we can do something."

"Busy doing what?"

Sage pressed her fingers into her eyes.

"Jesus, Piper, between you and Mom you act like I'm some hermit spinster." She snapped. "I have friends. I have dates. I have… stuff."

Like threesomes and two gorgeous men you aren't getting near. Not that they were hers anymore.

"Do you have a date tonight?" Piper asked, and she could hear the grin in her sister's voice.

"Goodbye, Piper. See you next weekend." Sage hung up. She flopped back on the sofa and let out a groan. She loved her family, she really did, but their constant pushing was annoying.

She turned her head and noticed it was getting late. She wondered what Ari was doing. Was he thinking about their night together? Or did he do this kind of thing all the time?

Ari wasn't the man she was going to marry, so she needed to push thoughts of him and Oliver aside.

No great love story started with a wild threesome.

Yet, her body had been burning all day with the desire for more. To put it bluntly, she was incredibly horny. Not for the rabbit, but for them.

Or rather Ari.

God.

They hadn't swapped numbers, so it wasn't going to happen. It had been amazing, and that was that. Maybe it was because Sage had gone so long without sex. Her body had just awoken. There was something incredibly sexy about letting such powerful men take control of her body.

Would she ever find that again?

How could she find the same excitement and passion in a man who wanted to get married? Someone with a great career and financial security. Someone she could take home to her parents, and who would pretend her family wasn't insane.

Someone who wanted babies and to build them a treehouse and go on a family road trip.

Oh crap.

She hadn't gone to the drugstore.

For whatever reason, Ari had been confident she couldn't get pregnant, and she was sure he believed that, but she wasn't taking a risk. She also wasn't immune to diseases.

Damn, she'd been irresponsible.

Next week, she would go for a checkup. Tonight she had to stop focusing on a man who was all wrong for her.

One she was never going to see again.

CHAPTER EIGHT

*D*arkness.

Blinding light.
Pain.
Pleasure.
Noise.
Silence.
Then the cutting began.
Again.

Callan had lost all sense of time, but he knew at this point he'd been held captive for months by whatever medical facility had him. Where he was, he didn't know. A few times, he'd sensed he was being moved, but during those moments, his physical senses were weakened.

Some days, he could barely think a clear thought and wondered if he was going insane. Then clarity would return, and they'd torture him, before he lost focus all over again.

It hadn't been like this in the beginning.

When he'd first been taken, they had interrogated him. Just questions at first, threatening his friends and family if he didn't answer. Then they had said they were going to harm the royals. It had messed with his mind to think he could be responsible for any harm that came to the Moretti family even as he knew they were powerful vampires. Yet, he wasn't a small guy, but they'd stopped him in his tracks and here he was.

So how had they overpowered him?

Callan was strong, standing over six feet and three inches. He might be a boring accountant working at a desk most days, but he had a gym in his house and worked out regularly. His body was a temple and all that.

Now it was a fucking mess.

A science experiment.

The humans in white coats, and some in suits, had him connected to a machine with tubes in his arms, legs, and neck. They wanted to know about Callan's race.

About vampires.

After a while, it became obvious they already knew a great deal and when he didn't talk, they simply began taking a look themselves. With knives. Because he was a vampire, Callan simply healed, allowing them to cut right back in again—something they saw as a great benefit. There was no cleanup, and they got more samples to work with the next day.

So yeah, he had heard their chatter, and either they hadn't cared, or they really did just see him as a caged animal and had forgotten he could speak English.

Assholes.

He hated them with every inch of his being. Given the chance, he would rip them all limb from limb. Just as they'd done to him.

Callan healed all right, but that didn't mean he wasn't in pain. Being cut hurt a vampire, just as it did a human as far as he knew. In the early days he'd still had hope of escape, so had told them he could die if they cut into his heart. Now he wished he'd let them kill him unwittingly.

They obviously didn't want him dead.

From time to time, he was intravenously fed blood, which kept him barely alive.

Every day, people came to take samples of blood, flesh, and whatever else they wanted. Then leave. There wasn't an inch of his body they hadn't studied in the most atrocious ways. Yes, even his cock.

Callan had wanted to scream when he'd hardened at the videos played to him, then been helpless as a woman jerked him off with a complete lack of emotion.

He'd lain prone listening as a team studied his semen sample at a nearby station. It was a total demoralization of him as a living being.

The lowest moment had been when they'd fed him and given him a room with gym equipment. Callan had believed they were rejuvenating him, to let him go. He'd eagerly drunk the blood, slept—though poorly—and worked out. Then one day, a week later, he found himself strapped to a steel table with tubes.

Again.

He'd barely been able to speak, but when he asked what happened, one lab assistant had shared they had been testing his strength and physical abilities.

Callan had tried to teleport out a million times, and each time failed. Why he couldn't, he still didn't know.

He didn't know anything anymore.

But he had a lot of questions. Why had no one come for him? Why were they doing this? Did the world know about vampires outside this nightmare of his? Were there others like him here? Would they ever let him go?

Callan needed this nightmare to end. He'd lost all hope and was losing his mind.

Now he just wanted to die.

CHAPTER NINE

Sage stared in the mirror. She'd wrapped a large white towel around herself after her shower and was contemplating whether to go to bed early or join her roommates in the living room to watch a movie.

Her living room.

One glance at her bed and she decided Netflix while she was cozy under the duvet sounded far more appealing.

But that wasn't why she was staring at herself. Sage was wondering who she had become now. After last night. She let the towel fall to the floor and cupped her breasts. Her thumb flicked her nipples and her pussy twitched eagerly.

Lying to yourself was hard.

Sage wanted more of what she'd had last night. It was lucky she didn't have Ari's phone number, or she would've texted him.

God, she didn't want to be that girl. The one who didn't realize it was just a one-night thing and wouldn't move on.

Because she wasn't.

Neither Ari nor Oliver was the type of man she was looking for. Nothing about them matched her *Life List*.

Yet she craved their touch.

Truthfully, it was Ari who had been on her mind all day, not Oliver, but Sage knew she could not say no to either of them.

She felt different.

Perhaps last night had changed her. She felt more liberated, sexually free, and confident. Sage had decided she was going to ask Carl out next week. If he said no, then she'd go on Tinder or some dating app and start dating.

Two men.

Wow, she still couldn't believe that had happened.

One day, she was going to tell Piper, who was far more adventurous than her, and couldn't wait to see her response.

"Sage! Door!" Tony called.

What?

Sage pulled the towel back on and poked her head out the door.

"Who is it?" she asked, but it was too late. The visitor had pushed through the front door, passed Tony, and was making a beeline for her.

"What are you doing here, Piper?" Sage asked, glaring at her sister.

She knew exactly what Piper was doing here. Her nosy parker sister had come over to see who she was going out with. Unfortunately, that was a big fat *no one*. Sage couldn't wait to hear her excuse.

"I need my blue earrings. You borrowed them, remember. I need them urgently so saved you the trouble of bringing them to me," Piper replied.

Sage frowned and dropped a hip. "Seriously? I've had them for six months and you want them now? Tonight?"

Piper stared her up and down. "Thought you were going out? Out to the living room?"

Sage strode across the room and opened her jewelry box. Digging through, she found the blue earrings and stomped back over to her sister.

"Here," she said, shoving them into Piper's hands. "Now go. I have to get ready."

Sage was grateful she hadn't been curled up in bed with her trackpants and Netflix. It was one thing to lie, another to get caught. Not to mention it made her look like a complete loser. She could tell her sister what she'd been up to, but there was still a big divide between them.

Piper took the dangly blue gems and sat on the edge of the bed.

"Piper," Sage sighed.

"Get dressed. I'll just sit here and chat to you," Piper said. "What are you going to wear? The black dress or the silver one with the low back? I love that one."

Damn it.

Piper knew she was lying.

She'd always been impossible to lie to.

"I'm not getting dressed in front of you," she said, although she'd done it thousands of times in her life.

"Ugh, Sage. Come on. When are you going to forgive me?"

Sage crossed her arms.

"I'm not having that conversation right now. Can you please leave so I can get ready? I said we can catch up next weekend."

Piper's shoulders sagged a little and she let out a little sigh. Sage had said she'd forgiven her, but they both knew they had only been words. Perhaps it was time to give her a second chance?

Maybe.

"Look, forget it," Piper said, standing up.

"Wait." Sage chewed her bottom lip. Maybe she could throw her an olive branch and tell the truth about tonight.

Piper raised a brow.

"I have a confession."

CHAPTER TEN

Ari stood outside Sage's house and cursed. What the fuck was he doing here?

He'd already had Sage—every delicious inch of her—so why on earth was he back here? Especially when members of the Moretti family were on their way to Seattle, and he had a tortured vampire to find and a science lab or two to destroy.

All day he'd tossed and turned, trying to sleep, then ended up jerking off. Twice.

He'd been a seriously grumpy asshole to his team and when Oliver had given him a sideways look, Ari had forced himself not to remove his new head assassin's head from his neck.

That's what he was doing here.

Collecting his fucking sanity, which he'd clearly left behind.

It was probably between Sage's legs. Which was exactly where he wanted to be.

Patience wasn't a fucking virtue—that was a huge lie.

He wanted Sage, so here he was.

Except it wasn't just her pussy he was after. His mind had wandered to taboo places. He'd imagined her as his queen, swollen pregnant with his babe and creating a world he'd never dreamed possible.

House of Moretti.

He'd see a world where they created a new line of vampires. It had been beautiful and full of love and laughter.

And it had been terrifying. This was the sort of dangerous thinking that fucked him up.

Sage wasn't his damn mate.

Ari had leaped out of bed and slammed into the wall—which Matteo was currently repairing—and then eventually ended up in the training center where he couldn't break anything else.

So he'd decided that he just had to fuck her a bunch more times and that would resolve his temporary insanity.

Not letting himself think about it another second, he ran up the stairs and knocked. Then waited.

A man opened the door, then recoiled.

Yeah, he got that a lot. He had a powerful presence that was overwhelming for some humans.

"Hey, can I help you?"

"I'm here to see Sage," Ari announced.

"Sage! *Another* visitor," the guy called out, then gave him a sideways look before wandering off, leaving the door open.

Another?

Did Sage have a guy here? Ari felt his fangs itch to press through his gums.

Jesus, settle down.

Sage appeared in the doorway. His heart began racing and his fingers burned to touch her. It didn't help that she was wearing nothing but a large white towel with her hair tied up.

"Ari," she breathed.

He didn't give a fuck who saw. He took a step and wrapped his arm around her lower back and pulled her against him. His lips dropped to hers and he kissed her.

Hard.

"Hello, Sage," he whispered against her lips.

A throat cleared behind them, but he didn't look up. He was mesmerized by the goddess in his arms. There could have been an earthquake and he wouldn't have given a fuck.

"What are you doing here?" she whispered.

"Ahh, hello, are you going to introduce me?"

Finally, he pulled his eyes from hers and glanced behind Sage.

Jesus.

Ari stared at the woman, then lowered his eyes back down to Sage, who was still in his arms. Then looked back and down again.

Ari was a twin. He knew twins. Though not identical, he and his brother were born two minutes apart. These two women were sisters.

Not twins.

If he had to guess, he would say Sage was slightly older, but not by much. A year, maybe two.

But while the dark-haired woman looked similar to Sage, their energies were polar opposites. Her smirk seemed like it was permanent, and the way she stood with her hand on one hip screamed of sass.

Sage leaned into him in what he could only describe as a possessive move. He wanted to purr.

Still, it was an interesting reaction. Sage wasn't a dominant personality, but she also wasn't insecure. That simple movement had indicated there was a history between these two, and if his instincts were right, Sage had been hurt.

Normally, human family bullshit didn't interest him in the slightest, yet right now he was feeling very protective of his little human.

What had this woman done to Sage? Ari wanted to know.

"This is my sister, Piper," Sage said with a long sigh. "Piper, Ari."

No kidding.

"Hello, Piper," Ari said, keeping his voice neutral as she ran her eyes over his body with a courage he'd rarely seen in a woman. Then her eyes landed on his crotch.

Good grief.

"Nice to meet you," Piper replied, "Sage, you have been keeping some *big* secrets."

Groan.

This woman was trouble.

"I didn't know you had a sister," Ari said, tightening his grip on Sage's hip. Piper's eyes moved to his hand and watched everything.

Interesting.

Their eyes met again, and Ari found within them some interesting emotions: distrust and, even more interesting, disbelief.

Disbelief that he would be interested in Sage? Disbelief they were in a relationship? Not that they were. Either way, he was curious to understand why her sister would be so stunned. Sage was a gorgeous and intelligent young woman.

"I had a twin brother," Ari said and wondered how the hell that had fallen out.

"A twin?" Piper's eyes lit up.

"He said *did¸* Piper," Sage admonished, then lay a hand on his arm. "I'm sorry for your loss."

Despite everything, and the centuries since his death, Ari still loved Giorgio very much. No one on earth could ever understand what they'd experienced together, being the first vampires.

Still, he was surprised he had shared that. He rarely spoke of him, let alone just spat it out like that.

Ari's eyes dropped to Sage's, and the warmth in them shot straight to his heart. It had been a long time since he'd felt a woman care for him the way Sage was doing right now.

"It was a long time ago," he replied, pulling her against him.

"Oh, I'm sorry," Piper said, dropping the sass, and for a moment, he saw another side to her. "That would have been heartbreaking."

He nodded.

Sage turned into him and tucked her towel closer around her. He hated she was being so modest around him. He shifted a lock of hair behind her ear and gazed down into her wide eyes. Her pupils dilated as a flush hit her cheeks, sending a rush of heat through his body.

"I should let you both get going," Piper said, and Ari narrowed his eyes in question as Sage blushed.

So, she'd lied to her sister and said they were going out tonight? Well then, she would get her wish. Their eyes connected and unsaid words passed between them. She mouthed, *I'm sorry,* but he wasn't.

"Yes, and someone needs to get dressed," Ari said, smacking her bottom.

"Right," Sage replied, backing away, narrowing her eyes at him.

"I'll call you tomorrow, sis," Piper said, planting a kiss on Sage's cheek and then dashed out the door with a wiggly finger wave. Ari followed Sage into her bedroom, giving her roommates a cursory glance, and shut the door.

"Hi." Ari cupped her cheek and Sage looked like she was waiting for his questions, but he had none. Everything he wanted was right here.

"Hi," Sage replied when he didn't continue.

"I need to taste you." He lowered his mouth and took possession of her lips, and she responded hungrily.

"Delicious... but I wasn't meaning that." Ari nudged her down on the bed and discarded the towel.

"You never said what you were doing here," Sage said, her voice hitched.

"I'm about to show you," he replied, kissing her lips once more. "Then I'm going to take you to dinner."

Was he? Dinner? Like a date?

So, he dated now?

Apparently so.

Ari moved down her body. "This is just the first course."

CHAPTER ELEVEN

Twenty minutes later, Sage was dressed in her favorite little black dress and slid into the leather seat of a limousine.

Ari stepped in next and positioned himself in front of her. He nodded to the driver and then the privacy screen slid into place.

Sage swallowed.

"Did you think about me today?" Ari asked her.

"Yes," she replied.

"Good thoughts, or naughty thoughts?"

Sage wished she could stop blushing in front of this man, but everything he said caused a reaction. "Both," she replied honestly.

His eyes blazed with flame as the car began moving.

"Where are we going?" she asked.

"Take off your panties and spread your legs," he said, ignoring her question. "Then I want to watch you touch yourself."

Her mouth parted slightly. Ari had just had his mouth on her and now he wanted more? He was insatiable.

Then again, so was she.

"Now, Sage," Ari growled.

She put her purse on the seat beside her and slowly slid her dress up, tucking her fingers under the lace of her black panties and tugging.

"Pull up your dress so I can see your pussy and spread your legs."

Oh, God.

The way he spoke, and the way he looked at her made her instantly wet. She began to tremble. Not in fear, but desire.

"Ari, I—"

"Don't think, just do it," he instructed. "Eyes on me."

The cool air hit her sensitive flesh and when her fingers connected, she drew in a small groan. Ari stared back at her like she was the seventh wonder of the world until his eyes dropped to her vulnerable flesh.

"Fucking gorgeous."

She watched his cock harden.

Jesus. This man was pure sex.

"Run your fingers through your pussy and I want to see them glistening with juice." His voice was thick with hunger. She let out a little moan when she brushed her clit and began to circle it. God, she'd been worried she wouldn't come again so quickly but she'd been wrong.

Her body was on fire.

"Slow down. You're not coming yet," he said. "Just do as I say."

She groaned in frustration, made worse when Ari pulled out his cock and began stroking.

"You see what you do to me?" He ran his thumb over the swollen end. "I'm ready to fuck you again already."

Her mouth watered as her heavy lashes dropped downward. She needed him inside her like a drug.

"Your pussy is so beautiful. Did you touch yourself today while thinking of me, Sage?"

"Yes." She barely whispered.

"Good girl. You are so much naughtier than I thought. Now, do you want to suck me or ride me?"

Sage's arousal flared even more as her finger strummed her clit. Her teeth clenched her bottom lip. "Oh, God," she cried, ready to come.

"Stop," Ari said and her eyes flew open. "Down on your knees over here. Now, Sage."

Reluctantly, her fingers fell from her pussy, and she dropped to her knees. Ari cupped her chin and tapped his large swollen cock on her lips.

"Lips open. That's it, suck the end of it. Yes, fuck." Ari groaned and then inserted himself completely inside her mouth.

Sage wrapped her lips around his cock. He was hot and salty, filling her mouth. A hand pressed to the back of her head, and he went deeper.

"Shit, yes." Ari groaned. "Fuck me with your mouth, Sage. God, I've been imagining this all day."

He had?

She moved up and over his cock, sucking, licking, and stroking it. After a minute, she reached down and began rubbing her own flesh. A moan escaped her, and Ari glanced down at her.

"Greedy girl," he said, lifting her with surprising strength onto the seat beside him. He spread her thighs and then his mouth was on her.

Sage cried out, uncaring who heard her.

"When you are with me, and unless I tell you, this is my pussy." He lapped and pulled her flesh with his lips. "You understand. You don't touch it unless I tell you."

Sage didn't agree at all, but right now she'd say anything for the release she needed.

"Yup, cool, oh my God." His thumb joined the party on her clit. "Ari, God, fuck, I'm going to come."

Two fingers slid inside her and she arched off the seat. Fireworks exploded in her brain as her orgasm flashed through her. Ari didn't stop. He continued to run his tongue over her sensitive flesh until he sat and lifted her onto his lap, gripping her hips. "Hold my shoulders."

Sage took control of the speed as she lowered onto his thick cock. The zipper on the back of her dress slid down, and then he pulled the garment off her.

"Oh, godfuckgod," Sage cried as he filled her completely.

"Sage." Ari moaned. "Fuck, you feel amazing."

He took one of her nipples in his mouth and her body roared in response.

"Ride me, fuck me, Sage," Ari demanded, as he moved her up and down his cock. "That's it."

She gripped his wide, muscular shoulders and gasped as she held his hungry eyes.

"Feel good?" he asked, and she nodded. "Do you like fucking me, Sage?"

"Yes," she cried.

"Clench me with your pussy," he ordered, and she tightened around him, while grinding into his body.

"Oh, God."

"Take what you need," Ari said.

"Ari, fuckfuckfuck." She cried out, her body trembling as the orgasm began and he tightened his hold on her, thrusting harder and faster.

"Jesus." He growled, gripping her head and crashing his mouth onto hers. He released into her and let out a cry that sent shivers through her entire body.

Sage slumped onto his chest, wondering if this was normal to desire someone in such an all-consuming way, and she didn't think she was alone in that thought.

THIRTY minutes later, they arrived at their destination. Sage had tidied herself up and was pulling on her coat when the door opened.

She glanced up as she climbed out. "Oh," she exclaimed.

"I hope this is okay." Ari placed his hand on her back as they both stared at the Seattle Art Museum with its large black sculpture. It was well known to locals as the Hammering Man.

Sage smiled at Ari. "Yes. I haven't been here for years. I'm just surprised."

"Because I don't seem like the history type? Trust me, Sage, history is my forte." He smirked.

She took his offered arm as he led her inside the museum, curious to know more after that comment. He didn't look like a man interested in history. War history maybe.

"It's not open for long, but I thought we could look around before dinner." Ari bought two tickets and directed her to the first exhibition.

"You seem to know your way around," she observed. "Do you come here often?"

His hand slid down her back when they stopped in front of a sculpture. He stood gazing at it a long moment before his eyes slid to hers. "From time to time. It's important to remember the past, don't you think?"

"Yes, I guess it is." Sage looked at the sculpture again. She took in the large quiet space and watched Ari wander around.

In a strange way, he had a similar old-world energy about him. Not old-fashioned, it wasn't that. He had a sort of quiet, solid depth to him that was hard to put into words.

It was just a vibe.

She chewed the inside of her cheek, realizing there was more to him than she'd first thought. Not that they'd had much time talking. Most of it had been spent undressed and pleasuring each other.

And she had zero complaints about that.

She was looking forward to their dinner so she could ask some questions. One thing she wanted to ask about was his accent. He sounded American, but with a blend of other accents she couldn't place. It wasn't horrible, in fact it was sexy and only added to his allure.

"Where are you from?" She spurted out.

So much for waiting for dinner.

Ari turned from across the room and stared at her.

"Your accent. What is it?"

He walked toward her like a predator and took her chin. "I am from Rome."

"Italy," Sage said.

"A long time ago. Come, we will finish with the next exhibit and then head to the restaurant." Ari led her across the room.

She wondered exactly how long ago it could have been given Ari was in his early thirties at most. Her curiosity was deepening, but Sage had to remember this thing between them was just short term. It had been one night initially, but clearly, both of them hadn't quite quenched their thirst.

That was it.

After tonight, she was unlikely to see him again.

Still, the more she watched him, the more questions arose. His gym explained his well-defined body, but he appeared to have great wealth. The way he dressed was more informal than a businessman, but it was expensive.

Then there was the limousine. He'd booked it while she was dressing as if it was no big deal, and the heavy watch on his arm had likely cost the same as a mortgage deposit in some states.

But there was something else about Ari which screamed of wealth. It was less tangible. Sage had seen it in some of the directors at her company. The sharp glint of power in his eyes.

Smart.

Powerful.

Dangerous.

Sage swallowed as her nipples hardened. Ari was a very interesting man, and while she knew this was going nowhere, she found herself wanting to know his life story.

Why was a man so powerful and attractive alone?

CHAPTER TWELVE

He hadn't thought this through at all. Sage was an intelligent woman. Of course she'd have questions. Yes, he could wipe her memory and start shuffling shit around upstairs but that would complicate things if he wanted to spend time with her. And he did.

Why?

Honestly, Ari didn't have an answer. He found Sage extremely beautiful and wanted to know more about her. He also had an irrational need to know if she was eating, sleeping okay, safe, and... single.

To clarify, Ari didn't want another man to get his hands on her.

He had never before felt this possessive over a lover.

Ari took Sage's hand and led her inside Canlis—Seattle's finest dining restaurant overlooking Lake Union, with views of the Cascade Mountains. He wondered if she knew it was one of the top restaurants in the United States.

"Ari," Sage whispered. He glanced down at the tug on his hand. "Everything okay?"

"This is..." She stared at her dress.

So, she did know and was uncomfortable.

"Don't do that. You look fucking gorgeous," he said, pulling her up against him, and cupping the back of her head. "Do I need to remind you how quickly I had your panties off earlier? Twice."

He was treated to one of her beautiful blushes.

"Totally not the same thing. Everyone in there is—"

"Everyone in there is of no interest to me. Do you want to go somewhere else?" He'd paid five thousand dollars to secure the last-minute booking, but if it made her unhappy then he was willing to leave immediately.

"No," she said quickly. "I just wish I'd worn something else. I had no idea you'd bring me to a place like this."

Ari glanced across the water, thinking for a moment. If Sage was going to feel uncomfortable, she wouldn't enjoy it. He ran his hand over her forehead and smiled.

"I'm sorry I wasn't more intuitive about this. I rarely take women out." As Sage shook her head to dismiss his apology, he lowered his mouth to hers gently. Then, as his eyes met hers and their lips parted, he delved into her mind and whispered. *"You look beautiful. You feel beautiful in your designer dress and your every step is one of confidence as we step inside together."*

Sage blinked. A smile formed on her lips, and she took his arm, and they walked inside where they were seated by the window with views over the sparkling lake.

"Mr. Moretti, we have the wine you requested," the server said. "The 1995 Bruno Giacoa Collina Rionda. An excellent classic red, sir."

"Grazie." He slipped into his native dialogue.

"So you really are Italian?" Sage said.

"Why would I lie?" He grinned. "I told you, I'm from Rome."

She'd surprised him at the museum with her question, but his response had been more shocking. Ari had wanted to tell Sage everything. About being born in the Roman era and his home back in 500AD, and his mother and twin brother, and all the things he'd seen along the way.

But he couldn't.

Her questions were normal to ask on a date. Unless you were asking them of a fifteen-hundred-year-old vampire.

Ari wondered what the scientist in her would think of him being the oldest living being on the planet. A shiver went through him. While there were bad scientists in this world who would tear him apart to discover his secrets, Ari would enjoy surprising and delighting Sage and her clever beautiful mind.

Those other scientists could rot in hell. They would never get their hands on him. It was a stark reminder of what he should be fucking doing instead of wining and dining this beautiful human.

He let out a little groan.

If he could take Sage home and tie her to his bed post, he would. He'd love to come and go, pleasuring her at will, making her into his little sex slave. It was unlikely Sage would be submissive enough for that.

He smirked to himself as he lifted his wine glass and watched Sage peruse her menu.

None of them took females into The Institute. Not only was the place full of vampires, weapons, and top-secret information, but his identity had been hidden for centuries.

Now the Moretti's knew he existed.

Still, the less people—or vampires—who knew about the location of the mansion, the better.

So, the rule remained.

It was for everyone's safety.

"So how long has it been since you left Italy?" Sage asked.

"I have been in the United States a long time. I've recently returned from a visit to Rome," he replied, bypassing her direct question.

Sage sipped her wine and stared at him over her glass. "Are you sure you're not a lawyer?"

Ari smirked. "Tell me about yourself, Sage. You have a sister. What about your family?"

"All my grandparents have passed on and neither of my parents had siblings, so we're a small family. Piper and I used to be close." Her gaze drifted away, then she glanced back at him and quickly added, "My mother is smothering but bearable. My father does everything to keep busy outside the house, probably for the same reasons."

"Tell me about Piper."

She shook her head, and he sensed a strong embarrassment rolling off her.

"Sage," Ari quietly demanded, and her eyes met his. "What did she do?"

She took a long sip of wine and swallowed. "She fucked my college boyfriend. The boy who took my virginity. I thought I was going to marry him." Sage let out a dry laugh and shrugged. "So, fuck her, but apparently I'm supposed to forgive her and just get over it."

Ari reached across the table and took her hand. "What a bitch."

Sometimes it was the simple things in life people wanted the most, Ari had observed. Sage needed someone on her side. What her sister had done was terrible. A complete betrayal. It was clear by her last comment that her family was pressuring her to move on so they could sweep the entire thing under the table.

Sage grinned. "Thank you." Then she sobered. "So your brother died?"

He nodded. "He..." Ari had to be careful what he said. "He was married and lived a good life."

"Oh, his poor wife. Did they have children?"

At last count Giorgio had approximately ten million offspring so yes, he'd had a few children. To his mate, only Frances.

"Yes, I'm an uncle." Ari nodded, thinking of Vincent and Brayden, and now little Lucas.

"That's so sad."

"The children are strong. They will be fine," Ari replied, thinking about how poignant this conversation was. He would soon be leaving behind his nephews and a part of him was starting to feel pangs of sadness about that.

While he had walked away from them, Ari had always kept a close eye on the royal family, knowing if something happened, he'd be there. As he was now, with this human experimentation monstrosity.

When the rebellion had risen, he'd known both Frances and Vincent were capable of dealing with them. Stefano Russo—the head of the rebellion—was a fucking dick, but nothing the Moretti royals couldn't handle. When they'd begun blowing up castles Ari had considered getting involved until suddenly the vampire race was exposed to humans.

Things had gone from bad to fucking ugly then, and now here they were.

"I'm sure you're very involved with your nephews."

You have no idea.

"I am now."

Sage raised an eyebrow.

"They are in Italy. I was visiting them."

"Oh, right."

"So, without wanting to sound like Oliver, tell me about your job as a scientist," Ari asked, and grinned when Sage blushed at the reminder of the night they'd all been together.

"It's boring. I'm just a lab assistant."

"Why do you continue working there if it's boring?" Ari asked.

It had confused him watching society evolve into this system of educating people and spitting them out at the end with credentials to work in a job and pay tax for the next forty years or more. That was it. Humans got up, went to work, came home, and ate dinner with their family and repeated it for five days. They had two days if they were lucky to do things they loved in their life, once the chores and shopping was done.

Life might have been simpler and less convenient centuries ago, but people had time to just be. To sit in a field or roam the earth and see nature and all its spectacular beauty.

That wasn't to say Ari didn't appreciate the luxury he now had. He did.

But he had choice.

Everyone had choice.

He saw people completely unaware of these choices after generations of education in this tax system. If there was one thing over his long life he'd seen and knew for sure, it was change.

Change was coming soon. For all of them.

Watching Sage mulling over his question, Ari felt a twinge in his chest at leaving this life knowing she would be navigating that change without him.

What the hell is wrong with me?

Sage lowered her wineglass. "It's hardly a glamourous job like some people have. I've been doing it for years, but I'm about to get a promotion. *That's* exciting."

"Congratulations."

"Well, not yet, but hopefully next week I'll hear back." She leaned forward. "It's top-secret, so I can't tell you anything or I'd have to kill you."

You could try, little minx.

Despite himself, Ari smirked. When was the last time a woman teased him? The more time he spent with this pretty human, the more he liked her. In truth, Ari didn't like many people or vampires.

Life and conversation were so repetitive no matter what damn century you were in.

Aside from Matteo, Ben and a handful of others, Ari had few vampires he could call a genuine friend or confidant. Yet he found himself wanting more from Sage. And dangerously, wanting to tell her about himself. He couldn't, but he wanted to.

Over the centuries, he'd come up with many fake job titles when out with women or in public. He'd pretended to be a stockbroker, artist, landscaper, and a poet. Yeah, that last one had tripped him up. The woman had asked him to write her a poem, so he'd had to wipe her memories.

Ari was as creative as a kitchen mop.

Except when it came to killing assholes. Then he got very creative.

"And how would you do that, my little *stellina*?" he teased. Christ, Sage was turning him into a cheesy Italian.

"What does *stellina* mean?" she asked and, for the first time in his life, Ari felt a tinge of embarrassment.

"Nothing. We should order." He picked up the menu while Sage pulled her phone out of her purse.

"Siri, what does *stellina* mean?" Sage asked the device. Ari frowned, lowered the menu and held her eyes as the digital device muttered away about the constellations and little stars.

She grinned back at him, clearly pleased with her new name.

"You're killing me, *cara*."

Fuck, there it was again.

"Siri, what—" Ari ripped the phone out of her hand, and she laughed. He placed it screen side down on the table between them. "You can search for them all tonight while you're lying between your sheets, wishing my body was on yours."

Sage frowned and he realized what he'd done.

"I have business to take care of tonight, but I will not leave you unsatisfied," he promised, reaching for her hand and flipping it so he could run his thumb across her palm.

She shivered under his touch.

"I think I'm pretty satisfied already after our drive here," she said as he released her hand.

No. Sage was wrong. She would want much more of him by the time he dropped her home. He'd make sure of it.

They ordered their meals and made their way through the wine, learning more about each other. Ari kept to the truth as much as he could.

"So, Oliver works for you," Sage said, and his body tensed. He wondered when she would bring him up and he wasn't prepared for the powerful feeling that arose within him.

"Yes," he replied. "Him and dozens of others."

He saw the heat in her cheeks. Sage had enjoyed Oliver. It wasn't a surprise—the vampire was extremely good looking and an excellent lover. He had a playful spirit many young women were drawn to. Ari wondered if Sage was ready to stop playing out her fantasies or if she wanted more threesomes in her life.

Or was she after something different?

Did she want to experience pleasure from a woman? Or a group of men in an orgy?

He could give her whatever she wanted, except he was beginning to wonder if that was possible. His need to keep her to himself was growing by the minute.

"Where do you live?" she asked, and Ari knew he had reached his limit with her questions. This is where he had to stop her.

"Medina," he answered, knowing she would never find The Institute mansion. The sweeping lakefront property was blocked from Google Maps and extremely difficult to find even if you drove past it.

And if Sage did become a stalker, which he knew she wouldn't, getting past his security system and vampires would make her a walking miracle.

Or dead.

"Fancy area." She was right. It was the most opulent area in the state and home to many well-known billionaires. The difference being, Ari was not known. But he was many times over a billionaire.

"Yes, I like nice things, Sage." His dark eyes roamed over her, and she looked like she was going to purr. He leaned forward. "*Cara*, do you wish to be discreet with the people living in your home?"

He was ready to take her home.

"My roommates?" she asked, eyebrows slightly rising. When he nodded, she shook her head. "No, they're not discreet around me."

He let out a small laugh. "Really?"

Sage shrugged. "Well, to be clear, we need to go into my bedroom rather than use the dining room table tonight and if you were bringing a friend, I might have to think on that."

Ari's eyes narrowed.

"So, you'd like to do that again?"

Sage let out a little cough and looked around.

"Yes or no, Sage?"

If she asked for Oliver, Ari wasn't sure how he'd react.

Bullshit.

He'd fill with fury.

More so because, while Sage was asking him lots of questions, it was more from a place of curiosity. He could tell she didn't see him as the type of man to be in a relationship with. To Sage, he was a man who had fulfilled her fantasy and could do so again.

"Maybe."

Bingo. His instincts had been correct.

This was good, right? He had nothing to offer Sage. So why did he feel like punching a wall?

"But? There's a *but* in there. Talk to me, Sage." Ari pressed, wanting to understand exactly what she desired.

"It's nothing. The experience was new to me and I'm still processing that it even happened." Sage didn't take her eyes off his. He could see she was telling him the truth, but also leaving something out.

Ari hadn't trained thousands of soldiers and worked with the most dangerous, powerful people in the world without knowing how to read both vampires and humans. Lies were complex. They were small and large. They could be right in front of you or hidden deeply, and everything in between.

And the thing about lies and secrets… everyone had them.

Everyone.

Ninety-nine percent of them were harmless. The one percent though, were dangerous as fuck. Which is why he got paid serious money to do what he did.

"Did you like Oliver?" he pressed, knowing he was torturing himself.

"Ari, please." She begged.

"Answer the question. Did he please you?"

She let out a little groan, which shot straight to his cock.

Fucking torture.

"I did like being with Oliver." She replied quietly. "But I didn't like how he left so abruptly. It felt cold."

Feelings washed over Ari. Feelings he'd never experienced before. They sat staring at each other, and he found himself unable to respond.

There was a vulnerability in her eyes, and innocence about how things should go, but regardless, she had bravely voiced how she felt.

Guilt rushed through him, knowing he was responsible for asking Oliver to leave, and not giving either of them the opportunity to finish things properly.

Sage wasn't the kind of woman to have sex without emotions. She wasn't the first human woman they'd come across like this either, but then again, he'd never kicked any of his males out until the female had been completely satisfied.

Did she have feelings for Oliver?

Sage hadn't shown any growing feeling for Ari tonight. There was certainly lust between them, but she'd not asked any of those chick questions about what he wanted in his life. Big red flag there.

Yet here she sat in front of him, filled with vulnerability as they spoke about Oli.

Ari gripped his glass with a tension he knew was about to—

Smash.

Glass exploded around them.

"Oh, shit." Sage jumped up.

"Fuck. Are you okay?" Ari climbed to his feet and pulled her out of her chair with a strength he shouldn't be exerting around humans. Right now, he couldn't give a fuck.

He checked her body for glass.

"Yes. Shit. It just gave me a fright," she replied as the server came running, apologizing as if it was his fault, and cleaning up around them.

Ten minutes later, they were in the back of the limo, heading to her house. This time, Sage was tucked under his arm while he stared out the window, wondering what the hell was going on inside of him.

CHAPTER THIRTEEN

When the limousine stopped outside her house, Sage wasn't sure what to do. Ari had been incredibly quiet since they'd left the restaurant, and she knew it wasn't because he was embarrassed about the glass breaking.

The man was so confident you could polish diamonds on him. On those abs, at least.

"Thank you for dinner," she said as the car stopped.

His dark eyes turned to hers, and his hand reached out and took her chin.

"*La mia luce stellare*, you think I would drop you at the curb? Come." He directed her out of the car as the door was opened for them.

Sage's heart pounded at his use of more affectionate Italian. In fact, she was close to swooning. She had to remind herself this big, tall Italian man was not looking to settle down.

I'm not here to ask you to marry me. Today or any other day. The words he'd said to her when they met.

Plus, she had her *Life List* to follow, and Ari really wasn't her type. Well, except in the bedroom, where he was absolutely everything she could have dreamed of.

Just because he'd taken her on a date didn't mean he'd suddenly become her boyfriend. Sage wasn't going to be that girl and suddenly fall in love with him. Plus, Ari shared his lovers, and that wasn't the type of man she was looking for.

Even if they did begin dating more, because of what she'd done with Oliver, it would be all kinds of awkward. Sage wasn't naïve; she knew some people lived in polygamous relationships. She just didn't know if it was for her.

No. She knew it wasn't.

Sure, from a fantasy perspective, it was hot as hell. She hadn't been lying when she said having both Oliver and Ari the night before was incredible. Her body still buzzed from the memory.

Tomorrow was Sunday, and she needed to finish her promotion application and get on with her life. Maybe she'd date Carl, or maybe she'd meet someone else.

Whatever happened tonight, if he wanted to come in or go home, she had a feeling it was the last time she'd see Ari.

She'd focus again on her life plans.

She crossed her fingers mentally at the promotion coming through next week, then she would give Tom notice. She wanted her home back so she could peacefully watch TV in her own living room and make a meal in her kitchen without having to clean up someone else's mess.

Ari finished talking to the driver, wrapped his arm around her, and directed them up the stairs. Sage pulled out her keys, and he took them and leaned into her ear to whisper, "That meant *my starlight*."

Her body shivered under his touch with need. "Say it again."

"*La mia luce stellare,*" he repeated, his voice thick.

"Very sexy." She smiled, leaning into his chest. "Are you going to come in?"

She just wanted a few more hours with him.

"Is that what you want, Sage?" When she nodded, he unlocked the door. "I cannot resist you."

They quietly made their way into her bedroom, and she turned to him when the door closed. Ari reached behind her, and her dress fell to the floor. With little effort he picked her up and kicked it away. Her eyes followed the garment as she let out a little gasp.

Then she was against his chest and Ari was gripping her chin. His mouth slammed down on hers with so much dominance it nearly blasted the air out of her body.

She clawed at his chest as their mouths hungrily explored each other's. They parted, and her bra and panties disappeared.

"*Scusate, mia cara*, I will replace them," Ari said, taking her breasts in his hands. Sage had no need for his apology. She wanted his mouth on her.

She needed it.

Boldly she pulled out of his arms and his eyes narrowed as she stepped back and lay on the bed. She widened her legs and ran a finger over her stomach.

Who was she?

If this was going to be their last night, she wanted him, and only him, tonight. She would do anything he wanted and make sure she enjoyed every single second of it.

"Sage," Ari growled. He climbed on the bed between her legs, running his fingers everywhere but there. She writhed and twitched and moaned.

"Ari," she begged. "Please."

"Where are your toys?"

Sage's eyes grew larger. "I like the one on your body, thanks."

His lips stretched into a smile. "You will have it, but first I want to play. Now, where is your vibrator? I know you have one."

She attempted to reach beside her bed, but Ari did it for her, opening the drawer and pulling out her purple rabbit vibrator with the clit stimulator.

"Is this what you use? At night, when you are alone?" He slid his fingers through her wetness and turned on the rabbit.

"Yes." She arched into his touch.

He ran the vibrator over her clit, and she let out a little mumbled noise. Over and over her flesh, he circled until he pressed it against her entrance. "Like this?" he said, adding pressure and the tip slid inside. "Do you do this as you imagine a man licking you, lying over you, desiring you?"

She nodded, her heart pounding and body trembling.

Ari slid the device in further, leaning over her as he'd just described, and suckled on her nipple. "And this?"

"Ohgod." Sage moaned. Now it was deep inside her, the clit stimulator on the outside reaching the right spot, taking the pleasure to a dangerous level.

In and out, he slid the vibrator slowly, changing the angle until she could barely think.

"And who do you imagine when you are about to come, Sage?" he asked.

"I, ahh." She couldn't get the words out.

"Do you imagine a man in your mouth and one in your pussy?" Ari asked, changing his position on the bed. "Is that what you desire, Sage? Two cocks, three?"

Sage's lips parted as Ari pressed inside her mouth, never easing his thrusts with the vibrating rabbit.

"I'm fucking your cunt and your mouth, Sage. That's it, good girl, suck me harder."

Ari hadn't pushed himself in deep tonight, just the tip, and she knew it was because he wanted her words. She moaned around his hard, thick cock, then he pulled her off him.

"Tell me what you want, Sage, and I will make your fantasies come true."

She panted. "I want it all. Oh, fuck, Ari, please."

"Is it me you want, *mia cara?* Or another?" He demanded in a possessive-sounding growl as his cock slapped against her lips.

Sage felt completely out of control. Her body buzzed with desire, willing to do anything, but she knew one thing. The only man she wanted right this minute was Ari.

"I want all of you," she cried, "Just you."

He grinned seductively.

"Be honest, Sage. I can have a male lapping your juices while another fucks you. I would be in your mouth and pleasuring your breasts." He growled. "Say the word and I will organize it."

She moaned as he slid back inside her mouth, this time deeper.

"Suck me more, Sage, while you imagine all of them on your body, pleasuring you, fucking you," Ari said, and the rabbit pressed even deeper.

Her eyes opened, and she looked up at him. His eyes were on hers, flicking to her pussy, and he seemed so close to coming.

"Would you like that, Sage? To be filled with cock?"

Sage cried, and her mouth fell off his erection as her orgasm hit. Ari gave her a minute, but then entered her again. "Back in your mouth. Suck me off while I come. Yes, fuckkkk, yes."

Sage came again, this time harder than she ever had before in her life. Before she was done, the rabbit was removed, and her brain zeroed out as Ari lay down and pulled her on top of him.

How was he erect again already?

"Take me inside you, Sage," Ari instructed, and he slid inside her.

Her eyes widened as they connected, and they stared at each other. Ari's eyes were burning with desire, but she saw his possession and a little slice of doubt.

"You okay?" he asked, and she nodded. He ran his fingers over her forehead and moaned.

It felt far too intimate for what they were doing and Sage bit her lip, then clenched around his cock. "Oh, God, Ari, shit."

"Yes baby, you feel so good." He groaned and pulled her down and took her lips in his. As with everything else he did, he fucked her mouth in a passionate kiss.

Then they were on their sides and her leg lifted over his big body. He pumped into her again and again, both of them desperate for more.

"Ohfuckohfuckohfuck." She clenched around him as another orgasm rose within her.

Ari's eyes held hers with such intensity, she felt him in her soul. "Come now, Sage," Ari ordered as he thrust into her, throwing his head back with a primal cry.

THIRTY minutes later, Sage lay with a bunch of Kleenex jammed between her legs, splayed over Ari's enormous body. His fingers were mindlessly running over the top of her ass, and she was trying to stay as still as possible, so he didn't leave.

She wanted him to stay.

She didn't want this to be over.

There had been something more between them. A connection she knew had surprised them both. She'd seen the shock in Ari's eyes and how he'd glanced away from her trying to dismiss it, only to pull her in closer and hold her in ways a simple lover shouldn't.

Finally, he shifted, and she lifted her head off his chest and looked up at him.

"I will stay until you fall asleep," he said gently. "Then I will slip out."

She nodded and lowered her head again.

"Sage." Ari's voice had turned serious, and his fingers dug into her ass a little painfully, but she knew he wasn't aware. "I need to know. Do you want those things?"

Those things.

She knew exactly what he meant. Did she want multiple lovers? Did she want to repeat what she'd shared with him and Oliver and try new things with even more men? While his words had quickly brought her to orgasm, and experiencing it in reality was probably extremely hot, Sage knew it wasn't what she wanted.

Correction. She would absolutely do it.

Just not with Ari.

When she was with him, it was more. More intense, and she only wanted him there. He had different needs. Sage knew she wasn't the woman for him, and while she'd never pictured being with someone like Ari, she couldn't deny the feelings she had for him so quickly.

He wanted someone like Piper. And yeah, that really hurt.

"No," Sage answered quietly. "I'm sorry. It's just not for me." She felt, rather than heard, his sigh under her and figured he was disappointed.

"Go clean up and then we will sleep," he said, patting her bottom, and she went to the bathroom. When she returned, he was holding her phone. "Unlock it and I will give you my number."

Her mouth fell open.

What? Why would he do that? She could see by his expression this wasn't something he did often.

"Are you sure?"

"*Si*," he replied as she pressed her thumb on the button. "I want you to know you can contact me if you need me."

Sage frowned as he punched in his number, let it ring, and handed her back the device.

"You don't need to do this," Sage said, sitting on the bed. "I can look after myself."

He tucked her back in his arms. "Maybe I'm not done with you yet."

"Oh, yeah?" She smiled despite herself. "When do you think you will be? So I can plan around it."

"Hard to say," he replied, lifting her chin to his. "You are a surprise."

Sage's smile faded.

"I know I'm not what you want, Ari. We are very different."

His smile dimmed too. "Oh, *cara*, I am very different from you, believe me. I have lived a very long and unusual life compared to most."

Sage shook her head. "Stop making out you're ancient or something. You are, what? Five, seven years older than me? It's no big deal. How old are you?"

"Fifteen hundred and twenty-two years," he replied, and she laughed. "But I feel much younger."

Sage rolled her eyes. "Well, you're looking pretty good for that age. Keep it up Granddad. And let me know your beauty secret."

Ari pressed her down against the sheets and kissed her. "Blood. Can I taste yours?" He made his way down her neck, nipping it sharply. She giggled and jumped a little, then his knee went between her legs.

"I'm totally fine with that. I have a vampire fetish." She purred, playing along with the joke. "In fact, did you know they're probably a thing? Like, a real thing."

Ari's head lifted. She expected to see disbelief on his face, but didn't find it. Instead, his eyes had turned dark. "Do you really have a vamp fetish?" he asked.

She shrugged. "Sure. Big, powerful vampires—what's not to like?"

He let out a groan and pressed his erection into her. "You need to stop, or I will fuck you again."

Did he think that was a threat because she was totally fine with going again, although she was starting to feel sore. Sage's smile faded as his cock slid through her flesh, teasing and making her wet all over again.

"So, vampires are real?"

"I think it's possible." Sage moaned, struggling to focus. "You saw the news last year, right?" The head of his cock was at her entrance, circling, promising nothing.

"I did. I was told it was fake news."

"Ari, I can't focus when you do that." She arched, trying to take him inside.

"Answer the question and you can have it, Sage." He growled, kissing her jawline and down her neck. "Tell me about the vamps."

"Is this another fantasy thing?"

"Yes. Do you want me to bite you?" He growled and she went silent. The scientist in her wanted to yell, *hell no.* Human mouths contained more germs than any other animal on the planet. She didn't want him to bite her. And yet, the thought of him marking her, making her his in that possessive alpha way they described in vampire novels, was hot as damn hell. "Ask for what you want, Sage, that's how this works." Ari sucked on her nipple. "And soon, because I don't have much time left."

"Yes, maybe just a little bit." She groaned as he licked her neck and then suddenly, she felt *sharper than normal* teeth drag along her veins. "Oh, God."

Sage moaned as his cock pressed harder against her core and the sharpness of his bite increased. Then suddenly he flew off her.

"Fuck," he cried. Her eyes flew open, and she blinked at what looked like extended incisors.

Jesus, she was losing the plot.

Ari wiped a hand over his face, forcing his mouth closed, and dropped his head to her knees.

"Ari?"

"Give me a minute," he ground out.

Sage looked around the room, confused. Then he pulled her against him. "You okay?" she asked.

"I need to leave in a few minutes," he replied. "Sage, we shouldn't be playing with shit like that."

"Sorry," she said, embarrassed, and he took her chin.

"Don't. We were both playing. It's okay. I just don't want to hurt you."

Her heart fluttered. Those words touched her in a way they shouldn't. "You don't believe me, though. About the vampires?"

"Oh, I do," Ari replied. "And because of that, I really need you to forget—"

Next thing Sage knew, she was curled up, dozing off as Ari kissed her forehead, promising to call her.

CHAPTER FOURTEEN

"Dr. Phillips," Xander Tomassi said in greeting, as the video call connected to his head scientist. Douglas Phillips had worked for him since the beginning of Project Callan and was highly trusted.

Xander was in a safe house in Baltimore. The property was surrounded by at least a dozen private military contractors. Not that he could see most of them.

They were protecting him from vampires. Not that he'd told them that little bit of information. It would only put unnecessary fear into them, so he'd given some bullshit story about upset investors. The management of the security firm seemed uninterested, but Xander knew better. They would have done groundwork on him. It didn't matter. No one would find out anything about the actual work he was doing.

Even them.

They were aware they were being tracked and watched by powerful enemies and were doing their job, so Xander was feeling as safe as he could for now. He'd been told it was too risky to head back to Seattle right now, so they'd brought him to the Baltimore safe house.

Xander and a small team had been forced to stay in a very average four-star hotel with terrible service before the safe house had been made available.

It had been torture.

Well, aside from that one night when the receptionist swung by with a complimentary bottle of champagne after he'd expressed what a *great* job she'd been doing. Smart girl had read between the lines and lifted her skirt.

The security team had kept him alive so far, and that was more than he could say for Diego Lombardo. The Italian president had been a large investor in this project; in fact, it was through him Xander had initially met Stefano Russo and learned about the existence of vampires.

He'd despised him immediately—the guy was a narcissistic asshole.

Unsurprisingly, the narcissism had been Russo's undoing.

Revealing himself to Diego in the hopes of forming an alliance to overtake the vampire king, Vincent Moretti, Stefano had dug himself, and his race, into a hole he'd never seen coming. Diego and Xander, on the other hand, had seen enormous dollar signs. It had taken them a while to hatch their plans, but a year later, the project was almost ready to go into execution mode.

Initially, they'd known very little about vampires, but it had been easy to get information from Stefano. The guy loved to show off. He thought vampires were superior to humans and was happy to prove it. So, they'd played the dumb humans while he'd played right into their hands. Even to the point where they included him in some of their plans, where he could be of value. Stefano was blinded by the need to overthrow this Moretti king of his and become all-powerful.

The latter Xander could understand.

Xander had more power than most people realized. The pharmaceutical industry was rife with corruption, and there was little anyone could do about it. All the most powerful leaders and people in the world relied on their financial backing for, well, fucking everything.

Those with the money pulled the strings.

They were the true king-makers.

It didn't take much to follow the money to expose them, but people didn't want to know. Companies like BioZen relied on the masses to continue feeling they were powerless to do anything.

Thank God.

Because if they worked it out, the entire power structure of the world would crumble like a house of cards.

It had always been this way.

Xander shook his head and shivered. Imagine if no one bought into the lies anymore?

It could happen. People were starting to become more aware. It was causing a problem, but he had a solution.

Nearly.

As for Stefano Russo, Xander had been told by Diego that the Moretti royal army had captured him and his brothers. He didn't know enough about the legal system in their race, but he would be surprised if they were still breathing.

Now Xander was on their damn radar.

Until recently, the Moretti family hadn't known anything about him, but they'd discovered and destroyed the Italian laboratory where BioZen were experimenting on a fresh batch of new vampires. Inside had been a bunch of data which had stupidly included his name.

Fuck it.

His team had messed up. There should have been nothing to trace back to him or BioZen. It was why they were on the US army base to start with. The government was an investor and customer.

Not that it was common knowledge across government circles. Obviously, vampires were still hidden from the world despite his attempts otherwise, so he'd had to go along with it.

The Secretary of Homeland Security, Joe Nutler, had explained his involvement with them was highly classified and his small, handpicked team didn't officially exist. Which went some way in explaining why the bust order at the lab in Italy had come directly by the order of President James Calder himself. POTUS didn't know about the BioZen contract.

One day soon he would, and the president would be pinning a medal on Xander's lapel. At thirty-five, he was already very successful, and one of the most senior executives at BioZen. They were hugely impressed with what he brought to the organization, but only two of the directors knew what he was working on. In fact, there were only thirty people in the organization who knew about the project, and they were all under the tightest legal contracts. Basically, they couldn't breathe without permission.

Each employee had been scrutinized and undergone intense background checks, as had their close friends and family.

"Mr. Tomassi," Douglas replied, pushing his glasses up his nose. With his white coat, gray hair, and BioZen security badge clipped to his pocket, he looked every bit the mad scientist. "Welcome back, sir."

He allowed Douglas to believe he was back in Seattle.

"Thank you," Xander replied. "I'd like to progress to the next phase in the project, so let's jump straight into your update, so I understand how things are tracking there."

"Everything is on track here. The new team members start mid-week," Douglas said. "Then we can swiftly move the program into the execution phase when you give approval."

Perfect.

"Excellent," Xander replied. All the months of planning and experimentation on test vampires were about to begin paying off. Their end product would be a series of injections, which they were now ready to test on real humans. If their experiments worked, and it looked like they would, the treatments would make a human body, along with all its senses, much stronger. Around fifty times stronger than the average human being.

What they hadn't been able to replicate from their vampire test subjects was their skill in telepathy. While they believed it was strictly cognitive, they had been unable to truly find the source of its ability. It seemed... and he hated even thinking these words... supernatural.

So Xander was looking for the right neuroscientist to work with them. And by *right* he meant someone willing to park their scruples and contribute to the next advancement in humanity.

Super humans.

"Will we see you in the lab this week?" Douglas asked.

Xander didn't want to scare Dr Phillips with all the details of the risks involved with what they were doing. As far as his team knew, they had US government backing, and it was a secure, top-secret program.

Which it was.

Fortunately, they had the best security and technology money could buy. And they had a lot of money. In theory, no one could get in.

Especially not vampires.

Their teams had done their research and ensured it was as vampire-proof as one could get. Their systems scrambled regularly, sending anyone hacking down a bunch of rabbit holes. They'd also used tungsten to reinforce certain areas around the lab if they did get into the buildings. The steel was the strongest in the world and was able to resist vampire strength.

"Not right now. I'll video where necessary. For now, my priority is setting up the new labs where we can mass produce these enhancers and test a greater number of subjects."

Xander shifted in his chair and adjusted the screen.

"Have you secured a location yet? I'd like to express my interest in leading the next phase. Sandy could take over here in Seattle if you agreed. She's doing a great job," Douglas said.

Xander nodded and tapped his pen to his lips.

Douglas had proved to be an excellent head scientist on this project. He was professional and didn't let ethics get in the way of science and progress. He was the right man for the job.

Plus, he trusted him, and that was a rare trait these days. Especially with his paranoia.

"I should be signing something later today, but it looks like we'll have a location in L.A.," Xander said. "If you can convince your family to move out there, the job is yours."

Douglas let a small smile hit his lips. "Thank you, sir. I'm sure my wife and teenagers will be more than happy with the warmer lifestyle."

He nodded.

"Good," Xander said. "Let Sandy know she'll be stepping into your shoes shortly. I'll get HR to arrange the paperwork."

They ended the call, and Xander began scrolling through his emails. There were a lot of them. The remaining shareholders were uneasy after the news of Diego's murder.

Because it *had* been a fucking murder despite those vampires making it look like a suicide.

While the country grieved his death, the vice president stepped into his shoes, and Xander was left the job of appeasing his investors.

And honestly, he really wasn't great with people.

Diego had been the man for that.

Now he needed to find a new investor to get this lab and the product manufactured. BioZen had only been willing to fund a certain percentage of it.

But who?

CHAPTER FIFTEEN

Sage stared out the window as the bus made its way along Route 520 toward downtown Seattle.

What a weekend!

She still couldn't believe she'd experienced it, nor that she'd had the courage to go through with it. Having sex with two men at the same time had been nothing like she'd expected. Both Ari and Oliver had made her feel gorgeous and sexy, while seeming to gain great pleasure from her own enjoyment.

Her core clenched at the memories.

Not appropriate on the damn bus, Sage. Stop it.

As she shifted, her body and its little aches reminded her the pleasure hadn't stopped there. The next evening she'd spent with Ari had been a big surprise. It had been sexy and intense. She hadn't heard from him since he'd left in the early hours of Sunday morning, and after a little bit of pining Sage had given herself a lecture.

Ari wasn't the man for her. Deep down, she knew that. She had a feeling she could fall for him, and Sage didn't want to do that.

Liar.

Either way, she was ignoring her inner voice and focusing on the positives. First, she'd had a threesome! *OMG*. In a way, Ari and Oliver had changed her. Or rather, they'd brought her out of her sexual shell.

She felt different. Freer and more daring. She'd never thought of herself as gorgeous but, as she glanced down at her body, she realized she'd even dressed differently today. Her cleavage was a little more exposed; her skirt shorter.

It wasn't inappropriate, it simply showed off her slim figure and gave her a few more curves. Heck, she'd been complaining about Piper having all the curves, but she'd been hiding hers under sensible clothes.

Why?

Sage mentally shrugged.

It didn't matter. She now felt seen and adored and wasn't going to hide anymore. Perhaps she'd go online and do some swiping, then go on some dates.

If she got her promotion this week, she'd soon have the house to herself and maybe one of her dates might be a little wild. Not *threesome* wild, rather someone who liked their sex life a little more rum and raisin, than vanilla ice-cream.

Okay, fine, she wanted someone to slam her against the wall, rip off her panties and made her come while she begged for more.

There, she'd said it.

Ari fit that bill, but she also wanted to get married. He didn't. Hell, he couldn't even stay the night and wake up with her in the morning.

Red flag much?

The bus stopped, and she jumped off, swinging her bag onto her shoulder and wrapping her coat around her. There was a flow of commuters scanning to get into the BioZen building, so she slowed her walk.

At least they didn't have swipe cards. No one ever left their thumb at home. The security access level was managed by the Security Office and seemed to be tight—as one would expect in one of the world's largest pharmaceutical companies.

Sage finally got inside and went straight to her office. She was eager to send off her documentation for the promotion even if it did seem eager so early in the morning.

She pushed send and then grabbed her white coat, a little smile on her lips recalling Oliver's tease, and where it had led.

Her colleagues arrived, and the day started.

At lunchtime, she realized she had left her lunch at home.

Greaaaat.

The budget didn't exactly account for buying lunch, but she wasn't going to sit through the day hungry. So, she headed downstairs to the food court.

While the elevator made its way down, she wondered what Ari was doing, once again. Gym stuff, she figured. Had he thought about her? He had said he thought about her on Saturday, so maybe he was.

Why had he given her his phone number if he hadn't planned to text or call? Maybe he'd had his fill?

She sighed.

It didn't matter. Sage had already decided he wasn't the man for her. He wasn't a match to her *Life List* and so it was best if she just let him go and forgot about him.

The elevator opened and Sage made her way to the sushi bar. Her mouth watered at the thought of salmon with avocado and a nice miso soup. Once she saw the display of food, she leaned in closer wishing she could buy here more regularly.

Come on promotion. Please be mine.

She stood straight and went to make her way to the cashier but slammed into a big wall of a body.

Omphf.

"Oh, shit, I'm sorry," she said, hot liquid splashing her white top.

"Oh crap," a familiar voice said. "Damn, it's all over you. I'm sorry."

Sage stared up into Carl's good-looking face and smiled.

Well, what a coincidence.

"It was my fault. I'm so hungry I didn't look where I was going." She wiped her hand over the marks on her top, making it worse. In fact, the brush of her hands made her sensitive nipples harden.

She glanced up and Carl was staring at her chest. Heat flushed her cheeks. She pushed away her shyness and lifted her head to find Carl smirking at her.

"No one will see it under my lab coat." She shrugged

His head tilted. "I rarely see you out of it. You look... different."

"Oh, yeah?" She grinned, feeling cheeky. "Like Superman?"

Carl let out a laugh. "Much prettier than Superman."

She blushed. That wasn't something she was going to be able to stop in a hurry.

"Want to sit and eat together when you have your sushi?" Carl asked, surprising her.

"Yup." She pointed to the cashier. "I'll just—"

"Sure, I'll get us a table." Carl nodded.

Sage ordered her salmon sushi and put her change in her purse as she chewed her bottom lip. Something *was* different about her. The buzz and excitement she was expecting to feel when he showed interest just wasn't there.

She made her way to the table he was waving from, and they sat eating, talking shop to start. Carl worked in the finance team and considered his job even more boring than hers.

"It's not really very glamourous, is it?" She laughed. "What do you say when people ask you?"

Carl shrugged, finishing his miso, and stuffing his napkins inside the recycled cup. "Not much, to be honest. We're pretty hamstrung in what we can say."

She nodded.

Then she frowned.

"What do you mean?" Sage knew they were all under tight confidentiality agreements, but Carl seemed to be referring to more than just that.

"Honestly, I can't say more than that. The things we see, where the money comes and goes from. The profit margins. Sage, it's... I need to stop talking." He leaned back in his chair. Suddenly he smiled. "I'm glad we bumped into each other."

"Literally." She laughed, glancing down at her top.

"You want me to wash it for you?"

Sage shook her head. "No. It was an accident."

"Sure, but it will give me an excuse to drop it off and see you again."

Heat bloomed on her cheeks. "You see me here every day."

"What if I wanted to see you outside work?" he asked, and she noticed a hint of vulnerability.

Elbow on the table, she placed her chin in the palm of her hand and grinned. "Are you asking me on a date?"

"Only if you say yes. If you say no, then I'm being a gentleman offering to wash your soiled top," Carl replied, smirking.

"Okay," Sage said, wondering if Cupid was stalking her. First Oliver and Ari, now Carl. Not that Ari or Oliver were in love with her. Ari certainly wasn't—made clear by the radio silence.

Neither was Carl, but there was a possibility with him that didn't exist with the others. He was the kind of man she could take home to meet her parents and he'd put up with their church stuff on holidays and build a family with her.

Right?

No tattoos—although Ari's tattoo on his chest was so damn sexy, she often found herself circling the unusual Roman clock. Oliver had far more than Ari and, yeah, she had let her eyes wander all over his body when he'd stripped.

Still, her parents would freak if she took either of them home for the holidays.

"That would be nice, but I'll wash my top," she replied with a grin and packed up her rubbish. Carl took it from her and stood, pulling her chair out for her. "Thank you."

See. A total gentleman. Her mother would gush at that.

"Wednesday after work? We can head to the bar down the road."

Sage nodded and glanced at the clock on the wall. "Sounds good. I better get going. I didn't notice the time. See you Wednesday!"

Standing in the elevator Sage stared at the steel doors and felt odd. Like, she should be elated or more excited, but she wasn't. Her mind flashed to Ari, and she pushed him aside, but he wouldn't stay gone.

Ugh.

She knew exactly what was going on. This was simply science. When you slept with someone, the euphoria that struck wasn't real. Well, it was, but it was all a chemical reaction. During sex, the hormone oxytocin was produced in the hypothalamus—*aka* the brain—which made you feel extreme emotions like love and affection. It wasn't called the love hormone for nothing.

Sage knew oxytocin was addictive. People became hooked on the chemical. It went some way to explain why people stayed in relationships when there was abuse alongside great make-up sex.

But it got worse. Sexual arousal actually turned off the prefrontal cortex—the part of your brain responsible for rational thought.

So basically, she was acting like a moron, pining for a man who looked like he'd stepped out of an action movie starring the best-looking Hollywood heartthrob in town.

See? She was nuts.

Still, Carl had asked her out. This was good and it totally aligned with her *Life List*. Who knew where it would lead?

Sure, she didn't have butterflies in her tummy or get that same dangerous erotic feeling she had with Ari, but that was good. At least she knew he wouldn't be inviting another man into their bedroom.

Not that she'd hated it at all. Oliver had been... God, so fucking hot.

She cleared her throat.

Forget them and focus on Carl.

She'd wear something really nice on Wednesday and work out what to talk to Carl about during their date. Hopefully by then she would have heard about her promotion and have something to celebrate.

Wednesday could be a great day.

CHAPTER SIXTEEN

Brayden stretched out his legs.

"I don't like how spread out the team is." Craig grunted and pressed the button on the plush leather seat of the Moretti private jet to recline it.

"Yeah, you look stressed as fuck." Brayden snorted and took a quick look out the window. They were thirty thousand feet in the air, getting close to landing in Seattle.

"Fuck off, you know what I mean," Craig responded. "Especially with the females at home."

Brayden shook his head. They'd been over this a dozen times, but he understood where the commander was coming from.

"It's not perfect, but it was either that or bring them with us and we both know it would've been too dangerous. They're safe at home with Ben, Tom, and Marcus."

Craig returned his seat to the upright position and cursed. "That's another thing. Kurt needs back up. We should've sent Ben with him."

Brayden shrugged. "Or Marcus. It's over to you. Just remember baby Lucas, the queen and Willow remain in Italy. You made the right call. Kurt has the entire black team with him to protect the king."

Willow was his mate and also the princess of the Moretti royal family. It was important to protect the entire royal family, but the new little prince was a priority. Second, of course, to the king. Brayden, as the king's brother, was also a prince and captain of the royal army, so he could take care of himself.

The royal family had expanded in the past twelve months and if Willow had her way, it would again.

It pained him she was struggling with the knowledge it could take up to one hundred years or more before she became a mother. He felt guilty in some ways because Willow had been a human when they'd met and never wanted to become a vampire. Yet, as his mate, she had little choice. Despite the fact he'd given her one. Thank fuck she'd chosen him.

Still, her insistence they keep trying to make another little prince was fine with him.

Craig threw back his vodka on the rocks and let out a groan. "You would have told me if you'd disagreed," he muttered.

"Of course." Brayden smirked down at his phone where he was messaging Willow.

"This is why we need to grow the team," Craig said firmly.

"Yes, but don't go head-hunting my uncles' assassins while we're in Seattle. Not all of them will be like Ben. We have a good team of lieutenant commanders we can develop. They deserve the opportunity to train and apply. There are some capable vampires in that team. Dozens of them."

Unlike human military forces, vampires lived for a fucking long time. Brayden had realized for a while their development program was a bit shit. It wasn't like any of them were going to jump ship and go work somewhere else.

Working for the king in the royal army was a huge honor. They only accepted strong, hard-working vampires. Times were changing.

Once their greatest enemy was Stefano Russo and the vampire rebellion. Now, they'd cut off the heads of that snake, and while the rebellion still existed it was, for the most part, dealt with. Today, they were looking at an enemy far greater than they'd faced before.

Humans.

Which was laughable.

Vampires were predators and could snap the neck of a human in under a second should they choose.

Or drain their blood.

Or many other deadly acts using vampire powers and strength. But they didn't.

Okay, fine, some did—there were monsters in every animal kingdom after all—but as a rule vampires wanted to survive peacefully living and fucking just like humans, alongside them.

Now, though, with technology and science, humans had become more deadly and deceitful than ever.

Humans had recently discovered vampires existed. The populace thought it was bullshit thanks to Craig's mate, Brianna. The Moretti royal team now had a handful of social architects keeping that narrative running constantly, buying them time to hunt out those who were working to destroy their race.

Scientists.

Brayden would like to think fear was at the heart of it, but it wasn't just that. It was greed and power. As they had for many years, pharmaceutical giants had discovered an opportunity to capitalize on something, no matter the cost or ethics.

Vampires had no need of medicines, so he had neither compassion nor gratitude for the industry that, from his perspective, only perpetuated disease. Not healing.

It seemed like madness to him.

Still, Brayden's deep hatred came from the fact these humans had kidnapped and experimented on his vampires under torturous conditions.

The vampires they had saved from a laboratory in Italy had shared little, understandably, of their experiences. Their screams as they slept had said it all.

Brayden had one big rocket up his ass to stop these mother fuckers.

Now they'd discovered Ari Moretti—his fucking uncle—was still alive, Brayden felt their chances had increased substantially. Ari ran a business called The Institute—a private security company with deadly vampire assassins.

Ari had trained him when he was a young vampire. He was the best. Back then, Ari had been captain of the royal army, and one day Brayden had voiced his desire to fill his shoes.

Soon after, he had gone missing.

The vampire had been a confidant to him in many ways. He'd had a good relationship with his father, Frances, but it was Vincent who had been close to the king. Brayden didn't resent it. His brother had shadowed their father from the moment he could walk, learning to become a great king.

It was a role Brayden did *not* want. He had wanted to be a warrior like Ari.

When they weren't training, Ari was telling him about the past, how he knew King Giorgio and what it was like seeing the vampire race grow in size.

Brayden had listened and asked questions. Ari had been as patient with those as he had in his training. It had been

Ari who had pointed out to him he was a powerful alpha and should be mindful of his dominance with Vincent becoming the king.

His uncle was right. Brayden had realized he was more alpha than his brother. Back then, Frances had raised it with him just after he'd had spoken with Ari.

"I don't want to be king or dominate my brother. I want to stand at his side and support him when he reigns," Brayden had said.

"Then tell both your father and brother soon. Don't let fear fester," Ari had said, and when he looked back now, Brayden realized Ari had been speaking painfully from experience.

If only he had known Ari had been his uncle and not just a vampire working for his family.

He had loved him and now he knew why.

Brayden had recently spent time with his uncle in Italy before the vampire returned to the United States last month. Later tonight, Brayden would finally get to see where Ari had lived for the past few hundred years while he thought him dead.

Both he and Craig were looking forward to seeing the training center and discussing how they could work together.

First, they had to find Xander Tomassi and bust this fucking operation wide open.

Ben, Ari's former head assassin, had shot the Italian president dead after learning he was one of those responsible for kidnapping his new mate, Anna, and allowing her to be experimented on. He now lived and worked for the royal family in the Italian castle as an SLC—one of their most senior warriors.

"We could be here a while," Craig said.

Brayden dropped his phone after wishing Willow goodnight—okay, fine, he'd instructed her on using her vibrator with minute details—and nodded.

"It's a possibility," he said. "If that happens, we will bring them over."

Craig nodded.

Keeping Craig and Brianna apart was like trying to split two raging tigers. He knew it was the source of his friend's anxiety right now.

"Willow, Anna, and Kate need Brianna's pragmatism in our absence. Keep that in mind," Brayden said. Well, not Kate. The queen had a sound head on her, but she was a new mama bear right now and rightly so. Her attention was on Prince Lucas.

"I need Brianna's mouth on me, but whatever."

Brayden laughed. "Two weeks, man. Can't you survive that long without it?"

Craig looked him dead in the eye. "No. Not really. But you have to live with me for those two weeks, so you be the judge."

Christ.

He hadn't thought this through well at all.

Craig smirked and reclined his seat again.

"Asshole." Brayden said.

A middle finger lifted into the air.

CHAPTER SEVENTEEN

*M*other fucking fuck.

Of all the people on the planet, Ari had to meet Sage. Who worked at goddamn BioZen?

As a fucking scientist.

Sage hadn't given him the name of the company, but it had only taken one call to his tech team, and they'd confirmed it. Ari felt like a fucking fool for not connecting the dots, but when she'd mentioned the secret project team she could be joining if she got the promotion, a lightbulb had gone off. Well, that, and when she mentioned vampires.

And wanting to be bitten.

Fucking hell, he'd nearly sunk into her neck and her pussy in one swoop.

It hadn't taken much for his team to do a background check and find out who she was. Their access into BioZen's systems was limited, but they had found her HR file: Sage Roberts, laboratory assistant.

So, she hadn't lied to him about anything.

Ari was pretty sure Sage was about to step into enemy territory. The promotion was for a department called Project Callan, which was so locked down and impenetrable even his team couldn't smash the walls. It didn't take a mathematician to put these two equations together and get *Mother fucking fuck.*

Ari had promised to call Sage, but it was now Monday, and he still had no idea what to do about this.

Her file indicated she was the top contender for one of the three positions, so Ari was confident she would be notified in the coming days she had the job.

Sage would be thrilled.

He knew enough about her now to know she would be celebrating the new job and give her roommate notice. How would she feel about what she learned they were doing in this project team?

Sage had expressed excitement about vampires, but Ari knew the difference between a female who had a vampire fetish—she wasn't the first he'd met—and a scientist with a curious mind for discovery.

No matter which way he looked at it, in a few days, Sage would be working in the department doing experiments on vampires.

Fury simmered in his veins.

He shouldn't care. She was just a female he'd been fucking. Nothing more.

Yeah, right.

He was already far too emotionally involved with the human than he should be. And fucking hell, he'd nearly bitten her. It was no big deal—it wasn't like doing so would change her or make her his mate. It didn't work like that. But getting the taste of her on his lips was dangerous because Ari knew he'd want more.

Everything about Sage made him want her more.

Fuck!

Now he was about to find out who she really was. Fictional vampires might excite her, but when she faced running experiments on a living one, how would she feel?

It was killing him to know the answer.

The reason he hadn't acted yet was because he knew his relationship posed an opportunity he was struggling to accept. Sage was now an asset. An opportunity to get inside BioZen and destroy this entire operation. They could use her to further their information and gain access to BioZen's systems at the very least.

Ari ran his hand through his hair as he paced the floor in his living room.

There was no question here. He had to do this. If any of his vampires had this information and didn't share it with him, he'd bust their fucking ass. Still, it meant putting Sage in potential danger and even though he was yet to learn where she sat ethically with this project, he would never let anyone harm her.

Ari knew his feelings toward her were unusual, but he refused to read into it. He'd been down that track before. Yet, when Sage had shown her feelings of Oliver at that restaurant, he'd literally lost control, smashing the wine glass.

Ari was an ancient vampire. He didn't lose control.

He *was* control.

Now, instead of possessing the sexy little female, he had to be patient and let things unfold this week. Once they knew her position on the BioZen experiments, Ari would decide what to do with her.

Because if Sage chose to take part in them, she then became his enemy. If she was, she and all of them would die.

Fuck.

Ari thrust his hand through his hair and growled loudly. He'd already punched two holes in his walls, so was trying to keep from needing more repair work.

Yeah, he knew he was ignoring the signs.

Ari had given up hope of ever having a mate, and while he was trying to keep his head straight, his response to Sage was powerful even he had to admit there was a possibility.

There would be no way he could kill his mate.

Could he simply take her now and turn her? *Sure.* Would he? *No.*

Sage was an asset first and foremost, until he knew for sure she was his mate. That would take for his eyes to show the vampire black ring around his iris.

Plus, he wanted to see what Sage chose. It was the only way he would ever know the truth. He'd long ago stopped trusting blind instinct when it came to deciphering another's set of morals.

Words meant nothing.

Actions told you everything.

Ari ran a hand through his hair again. God, he wanted to know what Sage thought. Would she comfortably lay him out on a table and stick chemicals in him to discover how he worked? Or would she walk away from the job, unable to stomach it?

She's a fucking scientist, moron, of course she'd do it.

"Sir," Matteo said in greeting after knocking. Ari turned and the man's smile faded. "What's wrong?"

Ari shook his head.

If there was anyone he could talk to, from a personal standpoint, it would be Matteo. The man was seven hundred years old and had worked for him for over two hundred of those years.

Matteo knew everything. Well, most things.

He was more than just an employee who took care of him, from his wardrobe to serving his meals. Back in the last century his title was man servant, or rather vampire servant, but they'd never bothered with titles. Matteo simply assisted Ari with life shit while he was busy catching the bad guys.

Washing his briefs was the last fucking thing he needed to worry about when things were getting ugly. Plus, Matteo seemed to be able to pack a suitcase like a goddamn magician and never forget a thing.

Every time Ari waved him off and did it himself, he'd have to buy a goddamn toothbrush and pair of socks. Fifteen hundred years and he could fight any male on this planet to the death and he couldn't pack a fucking toothbrush.

"I find myself in a pickle, Matteo," Ari said, planting his big body in an armchair while the vampire shut the door.

"Do we need the Macallan?" Matteo asked, raising a brow.

Ari smiled and shook his head. "No. I'm not sure it's going to fix this one."

Matteo sat on the end of the sofa nearby and crossed his legs. He was a tall vampire, slim compared to the warriors within the mansion, and very discreet. He was an unmated vampire and seemed to be more at peace with it than Ari.

"It's a female," Matteo said, surprising Ari.

Ari's gaze flew to his. "Why do you say that?"

Matteo shrugged, and a small smile hit his lips. "They are always the most complicated, I have observed."

Ari decided to share his feelings and inner thoughts. It wasn't something he did often, but he needed to talk.

"Her name is Sage. She could be our enemy, but my body aches for her in ways I've never felt before," he said. "I don't want to assume anything here, Matteo, but if she is my mate, this is a bad situation."

Matteo's brows rose.

"What?" Ari asked, frowning.

"Is this the female you shared with young Oliver recently?"

Ari nodded.

"He had a taste, that was all. I found myself unable to let it proceed." He glanced down into the fire roaring in front of him.

"That does raise some questions, sir." Matteo nodded. "You are right to be considering her."

"It gets even more complicated. I've just discovered she works for BioZen." He rubbed the scruff on his face.

"Oh, dear," Matteo replied, his English accent from centuries past creeping to the surface.

"Yeah."

"You will know in time. When will you see her again?" Matteo asked.

"I have no plans. I'm terrified I'll change her or kidnap the poor girl," Ari said. "I want to protect her and shake her demanding answers."

They both sat staring at the fire. Ari wasn't expecting Matteo to solve his problem. Just his steady presence as he talked was soothing.

"When is the prince arriving?" he asked.

"I'm not sure. Shall I call Travis?" Matteo asked, referring to his team manager.

"No need. I'll telepath."

Trav—when are our Moretti guests arriving?

He'd left it with his team to co-ordinate with the royals on their arrival and requirements while in Seattle.

They will be here in about an hour.

Okay, get the team together in the logistics room in ten.

Yes, sir.

He turned his eyes back to Matteo. "Is the mansion prepared, and all employees briefed?"

He had no doubt, but as the director of The Institute, it was his job to ask these questions and make sure everything was as it should be. While he was looking forward to hosting the royal, the work they did for private clients around the world needed to remain highly confidential.

Matteo nodded, then pressed his lips together in a small smile.

"Speak your mind," Ari said.

"I am happy, sir, that's all. You have always spoken affectionately of the prince."

It was true. Brayden and Vincent were his nephews, but Brayden had been a true soldier who had won his heart. As a little prince Brayden chased after him with his wooden sword desperate to train. Ari had taken great pleasure in playing with the young prince, knowing it would serve him when he got a real sword of his own, but also enjoying time with his relative.

Not that the prince had known Ari was his uncle.

Brayden had been cheeky but skilled, even as a little ankle kicker—which he used to his advantage. He had fond memories of them wandering fields after training and talking about the old days. As the prince grew, his playful nature remained, and he attracted a lot of females.

Yes, Brayden was a playboy, but he was also strong and dominant. More so than any other vampire Ari had ever trained. Including his father and brother.

Stronger than Ari? No.

His blood was pure Moretti. No one, since Gio had passed, was stronger than Ari Moretti.

Now he was hoping to mend the broken tie with Brayden. Four hundred years was a long time to disappear from his nephew's life. He'd had good reason, but no living soul could truly understand what he'd suffered. Especially Brayden who Ari knew he'd hurt.

ARI stepped into the logistics room, looking around at his senior team of assassins. Most people would crap their pants—even if they believed them to be human—if they knew what these predators were capable of.

Most were heavily tatted up and cut like the deadly warriors they were. Their heights and weights differed, but all of them were fast, powerful and wouldn't hesitate to take the shot.

He knew that for sure, because he'd trained each and every one of them, and hand-selected them for this team.

Travis, assassin and team manager, was responsible for a lot of organizing, which was akin to herding cats, poor guy. Oliver was his head assassin and second in charge.

The vampire gave him a quick nod, which he returned as he took his seat at the head of the table. He pushed the seat back to prop his ankle on his knee.

The room hushed.

He'd have to speak with Oliver soon. The guy deserved to know why he'd dismissed him. Ari just didn't have an answer for him.

Yet.

"'Sup boss," Jason asked.

In total, he had thirty highly trained and deadly assassins. On his senior team, in addition to Oliver and Travis, were the four team leaders: Jason, Alex, Logan and Elijah.

At any point in time, his assassins were out doing jobs around the world, so it was rare they were all here at The Institute at the same time. Still, the mansion was a bustling hive of other staff from housekeeping, tech teams, chefs and kitchen staff, admin vamps, and so on.

He also had engineers, mechanics and weaponry experts keeping their equipment top notch, pilots and air crew all located here and around the world.

Most were vampires, with a few humans for jobs they needed done in daylight. The latter were completely unaware who they worked for.

Ari pushed a few buttons on the panel in front of him and the lights dimmed, and a screen fell from the ceiling.

"Prince Moretti will be here within the hour," he said, and a bunch of heads nodded. "And as you know, joining him is the commander of the royal army, Craig."

"Big fucker," Oliver said.

Ari nodded without turning. Oliver was right, Craig was a big vampire. And powerful from what Ben had told him. He had questions about that, which he'd ask the prince one day.

"I've met him," Alex said, smirking. "He won't remember me though. Well, he might remember my cock."

Ari glanced up as the others gaped at Alex. "Explain."

"I attended one of the prince's infamous orgies when I was traveling to England a few centuries back," Alex said, "Don't ask me how I got an invitation, but I slipped in, and it was... yeah, fucking hot."

Jason whistled. "Fuck man, you never told us that. I want details."

"Later," Ari said, remembering those days well. "Let's stay on topic." Then he added, "And please tell me I don't have to—"

Alex smirked. "I won't say anything. Unless he does."

"You know he's mated now, right?" Logan asked.

"To that gorgeous redhead? Yeah, the entire vampire race knows who Brianna is," Alex answered.

"Yeah, don't fucking mention that or you will no longer *have* a cock," Ari said, shaking his head.

"He can try."

Ari dropped his hands. "Listen, I've trained you all to be arrogant assholes for a reason. You are the best," he said. "But there are a few other vampires who are stronger and faster in the world, and you are all about to meet them. So put your cocks back in your panties, boys, and don't piss them off."

He held their eyes firmly.

The last thing he needed was his team upsetting Craig or Brayden. They deserved respect.

"Not to mention Brayden is your prince and Craig is the goddamn commander." It was a role Ari had held for centuries. "So, you will give them the same respect you give me."

"Got it," Elijah said.

"Now, on that. Just a reminder, the majority of the work we do at The Institute is for private clients. While we're collaborating with the royals to flesh out the BioZen criminals, we need to ensure our clients' information remains classified. Our other objective is to find the…" He hated using the term, but they had no name for the vampire. "First test subject."

Cue the angry mutters.

Ari pointed to the screen and their heads turned. It was a photo of a plane on a runway.

"Talk to me about this," he ordered.

"We found Tomassi's plane," Oliver said, referring to Xander Tomassi, the BioZen pharmaceutical executive they had tried to capture when he slipped through Ben and Oli's fingers in Italy.

"Location?"

"Baltimore," Oliver said. "We're tracking his movements but keep hitting roadblocks. Dude has the money to stay hidden. It's making it difficult."

"He knows we're onto him," Alex said.

Yeah, but they weren't. *Fuck it.* They needed to get inside the pharmaceutical company and destroy the labs, the data, and any trace of vampire experimentation.

And the assholes involved.

The problem was the company was a huge global operation, and the labs seemed to pop up and disappear all the time. They'd also been unsuccessful for months in finding the first vampire who'd been taken.

And all of them were feeling the pressure and emotions around that.

Knowing one of their kind was being tortured and fuck knows what else didn't sit right with any of them. Especially when they had the ability to help.

The royal army had destroyed the lab in Italy with the help of some human intervention, which Ari still wasn't completely clear on. The king, Vincent Moretti, had powerful connections which he and Gio had forged right from the beginning and seemed to be long lasting—even if it was handed from leader to leader or down through a bloodline.

Ari was hoping the king would loop him in more on Operation Daylight. The team forged to evolve vampires into human society, but so far, Vincent had kept a lot of the details to himself. As was his right.

Still, war was Ari's forte, not politics.

Frustrations aside, he knew they had the technology, resources, and determination to beat these evil fuckers. It was just a matter of time.

Time being the issue.

They didn't know what BioZen was up to, but it wouldn't be good. Ari knew now the humans had got a lot of information from the now deceased rebel leader Stefano Russo and that gave them a really good head start.

Meanwhile, life had dropped a cruel gem in his lap.

His little *stellina.*

Ari knew he had to share this intel with his team. And now. His molars ground and fangs threatened to spring out of his flesh, and he ran his hand over his jaw.

He turned to face the room.

"Oliver and I met a woman recently. Sage Roberts." Ari glanced at the head assassin who blinked, giving himself away.

He tried not to resent Oliver for enjoying his time with Sage, but he did.

Sex was a big part of a vampire's life. They fucked freely until they mated. From time-to-time, vampires chose to commit to one sexual partner but it wasn't common.

What was common was for the males in this room to share females and have group sex. They had little time between assignments, so if they hit the bars and found one or two they liked, then everyone was invited.

Ari glanced down at the table, imagining Sage sprawled out, her cream flesh ready and willing to be pleasured by all the males in this room. His fists clenched even while his pants tightened.

He wanted to please her, while keeping her to himself.

You know. So nobody died.

"Was she delicious?" Jason asked.

"Very." Oliver smirked. "Not quite virginal, but inexperienced enough to be tight and—"

"That's not where I'm going with this." Ari growled, his pants tightening further. "We've discovered that Sage works for BioZen."

"Jesus, really?" Oliver said, his eyes widening. "Oh, crap, the fucking lab coat."

Alex whistled. "She wore a lab coat while you fucked her. That's hot." Alex shifted in his seat.

God's sakes.

"Sage was not wearing... look, she works for Tomassi's company as a lab assistant. The tech team is monitoring her accounts and email. Alex, I want you and two of your team on her tail. For now, we keep an eye on her."

"What do you think she knows?" Oliver asked.

"She's up for a promotion. In a top-secret division. I'm sure you can all work that out," Ari answered.

Oliver cursed.

"So we track her," Oliver said, nodding. "This is actually perfect. We put a tracker on her and now we can get inside the organization."

Ari had known this would be the next step. He just didn't know how he felt about it.

Yes, he did.

He fucking hated it.

Tracking Sage would entail putting a chip just under her skin so they could follow and hear everything in her world.

"Correct. Sage Roberts is now an asset. We need to do what's necessary to access systems inside BioZen," Ari said, clenching his jaw.

Jesus.

He had no solid proof she was his mate, and the fact he wanted to teleport into her bedroom and take her in his arms, burying deep inside her, likely meant nothing.

Zip.

Nada.

Nothing.

Ari forced his feelings back and focused on the job. He would arrange to visit Sage one more time, plant the tracker on her and then say goodbye.

"I'll do it," Oliver said, and Ari froze.

Like fuck.

Oliver would plant the tracker and his cock while he was at it. Ari wasn't born yesterday.

Let me say goodbye while I do it. Oliver telepathed. *I never got to finish what I started.*

Ari wanted to fly across the table and rip Oliver's head off.

No.

Yet even as he replied, Ari knew it was a sound excuse to see Sage again and it was better he keep away from her. If Ari went, it would only form more of a bond between them—something he needed to stop. He held Oliver's gaze and nodded.

"Any other intel before we jump into our client work?" Ari asked. "Travis?"

Everyone shook their heads and tapped on their devices, pulling up their usual agenda. For the next hour, they went through their jobs while Alex, Elijah, Oliver, Jason, and Logan gave updates on their teams out in the field.

Business as usual.

If you called being a private security company with vampire assassins normal.

The room emptied at the end and Oliver stayed behind, as Ari had expected.

"Did you see Sage again?" Oliver asked.

Ari didn't answer to anyone, certainly not Oliver, but he deserved an explanation. Had he seen Sage again? Yes, he had. Every gorgeous inch of her.

"Yes."

"Fuck. And you're okay with me planting the tracker on her?"

"No."

Oliver nodded in acknowledgment. "But you can't do it."

Ari shook his head, then stood and walked to the window, watching as the dark sky began to lighten. "No," he said. "You need to know this is dangerous for you. I can't tell you how to do this job or not to touch her, but I asked you to leave for a reason on Friday night."

"Is she your mate?" Oliver asked. It was a fair question, but not one he was going to answer.

He turned. "We are not having this conversation. Plant the tracker and remember she's an asset."

"I'm not going to let her get hurt," Oliver said.

Ari walked a few steps until he was directly in front of the vampire. "She's not yours to protect." He growled. "If you touch her, you do so at your own peril, do you understand?"

"Are you forbidding me?"

Ari's head screamed. If he made that claim, it would change everything. He couldn't. Sage was an employee of BioZen. She was an asset. Nothing more.

Fuck.

Ari understood Oliver's need to protect her. All his assassins were dominant alpha males. There was no way they would sit back and let a female get hurt, especially one he'd been sexually active with in the way Sage and Oliver had on Friday.

He'd made Oliver his head assassin because he trusted him. Ari gritted his teeth and snarled at Oliver. "Get the job done."

Oliver turned to leave.

"Oliver," Ari said. "You would be wise to keep the details on how you do this to yourself."

The vampire nodded and walked out of the room.

In a few minutes, the shutters would lower, and the sun would rise, closing them in safely from its deadly rays. Sage would go about her day unaware of the decision he'd just made, which would change her life.

She'd wake and again there would be no phone message from him. Would she care?

At some point this evening, after she finished work, Oliver would bump into Sage, and he would plant the tracker on her. She'd be embarrassed to see him, so it was the perfect plan in many ways.

The tracking device had to be fitted under her skin in order to be undetectable. You didn't need to get someone naked or fuck them to insert it, but he was quite sure Oliver would. Ari would do the same thing if he was in Oli's shoes. Sage was a sexy woman he'd been cut short with, and he had no doubt Oliver was eager to sink into her again.

Ari couldn't stake a claim to Sage.

He could kill Oliver, but that wouldn't be helpful.

He just needed to keep himself busy.

Brayden and Craig would arrive any moment, so Ari headed to his office to prepare.

CHAPTER EIGHTEEN

"Your Highness," Ari said, taking the last few steps of the stairs to greet Brayden.

"Ari." The prince stepped forward and they slapped each other affectionately on the side of the arm and gripped. Both reflected the power from their Moretti blood.

"Commander, welcome to The Institute," Ari said, turning to Craig.

"Great place you have here," Craig replied, his expression one of respect, but Ari saw he wasn't letting his defenses down. Craig would always protect the prince first and foremost, and fuck niceties.

Ari respected the large vampire as he watched him take in every single detail around him. Ari's lips stretched into a small smile. "You have nothing to be concerned about here. You're guests. The prince is family," Ari said, then waved them into the room ahead of him. "Please join me for a drink and we can discuss what you'd like to see and then get down to business."

He poured them all a whisky, and they sat around the fireplace. All three of their large bodies took up too much space. The testosterone levels were off the chart.

"When Ben first showed up, I knew he'd been trained by someone of great skill, but I couldn't figure out where the hell he would have done it, outside the royal army," Brayden said, shaking his head. "You popped into my mind, but of course, we thought you were dead for over four hundred years."

"I want to see this training center," Craig added.

"I have nothing to hide. The only things off-limits are my private client files and data," Ari said. "After all this time, it is… good to be reconnected with my family."

Brayden lifted his eyes to him, and a thousand words went unsaid.

They both looked away.

Oliver. Join us.

"Your files are safe—we have no interest in those. We're in the United States for the same reason as you. To eliminate the vampire program run by BioZen and any other fucker involved," Craig said. "But if you have a gym I can use while we're in Seattle, that would be awesome."

Ari grinned as Oliver stepped into the room.

"Oliver is my new head assassin," Ari said, nodding to the vampire.

"We've met," Craig said dryly.

Ah yes, the two had met in Italy during the stakeout on Tomassi after Oliver had busted Ben out of the royal prison. The job hadn't gone as planned for either side, especially when Ben and Oliver had made Craig, Marcus, and Kurt give chase across town. They had lost their tail and Ari wasn't sure if the commander was impressed or pissed.

Oliver grinned at Craig, then greeted the prince. "Your Highness."

"Nice to meet you. Ben says good things about you."

"Only because I know too many secrets about him. Keep an eye on that troublemaker." Oliver laughed.

"I am," Craig said, nodding.

"Oh, please. You two are BFF's these days," Brayden teased as Craig turned his head slowly and raised his brows.

Ari pressed his lips together in a smile.

Brayden had always been a cheeky son of a bitch, and he was pleased to see the spark within him had not faded. There was a strong bond between the prince and commander and Ari knew it had served them well working together. Ben would fit in well with them, and that made Ari happy.

"You want to see the training center?" Oli asked, pointing his thumb over his shoulder. Craig was on his feet before the words had left Oliver's lips.

"Yup."

Brayden choked on his whisky. "It's been less than twenty-four hours. Do you have ants in your pants?"

Craig walked to the doorway and shrugged. "I have... stresses. Plus, I want to play with all the guns and shit."

Ari knew exactly the type of stress the vampire was talking about. He'd seen males separated from their mates, and it wasn't pretty. The little he'd seen of Craig and Brianna together was enough to show how extremely possessive and passionate the vampire was in relation to her.

Once mated, there was no one else in the bed despite how promiscuous one had been prior.

An image of Sage lying under him came to mind. His eyes darted to Oliver, knowing the vampire was going to see her in a few hours.

Ari grit his teeth.

"We'll catch up with you," Brayden said, giving Ari a quick glance, and he nodded.

"We won't be long. Go play with the metal." Oliver and Craig took off eagerly, and the commander began firing off questions.

"Hope you've got a big budget. Your commander is going to have a big shopping list when he leaves here," Ari said, laughing. "Another?" He walked to the crystal whisky decanter.

Brayden laughed and accepted the drink. "You know we do. Whether he gets all the toys is up to Vincent."

The Moretti family was one of the wealthiest on the planet. He knew because he'd helped create the wealth. Then he'd walked away and created his own empire. Nowhere near the royal family, but it wasn't to be scoffed at.

"Is that true?" Ari asked, following Brayden who had walked over to gaze out the large window which looked out across the mansion grounds.

"What?"

"That everything is Vincent's decision," Ari clarified.

Brayden glanced at him. "He's the king."

Ari turned back to the window, nodding. From what he'd observed, the two brothers were very close. Perhaps even closer than when he'd known them.

"He rules differently than your father," Ari said.

"Yes. Times have changed. The world has changed." Brayden sipped his drink. "We changed."

Ah.

Of course, they did. Beheading your parents changed a person. "I nearly returned. Then," Ari confessed.

Brayden stood staring outside, saying nothing for a long time. Then he turned. "I fucking hated you when you left." There was ancient fury in his eyes, held back only by his inner strength.

"I know."

"And that day. Fuck, Ari. Do you know who I wanted to talk to after I had to goddamn slice my father's head off?"

Ari swallowed. "I'm sorry."

Brayden cursed and tossed back his whiskey. "Did you know about their promise?"

"No," Ari said immediately. "Frances and I were not close, and it was clearly a private agreement between your parents. You must understand that now you're mated."

The prince was silent as he nodded, and they both reflected back to the deaths of the king and queen.

Brayden turned, and Ari faced him.

"What happened? Why did you leave? I know what you told Vince and I in Italy, but what has this been all about?"

Ari held the prince's stare for a long moment, his heart beating. Rarely did he let himself think too long about the past and his deep pain. Leaving his family, despite his reasons, had been the most difficult decision of his life.

"You must understand, little prince, there is no one like me on earth. I am the oldest living being. Gio and I experienced something no other has, or likely ever will. We were human once."

Brayden blinked at his use of the affectionate term from long ago.

"Together, Giorgio and I created this entire new race of beings."

Brayden shook his head. "Why was your identity hidden?"

That was the fifteen-hundred-year-old question.

"Look back on history, Brayden. Kings are born to power. It is their birthright. Usually, they're riddled with fear of being killed or someone threatening their throne." Ari turned back toward the window. "Gio was the only one able to procreate. Over time, he got used to his position of power and didn't want to share it."

"He said that?"

Ari shook his head. "That's the thing about time. Words are stretched out, recommendations given rather than orders. It was a case of *perhaps we shouldn't confuse vampires by telling them you are a Moretti*, so they are clear who the king is." Ari grit his teeth as all the feelings and memories came flooding back. "My role in court lessened slowly and one day people forgot I was a Moretti."

Brayden cursed beside him.

"Your father had even more fear. No, don't worry, I know he was a good king, but you and I both know I'm a far more powerful vampire than your father ever was." They turned to face each other. "As are you, Brayden Moretti."

"Shit," Brayden said and dropped his glass on the table nearby. "So, you left instead of challenging him?"

Ari let out a laugh.

"No. I never wanted the throne, just as you don't. Do you remember me telling you to make your thoughts clear to your father and brother?"

Brayden nodded. "You were protecting me?"

"Yes."

"So why? Why the fuck did you leave?"

"Imagine a strategy being put into play now, or in a few hundred years, to stop the race from acknowledging you as a Moretti," Ari said, sitting back in his chair, his arms splayed out on the frame.

"Fuck that," Brayden cursed.

"It's more difficult with technology. I dare say impossible, but you'd be surprised what people will forget when told."

"Vincent would never do that."

"No. I am pleased the two of you are so close. The king knows you're no threat, but if he did, things could change."

"They won't," Brayden said firmly.

Maybe.

But the prince had asked a question, and he hadn't answered it yet.

"Losing my identity and having no purpose was slowly killing me. One day, I overheard a conversation between your parents, which I won't repeat. I knew I could no longer stay in the castle, or in the family, and so it triggered my departure. Despite everything, it was still the right thing for me to do," Ari said. "I want you to keep that story to yourself."

Brayden nodded. "Of course. Do you know why you have never mated?"

"I don't know."

"And if you do?" Brayden asked.

Ari shook his head. "It may never happen. I have no answers now, just as I never have," he replied honestly. "Just like you, I do not desire to sit on the throne, but I am an original, Brayden. If I mate and have children, it will be a new line of vampires. Neither of us can deny that. It would be the will of God."

Literally.

But Ari could never share that with anyone. Not anymore.

The prince stretched his arm along the back of the sofa, glanced at his boots, and let out a groan. "Jesus. I don't want us to be enemies, Ari. I don't fucking want that."

"Neither do I," Ari replied. "And hopefully Vincent doesn't either. There are multiple human royal families across this planet. There's no reason we can't do the same. If it ever became a possibility."

"So, you would?"

Ari stared at his nephew, choosing his words carefully. Sage may be a potential enemy, but a sliver of hope had emerged within him that she could be his mate. He didn't know for sure, but for the first time in his life it was a real possibility.

If not, Ari was happy to depart this world.

But if she was, Ari wanted to plant a seed within Brayden's mind, which he knew would be repeated to the king. If there was one thing Ari had learned over the years, it was to make change one little step at a time.

"I am done hiding my identity, little prince. I am a Moretti. The remaining original. The time for that to be acknowledged is upon us."

The prince cursed.

CHAPTER NINETEEN

Brayden wandered through the halls of the mansion, taking in his uncle's home. It was huge, even for a mansion, with the tightest security he'd ever seen. Craig would be having a field day, and hopefully not beating up Ari's team too much.

He grinned.

Then his smiled faded and he ran a hand up the back of his head. Their conversation had been heavy as fuck. Ari's confession played heavily on his mind.

"Through here we have our logistics room," Ari said, opening a door and showing him inside. "Not much to look at with the screens off, but we have all the bells and whistles."

Brayden had been heavily involved with setting up their operations rooms across all of the Moretti castles, so he knew exactly the whistles and bells to which Ari was referring.

"You have satellite?"

"Three."

Whoa, okay.

"Friends in high places," Ari added. "Humans fuck up often, so it's wise to tap into those little mistakes. It's amazing what a little adultery pays."

Brayden raised a brow and grinned.

After a quick tour of the living quarters, they headed to the training center, and he found himself excited to see beyond the two enormous black doors. An eye scanner greeted them, and Ari stepped up. A laser flashed three times across his retina, then the doors whizzed open to, well, Assassin Disneyland.

It was the size of a football field.

"Jesus, Ari. You built this?"

"Yup." Ari nodded. "Hey, we built castles back in the day. This was easy."

Brayden stepped in further, taking in everything.

"Over here we have the gymnasium which you are both welcome to use while visiting," Ari said. "The track allows the teams to run at vamp speed in private—as you know, cardio is an important part of training."

"I remember." Brayden laughed. "I hated it."

Ari grinned and thumped him on the back in a fatherly way. How the hell hadn't he realized Ari was family?

"Yeah, but it paid off," Ari said, and they walked further into the room where a boxing ring was set up. Next to it was a dirt space he knew was for sparring.

Brayden's heart began to race, and Ari glanced at him. On the wall hung a wide variety of swords he had no doubt were in optimal condition.

"Boxing?" Brayden asked, glancing away from the shiny swords which called to him.

"Yeah, it's best to let them beat the fuck out of each other in there and release tension." Ari smirked.

Brayden laughed. "Smart."

He'd have to talk to Craig about that. They often had issues with testosterone overload with their soldiers. It was a common thing among vampires.

His eyes darted back to the swords. His uncle tossed one across the space, and Brayden caught it with ease.

"Game?"

"Absolutely." Brayden grinned, ripped off his jacket and pushed up the sleeves of his long t-shirt. By the time he looked up metal was on its way.

Clang.

"Don't ever look away from your opponent," Ari said.

Fucking hell. He'd forgotten Ari didn't mess about. Give the vampire a sword, and he turned into the devil.

"I couldn't even undress?"

"If this was war, you'd have no head."

"Fine," Brayden said, lifting his sword once more as they danced back and forth on their feet.

Soon they had a crowd.

Smash.

Clang.

Brayden met strike after strike, but the other vampire was damn strong and soon he had a bit of a glisten on his forehead.

"Concede?" Ari challenged him, swiping low.

Ah, no.

"Don't think so, old man." Brayden smirked. He caught the tip and flicked it. Ari leaped, flipped, and the sword was back at Brayden's chest before he could take a step.

Ari grinned and stepped back.

"Well, young prince, perhaps it's a good thing you are here. Time to brush up on your skills." He winked as Brayden frowned.

"How the hell did you do that?" Brayden asked, giving Craig, who was laughing, the bird.

Ari took the swords and handed them to a vampire who had run over to collect them. As Brayden had expected, every single weapon in this place was kept in optimal condition.

"How?" Ari repeated, then led him over to another area of the training center, this time with Craig, Oliver and another two vampires he didn't recognize. "The same way I did when you were a boy, when your father was a boy and when your grandfather and I were young, and I was a soldier in the Roman army."

And that was the only explanation Ari had ever given him. Then and now.

Brayden was introduced to Jason and Elijah, then Alex and Logan pushed through the door to join them.

"Show the prince our big weight area," Ari said.

"Your Highness, this way," Oliver said, giving him a nod.

Ari halted and pulled out his phone.

"If you will excuse me?" he said. "I will join you for a meal in the dining room in a few hours. Please help yourself to anything. The offer for accommodation still stands."

"Yeah, I think I'll just camp out in here," Craig said. "Who wants to spar in the ring?"

Brayden pressed his lips together, holding back a grin as the five powerful young vampires all froze. He shared a humorous glance with Ari.

"See you for breakfast," Ari said and left.

Brayden noticed Ari had never bowed or lowered his head to him, as other vampires did. He never had when he was younger or as he'd grown. It had never occurred to him until now.

Now he knew why.

Brayden was secure in his role as prince of the Moretti royal family, but after today, he had a strong sense the ancient vampire was taking back his position of power.

The one that had never been acknowledged.

His loyalty would always be with Vincent—their bond was unbreakable—but he could understand Ari's position and hoped all of them could exist as one family.

Somehow.

Brayden wanted his uncle in his life.

Aside from the damn vampire pulling on his heart strings earlier, Brayden could see a huge benefit in them integrating their operations and sharing intel. Vincent was a pragmatic king and had already shown he was open to a relationship with Ari by allowing them to spend time at The Institute.

Or rather, he hadn't stopped them.

Now, after his conversation with Ari, Brayden was concerned. He would relay it to Vincent and then give him time to process it.

Ari may pose a threat to them one day. Maybe not today, or in two hundred years, but one day he might, and it was something they had to consider.

It all hinged on whether Ari mated.

Unless he truly was destined to never have a mate.

CHAPTER TWENTY

*R*eally? *Not one message? Not one… ugh, it doesn't matter.*

Sage shifted the bags on her hips and pulled out her key.

I don't care.

She had a date with Carl on Wednesday, so why was she thinking about Ari? It was clear he wasn't going to call, so it was better to just let it go.

Tony and Teresa had been suspiciously vacant since Sunday morning when they'd asked if she was having company over again. Which may or may not have been as a result of the loud sex she'd had with Ari.

"Yes, we'll be staying in," Sage had lied, and by early afternoon the two of them had left to stay at Teresa's for the night. She had no regrets.

"Shit." Sage nearly dropped the bags of groceries she'd bought on the way home, as she reached into the lock with her key.

"I gotcha," a familiar voice said at her elbow.

Shocked, she did drop the bags this time, but Oliver caught them, giving her a ginormous grin.

"Oliver. Hi." Her face heated.

"Oh, I've missed those pretty pink cheeks." He ran the back of his fingers over her cheek, which Sage figured had now turned bright red.

"Are you going to invite me in?" Oliver asked.

"What are you doing here?" she asked. "I mean, it's nice to see you, but—"

"I lost a key, and it's kind of important, so I thought I'd check it didn't drop out of my pockets while we were enjoying ourselves the other night."

"Oh," Sage said. Talking about it standing out in the street felt totally uncomfortable. She pushed the key into the lock and opened the door. "Sure, come on in."

Oliver placed the groceries on the table and looked around. Then she watched him wander over to the dining room table. He turned and gave her a wink. "So how are you doing?"

"Good. You?" She smiled.

God, he was gorgeous.

He was just as she had remembered, but his thighs were larger, or perhaps they just looked larger in the blue denim. His chest, though, was just as solid and broad. Her fingers twisted in front of her while wanting to touch him again.

It was so confusing that she could feel this way even as part of her was dying to hear from Ari.

And then there was Carl.

He didn't make her feel this way at all. No butterflies, no racing heart, no twitching fingers.

Oliver bent down and looked under the table. "I'm very good. I, well, not so good. I need this key."

Sage frowned and walked over to start helping him look. "Is the key that important?"

Crouching, Oliver looked so out of place. His large thighs were stretched so taut in his jeans she couldn't tell if he was semi, or fully, hard. She licked her lips as she took in his giant body like he was a melting ice-cream.

"Eyes up, sweetheart." Oliver grinned.

"Sorry." Sage smiled, embarrassed. God, it was so inappropriate of her to be staring at him like this.

"And yes, this key is very important, it turns out."

"What does it look like?" she asked.

"Key-ish."

She dropped onto her knees in front of him. "Oli?"

"Yes, Sage?" He smirked but tried to be serious.

"Is there really a key?"

"Why else would I be here?" Oliver asked, reaching out to brush her hair from her shoulder. "Can you think of a reason?"

Sage's eyes darted around the room, then back to the gorgeous man in front of her. Oliver was different to Ari. Playful, cheeky, and dangerously so.

"Why did you leave?" she asked, suddenly, and Oliver slid to his knees, bringing them closer.

His eyes darkened. "I had no choice, but I'm here now because I had to see you again," he replied softly. "Do you want to finish what we started?"

Sage swallowed and tugged her lower lip between her teeth. She was so confused.

Why hadn't Ari messaged her? He'd said he would. And why the hell did it feel like she was cheating on him being here with Oliver?

And what about Carl?

Oliver brushed her hair off her face, and she felt her panties moisten.

Oh God.

"You're thinking about Ari," Oliver said.

She nodded.

He slid his hand around the back of her neck and lifted her to her feet. Sage felt mesmerized by Oli's size and presence. She wanted him, there was no doubt, but this entire situation was confusing.

"Sage, look at me," Oliver said and lowered his lips to hers, lifting her and carrying her into her bedroom. "I've been thinking about doing this since the moment I left."

Oliver's jacket dropped to the ground.

"Tell me to go and I will."

His hand went behind his head, and he ripped off his t-shirt.

Holy shit.

Sage had seen him before, but the entire night seemed like a blur. Oliver had a lot more tattoos than Ari and was slightly shorter. Which still made him tall as hell. His muscles were incredibly defined and golden.

"Touch me," Oliver said, and with no hesitation she reached out and ran her hand over his abdominal muscles.

"You are so hard."

"Oh baby, you have no fucking idea," Oliver ground out, closing his eyes, then he popped the button on his jeans and slid the zip down.

He was commando.

Out popped his cock, and Jesus, it was beautiful.

She licked her lips without thinking and Oliver groaned, cupping her face. "Yeah baby. You can have it all. But first, let's get these off."

Oliver lifted her off the ground and her clothes seemed to vanish in seconds. He nudged her onto the bed and pushed her back, spreading her wide.

"Oli," she said, half-sitting.

"Yes, gorgeous?" He slid his fingers into her pussy. "Fuck, you are soaking."

"What about Ari? Is this, okay? I mean, I haven't talked to him." Sage felt like an idiot.

Oliver watched her for a moment.

"Are you okay with it?" Oliver asked, leaning into her pussy and with his tongue licked her in one long delicious sweep.

Sage moaned and lay back, not bothering to answer. There was no way she could say no to Oliver, and it was how she'd met Ari. Neither of them had committed to one another, so she was free to date and sleep with whoever she wanted.

As was he.

She just...

"I wish he was here, too," she said finally, and Oliver moved over her, his cock eager at her entrance.

"If you want me to stop I will," Oliver said, "At any point. But fuck Sage, I really fucking want my cock inside you. Tell me you want that, too."

She couldn't lie.

Sage nodded, arching into him. "God, I really do."

Oliver pressed inside her and they both let out a loud cry. He began to move, his eyes on hers, as he thrust hard. "Fuck, you are gorgeous, Sage."

God, and so was he.

Sage gripped his biceps, well aware this was fucking. There was no love involved, as the two of them enjoyed the way they made each other's bodies feel incredible.

Yet with Ari...

Stop Sage, it's over.

She was on her knees with Oli wrapped around her when she came and felt a sharp sting on the back of her neck. She jumped, but his fingers found her clit and all thought vanished from her mind. Oliver pulled them down to the bed and rolled onto his side, catching his breath, and he smiled down at her.

"Would you look at that? I found the key."

Sage let out a small laugh. "How am I the key?"

Oliver stiffened and tilted his head, then lowered his mouth to hers in a kiss. "Incoming."

She frowned. She hadn't heard anything, but when she turned her head, there was someone standing in the doorway.

A very large and devastatingly handsome someone.

"Hello, Sage."

CHAPTER TWENTY-ONE

Ari locked his gaze on Sage.

If he looked at Oliver, he was likely to do something he regretted. As Sage began to sit, he held up a hand. "Don't move, you look fucking gorgeous just as you are."

He wasn't lying, she did. She looked like a fucking goddess.

Despite the overwhelming need to possess her, Ari didn't want to make Sage feel guilty for what she'd done. In some ways, he'd known the two of them would need to get this out of their system.

He finally glanced at Oliver, who was making no plans to move. Smart vampire. He was waiting for instruction and gauging Ari's reaction. Unfortunately for him, Ari wasn't going to show him how he truly felt.

If he did, Oliver would be dead.

Ari had to take responsibility for this situation. He could have stopped Oliver from touching Sage, but he hadn't. Therefore, he had no right to rip the guy's head off. And Oli was his best assassin.

The entire situation was fucked up.

Sharing females was something they did regularly, and he'd refused to admit she was, or could be, his mate.

Oliver didn't deserve to lose his life today.

Tracker's in.

Good.

You want me to go?

That's up to Sage.

Na man, it's up to both of you. Fuck Ari, you should have said.

Okay, so maybe he wasn't hiding his feelings as well as he thought.

Don't. I want her to decide.

"When did you get here?" Sage asked. "Wait, how did you get in?"

He looked over his shoulder and lied. "The door was unlocked. I just walked in."

Ari had listened to the entire thing and then teleported inside her house because there was no creature on earth able to stop him from being there. He needed Sage to know he cared and hadn't disappeared from her life.

Despite everything, he couldn't stay away, and that was a big fucking problem.

When he'd heard her begin to moan, he'd barely held himself back, but then Sage had said she wished he was there, and his heart had burst open like a giant dam.

"Damn, I'm so charming you forgot to lock the door, Sage," Oliver teased.

Ari held her eyes and knew he had to stake his claim on this female. He was ready to be inside her again, but it was time for her and Oliver to say goodbye.

This time, as lovers, forever.

His eyes darted to Oliver.

I'm going.

Say goodbye properly this time.

Oliver wrapped a sheet around Sage and dressed while Ari removed his jacket and leaned against the door. He knew she was confused about what was happening, but she would soon know.

"Thanks, gorgeous," Oliver said, planting the last kiss he'd ever get with her on her lips.

"Um, thanks back." Sage grinned, returning his kiss.

"Back in a minute," Ari said, following Oliver outside. They stood on the sidewalk.

"Where is it?"

"Back of her neck," Oliver answered, then glanced out across the street. "You listened, didn't you?"

"Yes."

"And didn't stop me."

Sage may be his for eternity, or not. If she was, once the mating bond kicked in, there was no way he'd have allowed it. But this was how their relationship started and he'd seen in her eyes at dinner on Saturday night a need for completion with Oli. Ari was wise enough to let it unfold.

Oliver had needed it too, and it had been the right opportunity to plant the tracking device.

Ari hadn't been able to stay away.

"I did it for her," Ari replied. "I've been alive long enough to know you can't possess another being."

Oliver stared at him for a moment.

"But you want to. Possess her, that is," Oliver said, then tensed at his reaction. "Fuck, Ari. Don't fucking kill me for saying that, but someone has to."

Ari turned for the door.

"Go home."

CHAPTER TWENTY-TWO

Piper sat in a car across the street from Sage's house and watched the harem of men go in and out.

Okay, fine, two men. But still.

Who the hell were they?

She had met Ari *whateverhisnamewas*, and now there were two men were standing on the sidewalk together.

Maybe it was because she was an investigative reporter for *Seattle Daily News* or she was just a protective sister, but something didn't feel right. For starters, Sage had never dated a man like Ari before. Her sister was pretty, for sure, but the man was a walking Adonis.

Now suddenly there were two of them?

What the hell had Sage gotten herself involved with?

Piper narrowed her eyes as Ari walked back into Sage's house and Number Two walked to a silver car, which looked as if it cost more than her house. He climbed into the driver's seat, and as it pulled away from the curb, she saw the badge.

Maserati.

Jesus Christ. These men were wealthy.

Perhaps she worked with them at BioZen?

Piper snorted.

In no universe did scientists look like these men. Not hers, nor Sage's.

Piper pulled out and followed the car. Unsurprisingly, she found herself in a more affluent part of Seattle. Keeping a distance, at least two cars behind, she wove through the traffic. Soon they arrived in Medina and the houses turned into mansions. Mansions into estates.

Yup, she knew this was where all the billionaires lived. So what the heck was Sage doing hanging with dangerous-looking rich dudes?

Drugs? No way.

She slowed as the car turned into a driveway and enormous gates opened. When they closed, she drove slowly past and took in the number on the post.

1199 Medina Coast Road.

Well, that gave her something to work with.

CHAPTER TWENTY-THREE

Ari walked back inside Sage's house and locked the door. He dead-bolted it. If her roommates wanted back in tonight, they were shit out of luck.

Sage was still propped up against the headboard with the sheet wrapped around her. Her auburn hair was wild and tossed off her face.

Goddess.

Her face lifted when she heard him, and she smiled uncomfortably. Observant, Ari noticed her weak smile didn't reach her eyes. He'd hurt her but there was no way she would tell him.

Ari sat on the bed. "*Mia stellina.*"

"Am I?" Sage asked.

"Yes." Ari ran his thumb over her cheek and smiled.

"Yet you happily let me sleep with your friends."

"Not anymore," Ari replied softly, but firmly. "You both needed to do that. To finish it."

"And now? Why are you here?" Sage asked, and he saw the frustration and vulnerability on her face.

Ari had no answers for either of them. In a few days, she could be his enemy. Or his mate. He was just as confused as Sage. Tonight, they had no answers, but he needed to be with her.

"For you," he said truthfully.

"Why?" Sage asked. "Why? What are we even doing, Ari? You show up randomly and it feels so intense with you, but then you disappear. I just don't get what this is."

He stared at her, unsure of what to say.

"I have a date," she suddenly declared.

Who the fuck with?

His eyes narrowed, and he felt his fangs itch. "Why?"

Sage frowned. "What do you mean, why? It's what people do."

"Cancel it," Ari demanded, knowing he had no right. "God damn it, Sage. I want to claim you as mine, but I can't."

He needed to stop talking.

He needed to get up and leave.

"Are you married?" Sage asked, her brows bunching.

"No. There is no one else," he said firmly.

Stop talking and leave her.

"So you want me, but you just want to fuck me?" she said.

Ari tilted his head as he ran his hand over her cheek. If only she knew he was a vampire. Fucking is what they did. If she was his mate, they would be doing a lot of it. She was trying to analyze him as if he were a human man.

He wasn't.

Not anymore, and he hadn't been for a very long time.

Ari wanted to take away her anguish, but he wouldn't lie to her.

"I always want to fuck you, Sage. Being inside you is absolute paradise. But there can be no one else in this relationship." He tugged the sheet down.

Her lips parted as it pooled around her hips, exposing her breasts. Ari ran a thumb over them as she moaned. He pulled the sheet right off her and pulled her down onto the bed, spreading her legs. Then he stood and began to undress.

"Arms up." He wrapped his belt around her wrists.

"I need to touch you," Sage said.

"You will. Right now, I need to have full control, so I don't *lose* control." Ari ran his mouth over her body until he came to her pussy. Then his tongue was inside, claiming and pleasuring her.

Sage writhed against his mouth until he knew she was on the edge.

He climbed over her and wrapped her thighs around his, leaning to take a nipple in his mouth. When he released his belt, Sage wrapped her arms around him and their mouths collided.

Fuck.

He thrust inside her long and deep, and together they cried against each other's lips.

"Ari, you feel so, God, I don't know," Sage said, her eyes burning with emotions he didn't understand.

"Feel all of me, Sage. Take all of me." He growled, thrusting deeper and faster, surprised he was able to hold back his vamp power and not hurt her.

He'd never hurt her.

Not if he could help it.

She gripped him so tight, just as Ari had wanted her to for days. As he went deeper, hot walls clenched his cock, and he let himself fly. His balls tightened and fire flared through his shaft as he filled her.

Collapsing, Ari pulled her out from under him and, panting, Sage snuggled into him. His heart raced from exertion and unexplained emotions.

Mine.

No, he couldn't claim her. Not yet. Or maybe never, but right now it was clear he couldn't stay away from her and didn't want to. Yet he had to step away and let her return to BioZen while he painfully waited to hear if she would become his enemy.

Sage leaned into him, and he kissed her gently.

They weren't done.

Ari pressed inside her again and moved rhythmically within her, enjoying the feel of her as their eyes remained connected. Neither of them were seeking release, they were simply relishing in the feeling of pleasure and connection.

Sage looked like a damn goddess, and he wanted to wrap her in his arms and never let go. It struck him that in all the kabillion years he'd lived, he had never done this with anyone.

Ever.

At some point he pulled out and Sage dozed off. Ari discreetly checked his watch.

Boss. It was Oliver.

What's up?

I was followed home from Sage's.

By whom?

Well, you're not going to believe this, but she has a sister and... well, it's best you get over here.

Shit.

He absolutely believed it. What the fuck was Piper doing following his god damn assassin?

Where are you?

Oliver gave him the address, which wasn't far. He had no car, so it would be a simple teleport.

I'll be there in five.

As he moved, Sage rolled over and snuggled her ass into him. He groaned, not wanting to leave, but he had no choice.

"Sleep well, *Bellissima.* I will see you again soon." Ari kissed her cheek.

"'K," Sage mumbled in her sleep.

FIVE minutes later, he was standing outside Piper's house. It was easy enough to find because Oliver's Maserati was parked outside. Wait, was that Alex's bike?

Let me in.

The front door opened, and he followed Oliver up the steps into a living room that looked the complete opposite to Sage's. Where hers was a mix of modern and comfort, Piper's was bright and starkly modern.

The two sisters were different in every way.

Piper turned and stared at him. "Who are you, Ari?" she asked accusingly.

Alex stood with his arms crossed, leaning against the kitchen counter. He had a smirk on his face.

"What happened?" Ari asked, turning to Oliver.

"She must have been outside Sage's house. I noticed her following me a few blocks from the mansion."

Ari turned back to Piper. "Why are you following my men?"

The female raised her brows at him with a ton of attitude.

"Answer my question."

Piper shrugged at him this time and he glanced at her bound wrists.

"Alex's handy work," Oliver said, nodding at the other vampire. "She was getting all slappy."

"You were kidnapping me!" Piper snapped.

Oliver widened his arms. "This is your house, sunshine. If I was going to kidnap you... never mind."

"You wouldn't have the balls," Piper snorted.

"Don't try me, sweetheart," Oliver growled.

"I'm not your sweetheart, asshole."

Ari watched the interaction with interest. Weird. Oliver was usually much more, well, charming, with females. Piper had gotten under his skin, which didn't surprise him.

"Okay, okay, tone it down, you two," Ari said, taking in the scene around him. Piper's top was pulled tight across her breasts and the buttons strained to get loose. It was made worse because her arms were tied behind her.

He could see both Alex and Oliver were hyperaware of the sexual energy Piper was emitting. The high kitchen stool she was sitting on pushed her short skirt up and all of them could see it was inches away from showing off her pussy.

Ari shook his head.

This wasn't good. The last thing he needed was Piper talking to Sage about this and thinking they were a bunch of kidnapping sexual deviants.

Okay, so the last bit she kind of knew already.

"I'll ask you one more time, what were you doing following Oliver?"

Piper glanced from male to male, her intelligent eyes taking in her options.

"You won't hurt me." She held his stare.

He took a step closer and crossed his arms. Ari was a powerful vampire, and there was no way Piper was immune to him. Even powerful human men couldn't ignore the predatory power that rolled off him. He gave her ten points for effort, though.

Ari watched her blink but push away her fear.

"I was going for a simple drive through the neighborhood. Batman over here thought I was following him. Not my problem."

"Batman." Alex snorted.

"Shut it," Oliver snapped, then turned to Piper. "Listen Barbie, you *were* fucking following me. Why?"

Fire blazed in Piper's eyes as she glared at Oliver.

Whoa.

This needed to stop now. "Untie her," Ari ordered.

"I didn't tie her up," Oliver snapped.

Ari raised a brow. His males never refused an order. Oliver looked away quickly.

"Let me," Alex said, pushing away from the bench. He purposely stood in front of her, stepping between her thighs and reaching behind her. It took him an unreasonably long time—given he was a vampire and could shred the thing in seconds—to untie it.

"Alex." Oliver growled.

He stood back as she shook her arms.

"Criminals. Who are you all?" Piper spat at Ari. "If you're planning to hurt my sister, you won't get away with it."

And there it was. The reason she was following Oliver. Ari smiled and Piper knew she'd given away her motive.

He uncrossed his arms and plunged them into his pockets.

"You want to know if I am a danger to your sister? That's an admirable quest," Ari said, and meant it. Especially given the answer was yes. He was a very big danger to Sage.

Far greater than anyone in this room understood.

"Then tell me your full name," Piper said, rubbing her wrists.

"Ari Moretti. These men work for me."

He had to respect the sassy human for going to such lengths to protect Sage. Given their history, he was surprised. He had a feeling Piper was reaching out to her sister to make amends.

Unfortunately, she'd chosen the wrong mission.

"What was *he*," she pointed at Oliver, "doing at Sage's house?"

Oliver coughed.

Yeah, no one was telling her the answer to that. Not the fucking part, or the tracking chip he had implanted in the back of Sage's neck.

"Are you a cop?" Ari asked.

"No, why? Are you a criminal?" Piper asked.

Ari laughed.

"No. How about a lawyer?"

Piper narrowed her eyes. "No. Are you a mafia boss?"

Alex snort-laughed and Ari had to hold back his own laughter.

"Is that an actual job title?"

Piper shrugged, "Sure. I guess."

Ari grinned. She was a sassy female for sure, but he couldn't help but begin to like her. Not in the same way he liked Sage, not even in the slightest. His feelings for Sage were off the charts.

"I'm an entrepreneur. I have a private gym. A very private gym with a very private clientele. These men work for me. When people go sniffing around our property or follow us, we take it very fucking seriously." Ari's voice turned serious. He was warning her off. The last thing he needed was a stupid human getting in the way of things right now.

"That sounds dodgy as fuck and doesn't explain why you were both at Sage's house so late at night. How did you meet her?" Piper asked.

"What is your goddamn problem, princess?" Oliver snapped. "We're friends with Sage. Do you stalk all her boyfriends?"

She narrowed her eyes at Oliver.

"Are you her boyfriend? Or is he, her boyfriend?" She directed her eyes at Ari.

Okay, this was going nowhere, and Ari was getting pissed. He delved into her mind.

"So, you're a journalist," Ari exclaimed as her eyes widened.

"Well, that explains why you can't keep your nose out of other people's business," Oliver said, shaking his head.

Ari let out a sigh. He'd had enough of the banter. "Go. I will see you at home," he ordered Oliver and Alex, without taking his eyes off Piper.

Piper's eyes flashed to Oliver. Then she snarled at him, and Ari smirked.

"Later, princess," Oliver said, giving her the bird.

"Asshole," Piper responded.

Alex and Oliver disappeared down the stairs and he waited for the door to close then began walking slowly around the room.

"You have no reason to be worried about your sister." He lied once more. "She is important to me." A truth. "And to my men." Another truth, but for reasons Piper would never know or understand.

"Sorry if I don't believe you," Piper said. "There is something going on and I'm going to find out what it is."

No, you are not.

"Why is it you think your sister is incapable of having friends and a boyfriend such as ourselves?" Ari said, cringing at the term. "Sage is a beautiful woman and while she may not be as sassy or bold as you, don't mistake those things as weaknesses. She is courageous and vulnerable, which makes her sexy as hell."

Piper stared at him.

"If you think she is weak, you're wrong," Ari added.

Piper frowned. "What, do you think you can read my mind?"

"Yes." He nodded. Over the years, he'd found telling the truth was easier for him and most humans never believed him, anyway. Just as Sage hadn't when he'd told her the truth about his age.

"Well, those things may be true, but I know you aren't committed to her."

She had him there. He wasn't. He had never committed to any woman, and unless Sage was his mate, he wouldn't.

"Sage hasn't asked for commitment," he replied truthfully. "Nor have I offered it."

"And Oliver. Has he fucked her too?"

"You will need to speak to Sage about that," Ari answered, impressed with the female's intuition.

Piper walked across the room toward him. He narrowed his eyes. What was she doing? She stopped inches from him, and her lips parted.

"So, is that what you guys do? Find women and fuck them?" Piper undid a couple of buttons on her shirt, and it was clear she had no bra. Her nipples were itching to pop free of the material.

"Walk away, Piper," Ari ordered her.

Piper reached to the side and unzipped her skirt. It slid to the floor. No panties. Ari's cock hardened as he looked down at her shaved pussy. There was no way any male could remain placid in this situation.

He could easily fuck her.

Ari took a step forward until she backed up against the sofa.

"Is this what you want, Piper?" Ari asked. "To hurt Sage again?"

Piper's eyes widened, and she pushed him away. "I wanted to see what you would do!"

"Sweetheart, I could have thrust inside you before you said no. Don't play with fucking fire you can't put out." Ari growled. "Get dressed."

Piper pulled up her skirt and her shirt closed.

"You have nothing to concern yourself with. Sage is a grown and intelligent woman," Ari said. "I will make sure she isn't hurt."

Piper crossed her arms.

"You're not on her *Life List*." She huffed. "So don't go getting any ideas. You aren't someone she will marry."

Ari blanched.

Her fucking what? Life List?

He kept his expression neutral. "You have no idea what your sister wants, or what I want," Ari said, getting in her face. "Stay away from my men. Next time, I won't come to save you."

Piper reared back.

Shit.

He needed to get out of here.

Piper was a naive human, and if he was bonding with Sage, this sassy brat was going to poke him until he potentially snapped. She had no idea Ari was close to ripping anyone's head from their body for even hinting Sage couldn't be his.

Ari was beginning to strongly suspect she was.

Which meant the next few days were going to be fucking hell.

CHAPTER TWENTY-FOUR

Ari walked down the hallway toward the tech office when he returned to the mansion. He'd received a message that they were ready to brief him on the full investigation on Sage.

This was the team who would listen to her every movement and sound. A part of him—a dark part of him—was pleased he could check she was safe and know where she was. Knowing his team would listen—not so much. If he knew Sage, and he was beginning to think he did, she would pleasure herself in the morning.

His jaw clenched.

There was nothing he could do about that.

He pushed through the door and found a handful of the team leaning over a monitor. "What's up?"

They all stood, and the one sitting swiveled on his seat.

"Mexico." Darren, his head tech, spoke. "We're just surveilling the Pratt case. Think we've found the missing girl."

He turned back to the screen when Ari nodded, clicked a few buttons, then stood. "Follow them and screenshot each point."

"Got it." One of the others sat in the chair.

Darren followed Ari into a private office and clicked a button on a device, activating the screen on the wall. Images and a live feed of numbers and charts appeared.

"What do we have?"

"Just what we told you earlier. Sage Roberts, BioZen laboratory assistant, works in their Mercer Street branch, near the Metropolitan Markets. Seventeenth floor, the animal health division." He tapped away.

Ari watched the images of Sage's office flick up on the screen.

"Once she goes to work in the morning, we'll be able to access the cameras in the more classified sections. Hopefully," Darren said.

"Can you go through her personnel records?" Ari prompted.

"Yup." Another screen appeared, and Darren nodded to the two vampires, Frankie and Dave, who entered the room. "'Sup."

"Morning, sir," they both said.

"Good morning. Sit," Ari replied. "And please shut the door."

Frankie nudged it and sat down beside Dave. They all gave Darren their attention.

"Sage started with BioZen three years ago as a junior lab assistant and has been slowly progressing in rank. Or whatever. Job title."

Ari smiled.

"And, yeah, that promotion looks to be hers. The details of the department, though, are classified."

A chill ran through Ari's body. He knew exactly what it was. Ari leaned back in his seat. "Anything else?"

"Honestly, she appears to be just a stock standard human as far as we can tell," Dave said, spinning his smartphone around in his hand. "Hitting all the security walls inside a pharmaceutical company is no surprise. They're corrupt as fuck, as we know."

Stock standard human.

Those words rattled around in Ari's brain.

No, Sage was not a stock standard human. Not to him. But she was human. Vulnerable and easy to kill. And she had somehow found herself mixed up in a dangerous game with predators and unethical humans.

Perhaps he could find her another job? Get her a promotion with another organization somewhere and completely wipe her memory. Maybe persuade her to become a fucking vet or something.

Ari rubbed his forehead. "Yeah, okay. So, our prep work has given us very little except a location and where she hangs her bag."

They all nodded.

"We'll have a lot more later this morning," Darren said.

Ari worked closely with these three on the regular. No matter the job, they were his experts who did a lot of the dog work to prepare the path for his assassins to complete their assignments.

If they fucked up, the job got fucked up.

They were the smartest of the smartest, which was why they were working in the best private security company on earth.

This job, though, was their most important job ever.

Ari didn't want to freak them out, but they knew what was on the line for their race.

They just didn't know what Sage meant to him, and he couldn't tell them. Not fully.

"Sage is important to me. The recordings are to be sent to my files and kept off the cloud." All three of them looked up, surprised. "Do what you usually do, but if I tell you to turn the connection off, you don't hesitate for a second. Do you understand?"

There was a slight hesitation, but they all nodded.

"Got it," Darren said.

"And her personal moments—I don't think I need to explain that—unless you think there's a fucking good reason, you go dark."

Frankie rubbed his jaw. "Honestly, that's trickier than it sounds."

"He's right. If we go dark, we don't know when to turn it back on," Dave added.

Fuck.

"Just be discreet," Ari said, standing. "And all intel goes no further than me or Oliver unless I authorize it."

A bunch of *yes sirs* followed him to the doorway.

"Get some rest. It's going to be a long day," Ari added, then left.

He needed to take his own advice. In a matter of hours, Sage would find out she had the promotion—assuming her records were accurate—and learn vampires were real. He had a feeling, after their discussion at dinner, that she wouldn't be shocked.

Ari was less concerned about that.

It was the decision she'd make once she found out that had him wanting to punch holes in every wall of his mansion.

Sage was a scientist. The discovery of vampires would be the biggest moment in her life—hell, in modern human history. Her desire for knowledge, and thirst to contribute to such a moment, would keep her there.

Unless he was wrong.

Unless her morals were solid.

God, he hoped he was wrong.

Ari might be distracted by his feelings for Sage, but he was still focused on the mission. They had to find this poor damn vampire if he was still alive, and Sage might be the answer they'd been looking for. Once they found him, Ari was confident the rest of the information would be close.

Could they get lucky, and find the heart of the project located in Seattle? Of all the places on earth.

Well, it would save on gas, so that was something.

Ari teleported to his rooms.

Matteo. He called telepathically, when an idea popped into his mind.

Yes, sir?

Send a coffee, bagel, and a single red rose to Ms. Sage Roberts in the morning.

He gave Matteo her address.

With a card?

Oh.

His off-the-cuff idea just got a lot more complicated.

What the hell was he going to say? *I just realized you didn't eat tonight and now I'm worried you're going to starve to death. We can't have that, or I won't be able to fuck you anymore. Or* he could be honest and say, *I can't stop thinking about you even though I only left you an hour ago. PS: Your sister is an asshole.*

I'll text you the note.

I'll make sure she gets it before leaving for work, sir.

Thanks.

Ari pulled out his phone and began to draft the note.

Mia stellina, you are always on my mind, breakfast, lunch and dinner. Christ, it sounded like a restaurant or after-dinner mint commercial.

Mia stellina, we interrupted your dinner last night, please accept my apology.

God, he was terrible at this.

Mia stellina, I wish your lips were on me instead of the coffee.

"Jesus." Ari cursed. How fucking hard could this be?

"Siri, show me romantic notes to women," Ari asked his iPhone, feeling like an idiot.

Sorry I didn't see any matching notes about romantic.

The fuck?

He began to type again... *Mia stellina, you are perfect. Ari x*

That would do. Ari pushed send and knew Matteo would take care of it. It may be the last time he got to tell her how he felt. But he fucking hoped not.

For the first time in hundreds of years, he sent out a request to God, praying she chose him over scientific knowledge.

A huge, long shot.

CHAPTER TWENTY-FIVE

Sage zipped up her boots, grabbed her handbag and headed to the kitchen to grab something for breakfast. She had about ten minutes before the bus arrived.

Fortunately, the stop was just a few houses away.

"Yes, fine, fine. I'll make sure she gets it," Tony said, pushing his way inside the house carrying a gift basket. "Jesus, couriers are pushy these days."

"What are you doing here?" Sage asked, looking at the clock. It was nearly eight.

"I left my swipe card here, so had to come home first." He groaned and sent her a look, which told her Tony thought it was her fault.

Sage ignored the look and glanced at the wicker basket.

"Oh, here." He handed it to her.

She placed it on the kitchen bench. She could already smell one item and it was making her mouth water. Hot coffee.

Butterflies tickled the insides of her tummy as she lifted the rose to her nose. Was it from Ari?

Sage had woken feeling a mix of guilt and confusion.

Having sex with Oliver again had been incredible, but it felt as if the fun they'd had together was now over. Sage knew they wouldn't do it again. Not least because Ari had staked a claim on her.

Whether or not he knew it, he had.

He'd asked her—correction, told her—to cancel her date with Carl and now she had come out of the sex haze that Ari seemed to put her in, she wasn't sure that was a good idea.

He still hadn't committed to anything but fucking her. Sage had to admit she loved every second with him, but there was more to a relationship that sex and he left before she woke up. Every damn time.

It was unlikely she and Ari had a future, so she was going on the date with Carl. Heck, he might end up being the man she grew old with. He ticked all the must-haves on her *Life List*, so she would be a fool to cancel.

Plus, her mother would love him. He was an accountant for crying out loud. She could gush about him to the church ladies for hours.

Sage pulled out the carefully positioned hot drink in a cute reusable cup and placed it on the countertop. Next to it was a square carton with a hot toasted bagel smothered in cream cheese and jelly.

Her mouth watered.

She had missed dinner last night and was starving, but it had been worth it. So worth it.

She lifted the blue folded card with little silver stars, and read: *Mia stellina, you are perfect, Ari x*

She let out a little gasp.

She hadn't picked Ari for a romantic.

"No good?" Tony asked, coming out of his bedroom.

"What? Oh, no it's fine." She waved him off. When he got to the front door, Sage called out. "Will you be home tonight?"

Tony turned and shook his head. "I'll stay at Teresa's again. Look Sage, I was going to wait until the weekend, but I think we're going to get our own place."

Hallelujah... wait, mortgage payments.

"Oh."

"Yeah, sorry, but I think this is just not working out anymore. We're a proper couple you know, so it's just different."

Sage frowned. "I'm sorry, what's different?"

Irritation ran through her. She knew exactly what Tony meant. Ari was the first man she'd brought home since Tony had moved in. Clearly, what they'd heard through the walls on Saturday had been a little too much for them. Sage knew they had been loud, but Tony's comment was inappropriate and highly judgmental.

More than that, it stunk of superiority. Why? Because Ari looked dangerous and had tattoos?

Asshole.

"Just, you know. Our relationships," he replied.

"Still not getting it," Sage said, letting him spell it out like the complete asshole he was.

"Being around what you're doing with that man, sorry, but it's just awkward."

No Tony. It's awkward because I had a real man—okay two, but you don't know about Oliver, so we'll forget that for now—who made me scream. Loudly. Multiple times. And you and your little girlfriend didn't like how irrelevant it made your vanilla sex seem.

Sage nearly laughed. She'd had enough of him and was glad he was moving out. If there was any doubt left in his mind, she was about to make it even more awkward.

"I get it. I've been hearing you guys for months. Totally... well, I think we both know how different our sex lives are. So sure, best you two find your own place." Sage sipped her coffee.

Tony went bright red, and she held his stare.

As for whether she was in a *proper* relationship, well yes, that had hit a nerve. It was just sex with Ari, she knew that. Perhaps things with Carl would be different, but for Tony to point it out was totally rude.

She glanced down at the note and heard the door close firmly.

Asshole.

Sage grabbed the bagel and coffee and ran out the door to catch her bus.

BY the time she got to the office, the bagel was toast (pun intended) and her coffee tumbler was empty. She placed it on her desk, tucked her phone into her pocket and slid her handbag into the drawer where it was secure.

Even though access to her office was restricted, with thumb print only, there were still a large number of people who could get in. The more restricted areas required retina and she wasn't permitted in those areas yet.

Sage logged onto her computer and began pulling out her test tubes and samples from yesterday.

Today could be the day she found out about her promotion. If she didn't hear from them by tomorrow, she'd start to worry.

Now Tony was moving out.

Sage was relieved. The loved-up couple had been slowly driving her insane for months. However, she had a big mortgage to pay, and Tony's rent was needed. If she got the promotion things would look quite different—it came with a hefty pay rise.

Ping. Ari Moretti.

Sage's heart tap-danced in her chest when she saw his name on the screen. She smiled stupidly and quickly swiped.

Buongiorno, gorgeous.

Good morning, thank you for breakfast.

It was my pleasure. I love knowing you're fed and happy.

Sage smiled. How sweet.

…

She waited for him to send whatever he was typing.

Would you like to fulfil one of my fantasies tonight?

Sage coughed in surprise and a colleague glanced over. She patted her chest and mouthed *sorry*.

There was only four of them in this sterile room and they weren't the rowdiest bunch of people. She was looking forward to moving on with her career and working with new people. Hopefully.

Her eyes dropped back to the messages. Would she?

Should I be nervous?

I have a feeling you will enjoy it. Have a good day, mia stellina.

You too x

Oh no!

She'd sent a kiss. *Dammit.* It had been automatic. Now Ari was going to think she was in love with him and probably run a mile. Ugh, maybe she should have said something sexier? She had no idea how to stext. Or was it sext?

God.

What did one say when signing off to a lover? *Nice penis and have a nice day?* She palmed her forehead and tucked her phone back into her pocket.

Better she focus on science. At least she was good at that.

Sage rinsed her Tupperware container under the water while her BioZen colleagues milled around, making, or eating, their lunch in the cafeteria.

"Sage!" Talia called out.

"Oh hey, you're back. I thought you were away another week," Sage said to her work friend. The two had hit it off immediately when they had started the same day. Talia worked in administration, but they'd both had to do the two-day induction together which had cemented their friendship.

"It's been two weeks, girl." Talia laughed. "Look at this tan. The Caribbean was amazing." She had recently married her college sweetheart and the two of them had disappeared to the tropics for a honeymoon.

Sage was jealous.

What she wouldn't do for a holiday in the sun. A vision of Ari lying on the sand, wet after swimming in the ocean, filled her mind.

Holy shit.

They'd never make it out of the room if they were in the tropics together, with his gorgeous muscular body.

"What have I missed?" Talia said, walking down the hallway with her.

Sage bit her lower lip and grinned.

"Oh my God, what?" Talia whispered. "Spill."

If there was one person on earth she could tell, it was Talia. They two of them swapped their naughty books, as they called them, and swooned over new book boyfriends. But it had taken a work function and about four glasses of wine before they'd opened up about some of the sexier stuff.

They'd dared each other to try some of the things and the next day giggled about it. Talia had a husband to try them with, but he wasn't open to it. And Sage was single.

Still, from time to time, they still joked around. Now Sage had a story to tell.

"Okay, come in here." She giggled and pulled Talia into a storage cupboard.

Talia's eyes widened. "Now I'm really intrigued."

Sage blushed as she found the words to explain what she'd done. "I slept with—"

"Someone? Oh my God, who?"

"Well, two someone's," Sage replied.

Talia stared at her and then slowly, her eyes widened. "Noooo."

Sage nodded, a small smirk on her lips.

"No!"

"Yup. Twice." She grinned, feeling really proud of herself.

"Holy. Shit," Talia said. "Tell me everything!"

Sage shared the story of how she met Ari and Oliver and the past few days of her life. She left out the part about her growing feelings for Ari and she didn't mention Carl.

"I need to see a photo," Talia said.

A photo? Sage had never thought to take a photo of Ari or Oliver.

"I don't have one, sorry," she said. "I'll get one tonight."

"Are you seeing both of them?"

Sage shook her head. "No, just Ari."

"Are they friends or roommates?" Talia asked, and Sage realized she didn't know all that much about either of them.

"No. It's... well, I don't know. They live in Medina."

Talia's eyes flew wide. "Oh. Do you think they're ultra-rich guys into weird stuff? Be careful Sage."

She frowned.

"Ari wouldn't hurt me," Sage said, knowing in her soul it was true. "He's quite protective in a way."

Talia pressed her lips together in that pretend smile friends gave you when they want to say *you are an idiot.*

Maybe she was. Sage was glad she had her date with Carl. It made her feel less stupid.

"Let's catch up tomorrow for lunch. I have to get back to the lab. Nice tan by the way." Sage grinned and raced off.

When she opened the office door, Sandy Longstar, Senior Scientist of Project Callan, was standing near her desk.

"Here she is," one of her colleagues said.

"Sage." Sandy smiled professionally at her, then held out her arm. "Follow me, please."

Her heart pounded. She knew this was about her promotion. In moments, she'd find out if she was successful or not.

They stepped into Sandy's office, and she closed the door.

"Thank you for applying for the new associate scientist position in Project Callan," Sandy said. "Management were very impressed with your interview."

Thump, thump, thump.

"We'd like to offer you the position," Sandy said.

Holy sh—

"However, there are a few more steps we need to take before it's official."

What steps?

"First, we need you to look through this contract and sign it. If you'd like to review it overnight, then you are most welcome," Sandy said.

Nope, she would sign anything right now.

"Wow, thank you very much. It should be fine. I can just take a few minutes, then sign it," Sage said, knowing she sounded eager but didn't care.

Sandy smiled at her.

"Once you've done that, we'll show you around the Project Callan laboratory and offices," Sandy said. "It's important you understand the strict level of security in this top-secret project, so please read the contract carefully."

Sage nodded.

"We're working with governments around the world, and I can share with you now that we've undertaken a thorough security check on both you and your family."

Oh? That seemed extreme given she already had a contract with BioZen.

"I see." She felt less sure.

Sandy handed her a large white envelope. "There are two copies in here. Please read and sign, then pop back in here when you are ready. I'll be here the rest of the afternoon."

"Thank you." Sage left, holding the envelope in her hand like it held her future in it.

Perhaps it did.

She found a small breakaway meeting room and shut herself in and began going through the documents. After reading all twelve pages, all she could ascertain was she was unable to share anything she saw, heard, or discussed outside the walls of the department. Not even with her colleagues. She would be given a higher security clearance.

She knew what that meant.

A chip.

As a scientist she was reluctant to agree to that, but then again, this was the way of the world now and she didn't really have a choice.

There were a lot of other rules, which seemed odd, but in the end, she signed and dropped it off to Sandy.

"Fantastic," Sandy said, shaking her hand. "Welcome to the team, Sage. What I am about to show you is going to change your life."

Sage tilted her head in interest but chewed her lip as Sandy walked to the door.

"Follow me."

CHAPTER TWENTY-SIX

"Dr. Phillips," Douglas answered.

"How quickly can you get on a plane?" Xander asked. "If I send the corporate jet for you."

He was reluctant to have the jet leave Baltimore, but he wanted Douglas to check out the facilities he was looking at in California.

Xander was ready to sign and get production started.

"Tomorrow," Douglas replied. "I assume this is to California?"

Xander nodded.

"Yes, I can spare a few days," he said. "I will check with my wife, but I don't see any issues."

Fucking pussy. Why did these men let their wives make the rules in their lives?

"Let me know by midday," he said and ended the call. Xander pressed a few more buttons and let it dial.

"Tomassi." A powerful voice greeted him.

"Good afternoon," Xander replied, a smile on his face for a change.

"I hear you have a vampire product I could be interested in?" the man said.

"Are you? Interested in vampire products?"

"I'm interested in destroying them, yes," the man said.

"Then I think we might be able to do some very good business together."

Xander reclined in his chair and grinned.

CHAPTER TWENTY-SEVEN

Ari sat stone-faced and clenched his jaw while he and his team listened to every single word of Sage's conversation with Sandy. The logistics room was packed with his tech team and assassins. Sage had signed the contract and was about, they assumed, to learn vampires existed.

Shit.

His heart pounded, and he knew everyone in the room could hear it and probably had questions. He didn't get anxious when they conducted operations.

But Sage was not an operation.

Hello… she was Sage.

Ari cursed. He should be fucking happy. This was what they wanted and needed, especially now they'd learned Callan, of Project Callan, was their missing vampire and there was a high probability he was being kept in Sage's building.

Earlier in the day Ari had barged into the logistics room after Travis had called him in urgently.

"What is it?" he'd snapped.

Oliver and Travis had been leaning over Darren and Frankie's screens. "Project Callan. We're ninety-nine percent sure it's our vampire," Travis said and Ari had cursed.

"Show me." He had dialed Brayden at the same time. "You need to get over here."

"What's up?" the prince replied.

"We've found the missing vampire," Ari said.

Callan belonged to the king. This was royal business, and Ari was doing his part by letting them know immediately. Plus, he wanted them to be a part of this.

"Be there in five," Brayden said, as Craig had cursed.

He knew exactly how the big guy felt. All of them had felt heavy knowing one of their own was trapped in the hands of experimental scientists. They just hadn't known where he or she was. For Craig, it was even more difficult. He'd been inside one of the labs and spent time with the survivors.

"Teleport into the lobby and my team will let you into the logistics room," Ari had instructed them.

"God damn it. That poor bastard," Oliver spat out while Travis ran a hand through his hair in that fucked-off way.

"Patience. We have to do this right," Ari said, feeling just like his team but needing to be a strong leader. "We have no idea what state Callan is in, or exactly where he is."

Faces were rubbed and boots kicked walls.

"Yeah, and they could also move him before we get in. We can't fuck this up," Oliver said.

"The problem is, getting in," Darren, his head technician, said when Brayden and Craig entered the room. Brayden had nodded at them and found a seat.

"What do we have?" Craig asked, getting straight down to business. Ari gave Darren a nod, and he'd updated them on the details.

"We're still digging while Sage is inside her office, but this is what we have so far."

"So far," Frankie had emphasized. "People think this shit happens in twenty keystrokes because of TV. It can take days or weeks, you know."

"We don't have days; we have to get that vampire out fast," Craig said firmly.

"Bring up the building blueprint and compare that with what intel we have," Ari said, nodding to his team. "Grab a chair."

"I'll lean," Craig said, and Brayden smirked as he pulled a chair around. For the next two hours, they'd studied the data and building and reviewed a number of different strategies.

"Go back to the other image," Brayden said, standing and walking closer to the screen. They all knew it wasn't because he couldn't see clearly. It was one of those unconscious things one did when they wanted to think.

Darren clicked a few things and the image of BioZen's building reappeared. It was an architectural layout of the floors.

"Something isn't right with this." The prince crossed his arms, lifting one hand to his chin. "Here." He used a finger to circle one area.

Oliver leaned closer.

"The bathrooms," Craig said, and Brayden nodded. "There are two sets in that section. No one needs to crap that much."

Travis snorted.

"It's not big enough for a lab," Oliver said, shaking his head.

Ari stood and stopped next to Brayden. Alex was likely right, but it still raised a question.

"We need to get into the cameras. You guys are on that, right?" Craig asked Darren.

The vampire nodded. "Yeah, but I have to tell you, these are some serious security walls we're talking about."

Darren shook his head. "I've never seen anything like it. Fucking pharma."

Craig pressed his lips together and nodded slowly.

"Well, we have a few more hours, so keep going," Ari said.

"How does this tracker work? Does it have a distance limit?" Brayden asked.

Darren shook his head. "Kind of. It's a little like a modem. It connects us when Sage is there and disconnects when she's out of range."

"So, we need to get a tracker into the building and leave it there." Craig shrugged.

Ari glanced at Craig. "Getting in there during daylight is the problem, and without being recognized. We have good reason to believe they know exactly who you two are." He looked at Brayden. "Not to mention we're not sending in the Moretti prince. We still don't know how they've been able to weaken vampires."

"I'll make that call if the opportunity arises." Brayden stared at him with his powerful silver stare and Ari shook his head.

"Don't bother with the prince shit. If he wants to throw himself in front of a bus, trust me, he will," Craig said. "I've long since given up."

Interesting.

So Brayden put his role as captain before his royal status. That was something Ari could respect even if it was stupid as fuck.

"If one of my vampires is being tortured in that building, I'm not going to sit back and paint my goddamn nails." Brayden planted his hands in his jacket pockets. "If our intel is tight and we are confident, then Craig and I are going in."

Oliver cleared his throat and Ari looked at him. The rest of the team had now joined them and appeared restless.

"Okay, everyone, settle down. We are not going in guns blazing." Ari looked at his watch. "Let's get comfortable and see what the rest of the day brings. Sage hasn't been offered the promotion yet. That will give us all the information we need to start making some decisions."

Famous fucking last words.

Now here they were listening as Sage walked through the BioZen building into the Project Callan division where they were now absolutely sure the missing vampire was being held.

His Sage.

His fucking Sage.

Ari glanced at the faces around him, noting the anticipation and hope lining their faces when all he felt was dread. He wanted to teleport over there and stop Sage from going in. If she was going to find out about vampires, he wanted to be the one to tell her. Ari wanted to show her they were living, breathing beings just like humans. They loved, they hated, they cried, they made love, they had families.

Instead, she was about to see a sample she would be asked to experiment on. A living being who had been used to obtain data through pain and suffering. Someone who had had all his freedoms and choices taken from him.

Ari rubbed his jaw for the hundredth time. He could barely breathe as they listened to Sandy rattle on about the contract and how exciting it all was.

Sandy would die.

They would all die.

No one involved with this project would remain breathing once they had all the information required to completely destroy it. Until they got to the root of it and learned all they needed, there was no point randomly killing off scientists. They'd just replace them.

Ari didn't go around just killing people—okay, fine, they did. That was what The Institute was hired to do. They caught the bad guys and eliminated evil from this world.

These people were evil.

Unless Callan was living the life in some swanky apartment and had given them permission to do what they wanted with him—he doubted it—then they were evil.

They had seen what these scientists had done to the others, and it was horrifying.

So yeah, Ari was happy to rip a few heads off.

His stomach lurched.

Sage may be about to join that list of enemies, and Ari felt like he was going to vomit.

He knew why. All night he'd been pacing the mansion, trying to ignore what he knew deep down inside.

Sage was his mate.

Or at least he strongly suspected she was.

He'd never felt like this about a female before and over the years of his life, he'd seen enough males carry on like a lunatic to know the signs.

Ari had given up hope his mate would ever come to him and, as the fates would have it, she could be about to become the most despicable enemy he could imagine.

Fuck you, Fate.

As far as they knew, a vampire only got one mate in his lifetime. Sure, he could have taken her from BioZen and never known what Sage would choose, but he'd lived a long enough life to know that sort of shit would fuck with your head. He'd never trust her. He'd always doubt her. It would eat at them until they hated each other.

In any case, if Sage *was* his mate, and they were bonding, then her death or separation from her would literally drive him mad. Either way, his days were numbered now.

Fuck that. She is mine.

He looked around the room and made a decision.

"Whatever happens, Sage is mine to deal with. You got that?" he said darkly. Everyone muttered quiet *yups* while Brayden stared at him for a long moment.

"Agreed," Brayden finally said, but Ari wasn't asking, so he simply looked away.

"Shit, not again." Craig cursed and ran a hand over his face.

Yeah, they knew.

Both Craig and Brayden had recently mated and knew the signs. They'd be feeling pretty bad for him right now, but they could fuck off.

Despite his pessimism, there was a possibility Sage would be as disgusted by this as they were.

First, she'd be shocked. They'd all seen humans learn about the existence of vampires and lose their damn minds, before their memories were wiped. Or turned if they were a mate. Then when she came face to face with Callan, the reality would kick in, what was being asked of her.

That was when the metal hit the road and he'd have his answer about his mate. Or potential mate.

The voices started up again and Ari leaned unnecessarily closer to the speaker.

"This area is where our offices are. You will have your own." The woman, Sandy, spoke. "You can move now or tomorrow if you have work to finish up."

"Thanks," Sage replied, and Ari thought she sounded quiet.

"You getting anything?" Craig asked Darren, who shook his head. "Nah, man, they're jumbling everything. How are they doing it?"

"No camera?" Ari asked.

"Every time I catch a connection, it drops," Frankie said. "Mother trucker. Let me try something else." Dave leaned in and the two of them seemed to be tag-teaming the keyboard.

Ari began pacing as they continued listening to Sage's tour and he felt Brayden's eyes on him. He ignored him.

"Okay, let's go in here and we will get your biochip put in," Sandy said, and they heard footsteps and a door swish open.

Ari's hands clenched and his eyes flew to Darren, but Craig spoke the words on his mind first.

"Are they going to find her chip?" Craig asked. "Is she in danger?"

Darren shook his head. "Unlikely they'll scan for one. They'll assume she's clean."

Ari's brows shot up. "Not real comforting."

Darren shrugged. "It's all I've got. The answer is yes, if they scan, they will find it."

Fuck.

"Or if they try to put it in the same spot," Oliver said, looking nearly as unhappy as he was. "I should have put it in a less popular entry point, fuck it."

"The chances of that happening are about a million to one," Travis said.

Dave snorted. "Not a statistician then."

"No, but I could snipe your head from a hundred miles so shut it, tech boy," Travis replied, smirking.

Ari rolled his eyes and Craig grinned.

"Focus." Ari growled.

He knew they all needed a tension break, but they could go out and fuck later. His Sage was in a potentially dangerous situation, and he couldn't leave the goddamn property to help her if something happened.

Fucking sunshine.

Over the speakers, they heard a little noise, which Ari recognized as Sage. He knew all her sounds, which only made him cringe. "Oh, that kind of tickled," Sage said with a little laugh. "So, can I get it removed one day?"

"Not really," a man replied. "We can just disconnect it, though."

"Sure," Sandy said, coughing and shutting the man up. "If you ever left, but I'm not sure you will once we show you what we are working on. Let's go through here."

Ari glanced at Darren, who mouthed, *we can remove it.*

"Oh, hi Dr. Phillips," Sage said, and Ari picked up a strong note of respect in her voice.

"Sage, welcome aboard. It's great to have you on the team. I've been impressed with your work in our animal health division and think you'll be suitably challenged in this project," the man, Dr. Phillips, said. "Please take a seat."

Chairs scraped and then there was silence.

"What I'm about to share with you will come as a big surprise," Phillips said. "A shock."

"Oh?" Sage replied. "Now I'm excited."

Ari cringed.

"Let me preempt what I'm about to tell you and say this *isn't* a candid camera moment."

"Okayyy." Sage let out a small, uncomfortable laugh. There were some clicks, which Ari assumed was a presentation of sorts being brought up.

His stomach curdled. One glance at Oliver and he saw the vampire wasn't faring well himself. Their eyes met.

Fuck, Ari. Oliver said.

I know. Fuck, I know. Ari responded.

Dr. Phillips cleared his throat. "Recently we became aware of a new species. Not uncommon, but this is rather different. The team and I have been working with a sample and researching this new life form."

A sample? Fucking asshole. That *sample* was named Callan. And Anna, and the other dozen or so vampires they'd kidnapped.

Sage made some ooh and ahh sounds.

Ari was fucking close to punching another wall while the vampires around him growled low in their throats.

"Give her a break, guys, she doesn't know it's a vampire yet," Oliver snapped.

"Is it a plant or marine life? This is exciting," Sage replied. "Although, as you know, my specialty is animal health, but I'm totally open to diversifying."

"You do the honors, Douglas," Sandy said, and they could all hear the smile in her voice.

Ari glanced across at Darren. "Douglas Phillips. Look him up."

"Sage, you will be working with the first team on earth to study the vampire race," Phillips said with great pride.

Ari closed his eyes and held his breath.

There was a long silence.

"What?" Sage finally said.

"Vampires," Sandy replied.

"Here?" Sage asked, her voice shaky. Ari stiffened as he waited for a reply, but whatever it was, it was not voiced.

"Holy shit," Sage said, shock lacing her words.

They'd heard it all before, but from here he couldn't comfort her or show her the full truth and it made every damn muscle in his body tighten to the point he thought he might snap.

"Remember your contract, Sage. Now you must understand the extreme nature of the security around this project," Phillips said.

"Are they dangerous?" Sage asked.

"Very," Phillips answered.

"Dangerous to you, motherfucker," Craig growled. "I'm going to rip your head off and feed it to the fish."

"I'll help," Oliver said. "Asshole."

The conversation and questions continued, but Ari got no real sense of Sage's feelings. If anything, she was in a state of shock and very quiet. Neither of those things he could fault her for.

"Tomorrow, we will show you our test subject and you will learn much more," Sandy said. "For now, that's a lot to process. Head back to your lab and start moving to your office. You start tomorrow."

Chairs scraped.

"Thank you. My mind is blown," Sage said. "Wait, did you say test subject?"

Someone must have nodded.

"I can't believe they're volunteering. Wow," Sage ignorantly replied, and Ari felt his heart twitch in hope.

"Well... we can go through all that tomorrow," Dr. Phillips replied.

The next thirty minutes was just noise and chatter as Sage returned to her office and received congratulations from her colleagues. Ari had heard enough. He stood and walked to the door. "Call me if there's anything of interest," he instructed everyone. "Take shifts and get some rest. You've all been up for a long time."

It was late afternoon when they would usually be asleep and though it wasn't their first daylight rodeo, this was a tough one.

He turned to Travis. "When are Alex and Logan returning?"

Tap, tap, tap.

"Indeterminable at this point. Their check-in is at midnight, so I'll update you then."

Ari nodded. "As soon as they are finished, tell them to get their asses back here."

"We have a team with us if you need more bodies," Brayden said, standing and stretching his back. "Let me know when you want to do a combined briefing and we're ready to move."

Ari nodded when Darren looked up for confirmation. He was pleased his team were clear on who the authority was in the room. The prince may be more senior than he in the royal family, but at The Institute Ari was the boss.

"Until we can access their security, no one is going inside. I don't know how long it will take. I'm sorry," Darren said.

Ari stared at the prince a long moment. "It's not my call, but I think you should bring the queen and your mates closer."

Brayden turned to Craig and then nodded.

"You think they'll make a move?" Craig asked.

"Yes," Ari replied honestly. "Or at least I don't trust they won't and until we know how they've been able to weaken vampires, I believe we need to take all precautions."

If the royals knew how it was being done, they hadn't shared it with him. Regardless, if it was him, he'd either return to Italy—which he knew neither of the vampires would do—or move them back under his protection immediately.

"They may not have anything planned," Oliver said. "But once we go in and get Callan out, then they may act. I've seen their security firsthand. They're good. Who knows if they have eyes on the queen right now? I agree with Ari. Bring your females close."

And that was why Oliver had been promoted to head assassin. Among other things.

"I'd add Ben to your list. Not that he's a girl. Don't tell him I said that." Ari grinned.

"I'll tell him." Craig grinned back.

Brayden cursed. "Shit. Then we might have to move in here. Our security isn't good enough where we're staying. But first I need to speak to Vincent. God, he's going to be furious."

"So, a new mood for him, then?" Craig said sarcastically, slapping Brayden on the shoulder. Ari let out a small laugh despite everything. Vincent was a strong and capable king, but he was known to be moody.

"You're just happy you're going to get laid again," Brayden replied, punching him playfully in the stomach. Craig didn't even flinch, his abs of steel doing their job.

Ari was impressed.

"Damn right I am." Craig grinned.

Ari glanced around the room. Things were about to change around here, and fast. Since the beginning of The Institute there had been a no-female rule policy, except for those who worked here. Which was about five female vampires.

If he was about to mate with Sage, things would need to change. Such was life. Ari had learned many centuries ago the way to survive in life was to adapt.

"This is probably the safest place for you to be," Ari said to the prince. "The king and queen are welcome, as are your mates."

"Thank you," Brayden replied.

"Time to pivot, team. The royals are moving in. Frankie, set up the Moretti party with any security access they require."

"Got it," Frankie replied.

Brayden nodded at Craig and the two teleported out.

"Travis. Update Matteo and Alice. Get ready for a new world with females in the mansion," Ari said.

He glanced over at Oliver when no smartass comments followed. His team were somber, and he understood why. This was some serious shit. The team knew Sage was his without him saying so. You didn't work this closely as a covert security team and not know your colleagues fucking well.

Sage doesn't deserve this. Oliver telepathed.

I'll make sure she's okay.

Oliver nodded. *Ari... is she your—?*

I think so. Keep it to yourself. Ari returned to his quarters as they telepathed.

They know, Ari.

Yeah, they did, but still, it was his private business and until he had a sense of where Sage's mind was at, Ari was going to protect her as much as he could.

If she thought she'd had a surprise today, he was about to be the cherry on the top.

Then the decision was hers.

CHAPTER TWENTY-EIGHT

Ari leaned against the side of his Audi Q7. Men in off-the-shelf suits walked past and gave him sideways glances. Maybe it was the casual jeans and black leather jacket—*Prada assholes*—or his enormous muscular body that was making him stand out?

Or it could be the Tom Ford shades he wore, even though it was dusk. But the sun had not yet fully set. And yeah, he was pushing it. While vampires could be outside at dusk, the lowering sun still drained energy and fucking hurt the eyeballs.It wasn't something a vampire could do regularly, but he was desperate to see Sage.

His windows had a special coating which protected him while driving, so he'd waited until the last minute to exit the vehicle.

He wanted to see her face.

He wanted to hold her in his arms.

He wanted to take her back to the mansion and make her his for eternity.

Ari slipped his hands into his pockets and watched the entrance into BioZen like his life depended on it.

It just might.

Two minutes later, Sage stepped out of the building and began walking toward where he was parked.

Illegally.

Sage's wild auburn hair flew out behind her. Black knee-high boots ended just shy of the top of her skirt, which was held down by the weight of her coat.

She spotted him and her eyes lit up. Ari's heart thumped and he forced himself to let her walk to him.

God she's beautiful.

When she was a dozen steps away, he couldn't wait any longer. Ari began to walk toward her until they he was right in front of her. He saw the strain in her eyes and before she could speak his mouth captured hers. She fell into his body, and he wrapped his arms around her. In hours she might no longer be his, but right now she was, and he was taking all he could get.

"Hi," Sage said, and he wanted to take away all her pain.

"Hello, gorgeous." Ari rubbed a thumb over her cheekbone, then led her to his car and opened the passenger door. He slid into the driver's seat and pulled the car away from the curb.

He reached over and took her hand. "How was your day, darling?"

"It was fine, thank you, sweetheart. How was yours?" She laughed, and it was like music to his ears. He loved being able to bring her some joy right now.

This could be their last night together and he was going to do as he'd promised; play out one of his life fantasies. He knew it would surprise her.

"Well," he said, putting both hands on the wheel and acting all serious. "It was okay. I had a lot of paperwork to do, then I had some HR stuff to deal with. But now I get to spend the evening with you, so life is good."

Sage was staring at him funny. He could see the underlying tension on her face, but there was time for that later.

"What shall we have for dinner tonight?" he asked.

"Err," Sage said.

"Let's get a takeout. Chinese? Thai? Mexican?"

"Wha—"

"Do you have Netflix?" Ari asked.

Sage's mouth clamped shut. Ari indicated and turned the corner, focusing on the traffic. Then glanced back at her when they stopped at the next red light.

"Honey?" he asked.

"Who are you and what have you done with bad, sexy Ari?" Sage asked, her brows bunched.

He grinned.

"This is my fantasy," Ari replied. "So, play along."

Sage's eyes flew wide. "Netflix and takeout are your fantasy? Are you kidding me?"

"Well, part of it. I've never done those things before. I thought I'd try it." Ari lifted her hand to his mouth. "Don't worry, *stellina mia*, I will ensure you enjoy yourself."

They decided on Mexican. Ari carried the Mexican takeout inside Sage's house and watched as she hung up her coat and handbag, then began to pull dishes and utensils out of the drawers.

He removed his jacket and boots, then wandered over to steal another kiss. Sage continued to give him curious glances, which just made him smile.

"Shall we eat at the table or sofa?" she asked.

"What would you normally do? To Netflix and *chill*?" he asked.

Sage laughed and pointed to the sofa.

"Where are your roommates?"

Sage directed the remote at the TV and the screen lit up. Next minute Netflix appeared, and she began scrolling.

He'd watched the network many times before, but playing house with a woman he liked? Never.

Rarely did he resent being turned vampire, expect when it came to a couple of really mundane things. Ari had spent his life alone, which is probably why the everyday habits of those returning from their day at the office and enjoying their spouse was something he craved.

It was the intimacy of it all. The feeling of belonging.

He had his routine, but they included his employees and assassins. Not someone who loved him.

So, this was his fantasy.

And there was only one female he'd ever wanted to do it with.

Sage.

"He's at his girlfriend's. This morning he gave me notice. He's moving out." she said, throwing the remote on the sofa.

"This is good, right?"

"Yes." She smiled. "Especially as I got the promotion today, so I don't need his rent money."

Ari stilled.

"Congratulations." he said, keeping his face devoid of emotion.

"Thanks," Sage replied, and disappeared into her room. It was clear she wasn't bursting with happiness and part of him felt there was hope. She exited a few minutes later wearing a pair of navy trackpants and a tank top. She sat on the couch next to him, crossed her legs under her, then reached for one of the plates.

"Welcome to Netflix and chill," she declared.

"It's less sexy than I imagined," Ari said, with a raised brow, then smirked, and got an elbow in the side for it. He twisted her face and pressed his lips against hers for a long moment before they continued on with their meals.

They ended up watching a show, something about a female called Emily in Paris who seemed to have boring sex with a lot of French men.

"Why doesn't she just tell the man she likes him?" he asked after the second episode.

"She does." Sage nodded profusely, as if this was important.

"She does? You've watched this already?" Ari asked.

"Mmm hmm." Sage nodded again.

"Why watch it again? That seems like a waste of time." Ari may have lived a long life, but watching the same show over and over seemed completely pointless. There was an abundance of everything in life—there was no need to do anything on repeat.

"If you like something, that's what you do." Sage shrugged. "Like drinking your favorite whiskey or, I don't know, hanging out with someone you like multiple times."

Ari stared at her.

"Is spending time with me a waste of time? You've done it more than once," Sage said.

No.

Ari moved fast, pulling her under him, and enjoyed the surprised little squeak she let out. Her cheeks flushed and big eyes stared back at him.

"Does it look like it? I have a million things I should be doing, and yet I'm here with you," Ari replied as he gazed down into her beautiful, big eyes. "The question is, why?"

Her tongue swept across her lips. "Why then, Ari?"

"I find you irresistible and enjoyable to be with."

"What are we doing?" Sage whispered.

"Netflix and chill, baby."

Sage closed her eyes briefly, then she smiled sadly at him. "I'm sorry. I just had a bad day."

Yet another opening for the conversation he needed to have with her. He let it pass. He just wanted five more minutes with her before everything turned to shit. His forehead landed on hers and Ari drew in a deep breath.

Sage wriggled underneath him. He let her sit up and watched as she ran a nervous hand through her hair.

"I'm sorry, Ari. I'm tired and need to process some stuff from today. Do you mind if I have an early night?"

"Sage," Ari said.

"I'm sorry."

"No, sweetheart. I am." Ari knew he was about to change both their lives. "We need to talk."

Her brows bunched in confusion. "About what?"

About how you've unwittingly gotten mixed up in dangerous things. About how I am about to tell you something that could lead to you losing your life or offer the chance for you to start a whole new one.

The choice was hers, but Ari knew he had to tell her everything.

"Vampires."

CHAPTER TWENTY-NINE

Brayden's phone rang, and he glanced up at Craig.

"Do me a solid and don't call Brianna yet," Brayden said. "Let me talk to the king, otherwise Willow will be on my tail thirty seconds after you speak to your mate."

Willow and Brianna were best friends, so there was no way the two of them wouldn't share the news they were being brought over to the United States.

"Fine," Craig replied, tapping the screen of his smartphone impatiently on his knee.

Brayden swiped the phone to answer as he walked down to the office. "Organize the teams to prepare a jet if you want to make yourself useful," he called out to Craig as he put the phone to his ear. "Vince."

"I'm not your fucking secretary!" Craig called.

Brayden nudged the door closed. Not that he usually kept anything from Craig, but occasionally he needed to have a private conversation with his brother. And today was that day.

"Jet? You leaving Seattle already?" Vincent asked.

"No." Brayden stepped up to the window and drew a breath. "The opposite."

"What's going on?" the king's voice darkened.

"We've found the missing vampire. Callan. Ari has an asset inside BioZen, so we are making moves to get him out," Brayden replied.

"That's damn good news," Vincent said. "What am I missing?"

Yeah, Vincent knew him well.

"We don't believe it's safe to leave the family in Italy. I want them here with Craig and me," Brayden replied. "Including Kate and Lucas."

"What's your plan?"

"We get them here overnight. Ari has offered us accommodation at The Institute. I think we should accept. His security is the best I've seen," Brayden replied. "Then, when you're finished in Washington, you get your ass to Seattle."

Brayden heard the king growl.

Asking him to fly the queen and their newborn across the world without either him or Craig onboard was a big ask. Kate may also have a few things to say about it, but Brayden knew it was the right thing to do.

These people—humans—had disempowered and kidnapped dozens of vampires and they still didn't know how. It meant all of them, including his warriors, were vulnerable.

At least if the females were close to them, they had a better chance of protecting them.

"I don't like it," Vincent said.

"Neither do I, but it's the best way to keep them safe," Brayden replied. "Let's get them on a plane and over here as fast as we can."

There was silence for a long minute until the king spoke again.

"Let me speak to Kate. She may prefer to fly into Washington."

Brayden rubbed his knuckle against his forehead and squeezed his eyes shut. He'd predicted this.

"Vincent, I am not having our king, queen, and the heir to the fucking throne, protected by a handful of vamps. Even if Kurt is there." He growled. "Absolutely not."

"Well, I'm the king—"

"Nope."

"Yeah, I actually am."

"I'm in charge of your security. The decision is final. They are getting on a plane. If you want to fuel up and get over here now, do it," Brayden said.

Brayden rarely put his foot down, but when he did, he meant it. Vincent was the king, yes, and he could tell Brayden—and any vampire - to sit his ass down and do what he was told.

But he wouldn't.

Their relationship, regardless of being brothers, worked because of the respect they had for the roles they played. The king knew Brayden was an expert at what he did, and every decision he made was for their family's safety.

That, and he never wanted to sit on the goddamn throne.

Plus, they were family, so he loved them and stuff.

Whatever.

"You want to tell Kate, or shall I call her?" Brayden added.

"I'll do it. Just text her the time," Vincent said. "She'll need time to prepare, Bray. You can't just uproot a baby."

Like he was the expert. The guy gagged every time he saw a dirty nappy. Clean ones too, now.

"Got it," Brayden replied instead.

"How's it going with our uncle?" Vincent asked.

Brayden walked to a large armchair and sat down. He needed to be honest with Vincent about the conversation he'd had with Ari, but he wanted to do it in a way that wouldn't damage their fragile relationship. Vincent didn't have the close history he had with their uncle, but they weren't strangers.

He recalled Ari's words.

"I am done hiding my identity, little prince. I am a Moretti—the remaining original—and the time for that to be acknowledged is upon us."

"Good. He's been very welcoming, and his mansion is incredible. You'll be impressed."

"Brayden, I'm not the editor of Home and Fucking Country magazine. You know what I'm asking," Vincent said.

Despite himself, Brayden snorted.

"You know, Vince, he's had a long damn life. His identity wasn't acknowledged. Why? It's so fucked up."

"Did you ask him?"

"Yes. He said our grandfather feared Ari would create his own line of vampires and threaten his reign," Brayden replied.

"Yet he has never mated or procreated," Vincent said. "So, why the fucking concern?"

Brayden logged into the VampNet while he was talking to his brother and saw Willow was online. He sent her a message asking her if she was free in ten minutes.

Yesssssss xxxx

He smiled at the reply and couldn't wait to see her face. Dammit, he couldn't wait to get his hands on her body and cock inside her. He lifted his eyes from the screen to concentrate.

"I think he's met his mate," Brayden said. "And Vince, you need to know, if he has, and they can procreate, he intends to start his own line of vampires."

The silence was deafening.

He held the space for the king to process what he'd just shared.

"Let's talk when I get to Seattle," Vincent replied.

Yeah, he'd need a lot of time to mull that over. It wasn't an immediate threat and there were lots of conversations to be had. He knew his brother and had no concerns he would act irrationally. Brayden would never have shared the information over the phone if he had. But it was important Vince knew before he arrived in Seattle.

"Okay. I've got Willow waiting, so I'll see you tomorrow." Brayden punched end on his phone and dialed the video in VampNet. "Hey sexy, do you miss me?"

Willow purred, her dark wavy hair all sexy and messy.

Brayden groaned.

"Are you naked?" He frowned. "Wait, where are you?"

Willow grinned.

"Turn the phone, Willow," Brayden growled. She pouted and turned her device, showing him Brianna and Anna, who were sitting in the hot tub with her.

Brayden shook his head. "Lucky, we didn't launch into phone sex."

"I would have closed my ears!" Brianna called out.

Liar.

"Take me off speaker, mate." He instructed Willow, giving her his bossy look. He wanted Craig to have the opportunity to tell his mate, otherwise he'd never hear the damn end of it.

"I'll get out," Willow said, and the camera went all over the show and there was some splashing and naked skin.

Christ.

With a towel wrapped around her, Willow stepped into the changing rooms and lifted the camera. "Shoot," she said. "Are you coming home, my sexy vampire?"

Brayden shook his head. "No, baby. I need you to come to Seattle," he replied, his tone serious now. "It's not safe for you to stay in Italy without full security, but don't panic. Just get packing for a few weeks and the jet will depart in around six hours."

Willow stared back at him. "Just me?"

"All of you. Kate and Brianna—but please don't tell her before Craig or we'll both suffer." Willow smirked. "I'm serious. Oh, and you may need to help Kate with Lucas."

"What about Anna?"

Brayden blinked.

"You're bringing over the big guns, right?" she asked, reminding him why he loved her. Willow was gorgeous and too damn intelligent for her own good.

"They're called Senior Lieutenant Commanders, not big guns," Brayden replied. "And, yes, Ben is going to escort you to Seattle, so I guess that will include Anna."

Jesus.

They needed a damn castle in Seattle now, too.

"Where are we staying?"

"At Ari's."

"With all the assassin people?" Willow's eyes widened.

Brayden stifled a laugh.

"It's the safest place, baby," he said. "Plus, I'll be with you most of the time."

Her bedroom eyes lit up, and Brayden felt his cock react.

"Good, I've been aching for you," Willow said, tilting her head seductively.

"Okay, don't do that. I have to ring the queen, and I don't want to do it with a damn erection." He added, "And leave that ache for me to sort out when you get here. No touching, princess."

She gave him a naughty smile. "It can be both."

Brayden groaned. "I'll see you tomorrow, baby. I love you," he said. "And Willow? Don't. Tell. Bri."

"Fine!" she replied. "Love you, sexy vamp."

He ended the call and walked back into the living area where Craig was pouring a glass of plasma. "Ring your girl," Brayden said, taking the glass of plasma off the counter.

"Dude. Get your own," Craig said, freezing as he went to put the bottle back in the fridge.

"I'm the prince."

"That excuse is getting real old," Craig moaned.

Brayden flopped down onto the sofa.

"The jet is booked, and the males are getting their shit together," he said, referring to their most senior warriors.

"So Tom is staying behind, right?" Brayden waited for confirmation.

"And Marcus," Craig said, dropping into the other armchair. "Unless you want him here? I think Ben, Kurt, and the green team led by Carlos are enough."

Brayden nodded slowly. "Anna is coming with Ben, right?"

"Yeah, so Ben just informed me," Craig said, rolling his eyes. "Little shit. But I get it. I hate being away from Bri."

Brayden nodded slowly. He couldn't shake the feeling this would be the start of a permanent move back to the United States. He wasn't sure how he felt about that. Being back in their homeland of Italy had been nice.

In the end, it would be Vincent's decision.

"Let's get our asses back to The Institute and sort the accommodation before they arrive." Not just for their mates—Brayden wanted to check out the rooms for the king and queen, and baby Lucas. "Ben, Anna and the teams can stay here, but I want our girls with us there."

"Brianna and I will stay here," Craig said.

"You sure?"

Craig nodded. "Let's just get the royal family secured."

Brayden stared at his commander.

"No. I want you and Brianna with us. Don't argue with me about this. You may not be royals, but both of you are essential members of the extended family," he said firmly. "Plus, there's no way I'm separating Willow from Brianna. She'd drive me and the entire mansion crazy."

Craig nodded knowing. "True, that."

CHAPTER THIRTY

"I'm sorry, what?" Sage asked, her mouth dropping open.

Vampires.

She had nearly canceled the date with Ari tonight after being shocked by the news that vampires existed. This time it wasn't a bunch of fake news on the internet—it was true. Highly respected scientists had presented images and facts to her this afternoon that shocked her.

They looked just like humans.

The rest of the afternoon had been a blur.

In the end, she hadn't canceled because her desire to see Ari again had been stronger. The moment her eyes had locked on his outside her office building, she'd felt calmer. He had taken the nervous edge off her and made her smile, but now she needed space to process all the thoughts forcing their way into her consciousness.

Sage couldn't talk to anyone about this. She was now a member of a high-level security team working to understand the inner functionings of a vampire. Apparently, they had volunteer subjects, and she was going to meet an *actual* vampire.

But Ari had just said he wanted to speak to her about...
vampires. Sage stared at him blankly.

What was going on?

"Sage." Ari repeated, and her eyes flew to his. "Sage,
stop thinking," Ari said quietly, placing a large hand on her
arm.

Vampire.

"I need you to stay calm and hear what I have to say,"
Ari said.

"You want to talk about vampires?" Sage asked, staring
at him. She tried to keep her expression blank.

"Yes." He nodded.

"Can we do that another night? Friday maybe? I am
really tired."

The intense way Ari was looking at her sent shivers
through her. He shook his head. "No, *mia stellina*, this
can't wait." He shifted his large body on the sofa away
from her. She frowned. She'd never seen him distance
himself from her.

She began to shake.

Something was wrong.

"Calm, Sage." A feeling of relaxation flowed through
her, but it felt forced.

"What is going on?" she asked, panic fighting for
dominance. "Why do you want to talk about them tonight?"

Her eyes darted around the room.

"Today you learned vampires exist," Ari said, and she
recoiled.

"What?" How the hell did Ari Moretti know that?

"You were also told there are vampires at BioZen to
undertake... experiments on." He ground out the words and
his eyes darkened.

Sage froze.

This was dangerous territory.

"Ari," Sage said, standing. "I can't talk to you about this. How do you know? Who are you?"

He nodded calmly, staying seated.

"Where did you get this information?" she asked, knowing she shouldn't, but it was clear Ari knew something and was here for that very reason.

Ari shifted on the sofa and leaned back into the cushions.

"I overheard your conversation," he replied. "I'm not going to lie to you about anything, Sage, but I need you to know a few facts before I leave here tonight. Facts that are going to shock you more than you already are."

Sage wrapped her arms around herself.

"I doubt it," she replied. "But I'm not comfortable with this conversation. Maybe you should go, Ari. I need to speak to my manager."

Ari let out a sigh and shook his head. "No. I'm not leaving. Once I've shared this information with you, the decision on how you proceed is up to you."

Sage blinked. Her brain was in do-not-compute mode. What did Ari have to do with any of this and how could what he knew surprise her more? Sage couldn't fathom how a gym owner had knowledge on the existence of vampires.

Unless they really were circulating in society. She narrowed her eyes and took a step toward him.

"Do you know any vampires?" She shouldn't be asking, but it might come in handy for their research, and he clearly knew something.

"Yes."

"Holy shit."

"Sage—"

"Can you tell me about them? Can I meet them?" she asked. "Wait. Are they dangerous?"

Ari stared at her as if deciding on his answer and she felt a chill run up the back of her neck.

"Are they?"

"Not all of them, but they can be." He nodded.

"Do they go to your gym?" she asked, and when he let out a little laugh, she frowned.

"Sage, sweetheart, I'm sorry." Ari shook his head. "You are the most gorgeous female I could ever have hoped for."

Sage lowered her brows at him. "Ari, what the hell is going on?"

"First, I need you to know I'll never hurt you. Remember what you told Talia today?"

What the hell?

Sage gasped. "You heard my conversations? Oh fuck, I'm going to get fired," she said, throwing her arms up in the air. "Jesus, Ari, do you have any idea what you have done? These people are... they're... you don't fuck with them."

Ari stood, and he seemed to suck all the air out of the room.

"Sage. I am a vampire."

She froze.

Then she burst out laughing.

ARI waited for Sage to move through her feelings of disbelief, then shock and arrive at panic. It was the usual process and didn't take long.

Her expression showed him everything. He could have dived inside her mind, but it was unnecessary. And this wasn't his first rodeo.

"Are you here to kill me?" she asked.

He frowned.

"What? No. Jesus, Sage." Even though he'd heard it from humans many times, coming from Sage, the question struck him in the chest.

"Is that why you had sex with me?" she asked, shaking.

Fuck. There was no way he was letting her believe that.

"I had sex with you because I like you." He answered honestly. "A lot, Sage."

"You're a vampire."

He nodded.

Sage's eyes scanned his body, and he watched her scientific mind working overtime as she fought against her fear.

"You've seen every inch of my body, and touched me everywhere, Sage," Ari said as her mouth dropped open. He hated the way she was looking at him right now.

"Oh, God." Sage's trembling increased, and he clenched his fists against the dominating urge to go to her.

"Stop, Sage," he demanded, and her eyes flew to his in surprise. "Stop your mind going to the worst-case scenario. I'm still me. I have never hurt you and I never will."

God, he hoped that was true. He would do everything in his power to honor that promise.

"Oliver?"

He nodded.

"Oh, my God," Sage said, and dropped to the floor. Ari flew across the room and scooped her up. She gasped and thrashed at him.

"Punch away, but I am not going to stand there and watch you collapse in front of me. Not when I fucking l—"

He stopped himself. He couldn't say it. Not yet. Maybe not ever.

Sage screamed into his chest.

"It's you I'm terrified of." Sage cried as she continued to punch his arms.

"Okay," Ari said, wrapping his arms around her and letting her tire herself out. His heart warmed as Sage found comfort in his arms. She may not be aware, but her body was calming as he wrapped around her.

It was a true sign she could be his mate—her soul letting her know he was trustworthy, even though her mind struggled with the reasoning.

Loud sobbing continued as her thumping began to subside.

"I have to… have to…" Sage tried to move off him, but Ari held her firm.

He had no idea what he was doing. He was just following his instincts, hoping it worked. Despite everything, even the risk to his race, the most important thing to him right now was Sage.

Watching her collapse had struck him in the heart like a fucking arrow.

"Let the panic pass," Ari said quietly, rubbing her back.

Hiccup.

"What if you kill me?"

"Then I couldn't fuck you anymore, so that would be stupid of me," he replied with a smile.

She glanced up at him, her eyes bloodshot and wet. "Are you mad?"

"Furious,"

"I don't mean that."

"I know, but when you're ready, I want to tell you why I'm so angry," Ari said.

"At me?"

"I hope not." Sadness spread across his chest as his eyes lowered.

"Promise I'm safe?"

"From me, yes. I will protect you with my life," Ari answered. "From those you work for, trying to harm my race? That is up to you, *mia stellina*."

Sage blinked at him and wiped her eyes with her forearm. He'd never wanted to kidnap anyone before, but my God, he wanted to just steal her away from this entire mess.

But he couldn't.

Sage was an asset. She was an earpiece and front door key for them into their number one enemy's home.

Ari cupped Sage's cheek. "I wish I could tell you what you mean to me." Even though he was waiting for confirmation of the mating bond, Ari already knew. Never had he felt so excited and terrified at the same time.

His heart was ready to shatter if Sage chose BioZen and science tonight. Or she might be the female for whom he'd been waiting fifteen hundred and twenty-two years.

If he had to wait a few more fucking hours, he would.

No, he wouldn't kidnap her, but if someone harmed her while this played out, he would take their life and then his own.

CHAPTER THIRTY-ONE

"Tell me then," Sage said, as she stared into the depths of Ari's eyes.

"I don't know how," Ari said. "This is new to me. Feeling this way. You are... special."

Sage scanned his face, looking for answers. What was he trying to tell her? Aside from being a vampire.

Apparently.

Ari smiled and wiped the hair from her face. "You want more information, Sage, not confessions of *amore*. Tell me what you want to know."

Amore?

Didn't that mean love? Her eyes widened. There was no way Ari loved her. They'd known each other less than a week.

Focus Sage. He's just told you he's a goddamn vampire.

"Fangs," she spat out. "Wait, aren't you meant to be super-strong?"

He grinned. "You don't think I'm strong?"

She chewed her lip.

"Okay, I'll save the jokes for another day," Ari said, slipping out from under her and standing up. "You ready?"

She nodded and tucked her legs underneath her, then grabbed a cushion.

He stared at the cushion. "Armor?"

"Yes. I feel safer."

"Good to know. I'll get my males some cushions." He smirked.

"Your gym guys?"

"About that... actually, let's focus on one thing at a time," Ari said. "Fangs or strength. Which one first?"

Part of her was hoping this was all a really bad joke, or she'd wake up. Sage knew it wasn't. "Strength."

Ari looked around the living room.

"Stand up," he said. "Everything else has girly ornaments on and I don't want to break anything."

Sage jumped off the sofa, keeping the cushion hugged to her chest. Ari walked to the end and, with zero effort, lifted it up, so it was standing on one end. She stared at him, unconvinced he'd done anything supernatural.

He shifted his hands for a better grip, then lifted it into the air.

Jesus Christ.

"I mean, steroids could do that," she said, blinking, looking for a rational explanation.

Ari replaced the sofa and sent her a look which resembled pity. Then he walked over and guided her to sit down next to him. They faced each other.

Shit.

"Wait."

"No, Sage. It's time," Ari said. His lips spread open and long enamel fangs slipped from his gums down past his teeth.

She began to tremble again. Her brain wasn't sure what to make of it. She could see the physical difference between a human mouth and his. It wasn't done by a medical procedure; she was pretty sure of that. There were clear veins and blood pumping through both the gums and teeth. They were alive and looked like little weapons.

"Don't touch," Ari said, his voice altered by the change in his mouth. "They can hurt you."

She nodded repeatedly.

"I've never felt them."

"Yes, you have. Once," he said. "It was an error on my part."

Sage remembered the sharp bite to her skin when they were in bed playing and joking about vampires.

"Do you drink human blood?"

Ari nodded. "To survive. We don't kill humans, and we have lived peacefully with your race on earth for over fifteen hundred years."

Sage blanched. "How? How is that possible?"

Ari smiled. "Now that is something I hope to tell you one day, *mia stellina*. And you will be the only living being who knows the entire truth."

Sage frowned in confusion.

"There is a lot I'd like to tell you, but one thing at a time. For now, we have a more urgent matter to discuss."

"More urgent than learning vampires exist, and the man I have been sleeping with is one of them?"

Ari nodded. "Yes. The two are connected."

"Oh, God. How?"

How much worse could this get? The look on Ari's face was grim. Even though he occasionally joked around with her, for the most part, he was a powerful and dominant personality. More prone to seriousness.

But this look was dark.

"BioZen has one of my vampires. They have been experimenting on him for months," Ari said.

Sage's eyes widened.

"Yes, he's a volunteer," she replied, her heart thumping.

"No, Sage, he's not."

CHAPTER THIRTY-TWO

Aside from Sage's commitment to denying as much as she could about their conversation, Ari was impressed with how she was handling it. Now, though, her reality was about to shatter completely. And this was just the beginning of what could be a very long journey into a whole new world, life and existence for her.

Ari understood as he'd had it happen to him many, many years ago.

"Sage, no vampire would volunteer to be experimented on. From birth, or... well, yeah, from an early age, we teach vampires to remain hidden from humans. We've always known what would happen if we were discovered."

Her eyes dipped away from his and he saw the shame.

"We need to talk about this, Sage. It is vitally important. I wish to fuck you weren't involved with this, but you are."

Sage shook her head.

Fuck.

"I am not allowed to talk about it, my contract—"

Ari's body tensed up like a nuclear bomb about to explode. Was this the moment she chose science? Would she choose information over the life of a living creature he'd just told her was being experimented on?

Of course, she would.

His heart began to splinter.

It was what scientists did every day. A rat, a mouse, any number of living beings. To them, a vampire was an unknown they would need to study.

Bile rose within him, but he'd always known this would be a possibility. Sage was a scientist. Sure, not all of them lacked ethics, but he'd hoped Sage was one of the good ones.

"Fuck your contract, Sage. I will protect you legally." He removed a major block for her.

Her eyes darted to his. "Oh, and how will I pay for that? And my mortgage? Tony is moving out and now you want me to lose my job. I can't risk talking to you about this top-secret information." She stood up. "Ari, I can't. You need to leave."

Ari shook his head as disappointment flowed through him.

It was like she wasn't hearing him.

It was time to be completely up-front about the stakes here. Then the rest was up to her. Ari had to accept, whether she was his mate or not, that the decision was up to her. If she chose to be part of the BioZen team and continue on, she was his enemy.

Ari parked his emotions and let out a sigh.

"Let me be straight with you, Sage Roberts," Ari said firmly. "The vampire BioZen has been experimenting on for months is named Callan. He has a family, and it's likely he has been in tremendous pain and suffering this entire time. He may not even be alive, but if he is, my team and I will be retrieving him."

Sage stared at him; her lips pressed together.

"You could assist us, or not. The choice is yours."

Her brows creased. "The men at your gym?"

Ari held her eyes for a moment, then decided it wouldn't make any difference to tell her the truth.

"I don't own a gym. I own a private security company with the most powerful warriors on earth. We work for wealthy and influential people, including humans and governments, all around the world," Ari said. "I can protect you. Or I can do this without you."

Sage's eyes darted around the room.

"I understand your fear. The industry you work in is powerful."

She shook her head and covered her face. He didn't know if she was crying, but it took everything in him not to go to her.

"Sage, *fuck*. Talk to me for God's sake."

"What can I say?" she said, flopping back down on the sofa and leaning her arms on her knees. She stared down at the floor. Ari used his foot to move the coffee table out of the way and crouched in front of her, leaving a little space.

She glanced at him. "So you're going to use your vampire power in front of me all the time now?"

His mouth opened, then shut. "Yes. It's who I am." He was pissed that she would even ask that. "If you choose to remain part of the experimental team, it won't be an issue because you will never see me again."

You won't live long in any case.

Not if she was his enemy. An enemy of the vampire race.

Crack.

Another part of his heart fell away.

Sage's mouth fell open. "You're asking me to leave my job? We only met a few days ago and have fucked a handful of times. I think that's a little demanding."

Fury was building within him as Sage focused on stupid human details. He realized she didn't have the same

231

context as him, and yet Ari was struggling to curtail his anger.

He didn't want to scare her and knew this conversation was coming to an end.

"I'm asking you to walk away from an evil environment hurting innocents," Ari said. "If you do, I will take care of you in every way. I give you my word. Forget about our sexual relationship, this is about something much—"

"More important?" Sage asked, raising an eyebrow. "Thanks for the clarity."

"That's not what—"

Sage's phone rang, and they both stared at each other.

Jesus.

"It's Mom," she said. "I have to answer as it's late and she'll freak if I don't."

"Answer it. On speaker," Ari said. "And stay in here."

He had to be sure Sage didn't tell anyone anything. Though his team was monitoring her, he'd asked them to turn it off while he was with her.

"Hey Mom," Sage said. "It's super late. Is everything okay?"

"It's only nine, Sage," her mother replied. "I'm ringing to see how work was today."

Ari watched Sage rub her forehead.

"Fine. Why?" Sage replied.

"Well… did you?" Her mother didn't finish her question and Ari frowned at Sage. Then her eyes widened.

"Oh. Yes. I got the promotion," she replied quickly. "Hey, can I call you back tomorrow? It's been a long day and I want to get to sleep."

"Congratulations darling. Listen, tomorrow we will celebrate. I have a bottle on ice, and your sister can come over. Your father is going to be so proud."

232

Ari felt a pang of regret for her. From today her life would never be the same. Her family might irritate her, but if she were his mate, she wouldn't have them in her life for much longer. Maybe for a few years, but as they aged, and she didn't, it would raise questions.

This was all assuming she *was* his mate and chose the right side.

If it turned out Sage was, he would turn her. She wouldn't understand now, but as an original vampire, her existence was miraculous, and he wasn't going to fuck around convincing her.

He'd change her and then ask her forgiveness.

If she contributed to the experiments on Callan or any of his vampires, she was an enemy, and that was something Ari would never be able to face. Thank fuck Brayden was in Seattle. If there was anyone he trusted to end her life, it would be the prince.

His hope was wavering. Sage hadn't acted as shocked and revolted by the possibility of live experimentation as he'd hoped she would.

She glanced at him. "Tomorrow night? Actually Mom, I have a date."

They did? Oh, the guy. Yeah, no, that wasn't fucking happening. He'd told her to cancel it. Ari raised a brow at her. *I don't fucking think so.* Sage looked away.

"Oh," her mother said.

"Hang up, sweetheart," Ari commanded her, a sliver of anger lacing his words.

"Mom, I have to go," Sage said, her eyes on him. "I'll swing by on the weekend, okay? I love you."

Ari stood.

"Oh, darling. That's so nice to hear. I love you too." Her mom gushed and when the conversation ended, Sage curled herself back in the corner of the sofa.

He let out a long sigh and stared at her.

"There is so much more to share with you, but for now, I think it's best I leave you to your thoughts and conscience," Ari said, frowning. "If you find yourself unhappy with what you see, text me. If you have any photos or information you can share with us, that will be helpful."

Sage simply nodded.

Ari took in the small human and clenched his fists, fighting the desire to teleport her back to his mansion and simply turn her.

He had to give her a chance. One small and very fucking important chance.

"Remember what I said, Sage. We *will* retrieve Callan and destroy BioZen's operation. If you choose to stay and be part of these experiments, I cannot protect you."

Her mouth fell open. "Are you threatening me?"

"No," Ari replied, his eyelids closing briefly, then he looked directly at her. "This is me, protecting my race while I tear my heart apart."

Then he teleported away.

CHAPTER THIRTY-THREE

"L et me take him," Willow said, lifting Lucas out of Kate's arms. "Whooo's Aunty Willow's favorite boy?"

"That would be Brayden," Brianna said, laughing.

"Whooo's Aunty Willow's *second* favorite boy?" she corrected while the queen laughed and began to pack up the ten million baby items she seemed to have to lug around with her. Willow hugged Lucas to her chest and bounced gently.

"Aguga mooova gah," Lucas said.

"Exactly, little prince," Willow responded. "I totally agree."

The jet doors finally opened and, predicably, two giant vampires came flying on board.

"Arrghhh," Brianna cried, throwing herself at Craig as if they hadn't seen each other in two years.

The truth was, it felt like two hundred. Being away from your mate was unnatural and uncomfortable. All three females had been driving each other crazy the past week.

"Fuck, Bri!" Craig said as he pressed her up against the sofa and… well, if she hadn't been a vampire, Willow may have been concerned about her friend's safety.

Willow's eyes darted to Brayden's as he stalked toward her. Hunger swirled in those silver eyes.

"My queen," he said with a smile and nod to Kate, then gripped Willow's hips, glancing down at her and Lucas. "Hey beautiful."

Willow wanted to purr as he lowered his lips to hers with force, while being careful not to squash the heir between them. Their kiss deepened.

"Gah! Gooooey." Brayden released her mouth and glanced at Lucas.

"Hey little man." He kissed him on the forehead. "We're going to have a talk when you get a little older about cock-blocking."

"Brayden Moretti!" Kate snapped.

"We can't say cock either? He has a cock." Brayden frowned, his eyes darting between her and the queen.

"It's a penis, Brayden," Kate replied.

"I know what it is. Thanks for the biology lesson." Brayden winked at Willow, and they shared a grin. "Please tell me when we have little princes and princesses, we will let them curse and say vagina and other things."

Willow grinned at him. She would let him do whatever he wanted if he impregnated her. Every day she wondered if she was with child, but she needed to stop so it didn't drive her mad if she wasn't. Sometimes it took over a hundred years.

"Yeah, silly question." Brayden smirked.

"Can someone please take a few of these bags? I have no nannies because of these ass... annoying humans," Kate said, and Willow watched Brayden smirk at her near slip-up.

"Craig. Bri." Brayden ordered them. "I've got the queen, princess, and prince. You two take the bags."

Willow handed Lucas back to Kate, and then finally he wrapped his arms around her and lifted her off the ground. The feel of him against her made all her senses calm.

An hour later, they were being escorted to their rooms. Willow had met Ari in Italy, but the powerful vampire was not here. Instead, Oliver, who had taken Ben's old job, and another scary assassin dude, Jason, were showing them to their accommodations.

"Ari said you can choose whichever rooms you'd like," Oliver said.

"We've checked them out, Kate, so it's over to you," Brayden said, turning to the queen. "These two are right next to each other so you can take this one and Willow and I will take the other."

Kate walked through the door they were standing next to and glanced around. "This will be fine. I can set up the bassinet over here. And... yes, thank you, this will be fine."

Willow knew the queen was extremely unhappy about uprooting baby Lucas, but they'd had a talk on the flight over about it being more important that they were all safe and alive.

Powerful vampires they might be, but now the humans had some ability to disempower them, the whole power balance had changed.

Typical.

Just as she'd gained superpowers.

"We'll help you get things set up," Willow said to Kate. "When is the king arriving?"

"He'll be arriving this time tomorrow," Craig said. "We're down the hall, so see you in a couple of hours."

Brayden glanced down at her, heat in his eyes.

"Go. I can unpack and put Lucas down. Go shag your mate," Kate said, waving them off.

"She said shag." Brayden smirked, and Kate gave him the finger. Willow giggled and glanced at the assassin males.

"We'll leave you to it," Oliver said, pushing against Jason's arm. The male was checking Brianna out.

Oh boy.

This wasn't going to end well. Her sexy red-headed friend had quite a following of fans, much to Craig's frustration.

"Word of advice," Willow said, leaning forward. "If the commander catches you looking at his mate, you'll be rabbit food."

Jason's eyes darted from hers to the prince.

"Okay, let's go," Brayden said, guiding her down the hallway. Then he called over his shoulder. "The princess is right, by the way."

Willow grinned as the door closed behind them and huge arms scooped her up.

"Mate." Brayden growled into her neck.

CHAPTER THIRTY-FOUR

Sage lay awake, staring at the ceiling for hours. At one point, she began crying. She didn't really understand why she was sobbing, but she felt a great sadness and loss.

Of what?

It was like she'd lost her virginity or some damn thing. Everything she knew about life was untrue. How could a species live among them for so long undetected? Especially with technology and surveillance.

How did she know vampires weren't to blame for the millions of missing children, or serial murders, or any number of other things? Sure, they could have wiped out humans. But then again, why would you destroy your food source?

Fucking hell. That just scared the hell out of her.

Yet, Ari and Oliver had never hurt her. They had pleasured her.

Sure, Sage, haven't you heard of animals playing with their food first?

Ugh.

As a scientist, she'd been trained to ask questions, but she had no data. What Ari had showed her tonight pointed to vampires being predators. Yet what was the point of being terrified of something that had existed long before anyone knew?

And so the monkey mind continued for hours.

Sage realized that wasn't why she was crying.

Not really.

The way Ari had left, his words had cut her to the bone.

It made no sense that she wished his arms were wrapped around her when he was a vampire.

And yet she did.

She was scared and had no idea what to do. She couldn't just quit, or she'd lose her home. She knew that's what he wanted her to say, and she couldn't. Sage needed to see it with her own eyes. Processing all of this was taking some time. She was upset he hadn't even given her a moment to come to grips with everything.

And he'd done it cruelly.

Part of her understood what he must be feeling—kind of—she had no idea, really. What she needed was time to work it all out in her head.

Accepting money and support from a man—vampire—she'd known for thirty seconds wasn't an option. Especially one who appeared to have told her so many lies.

Ari didn't own a gym. He owned a security company dealing with dangerous people and it was full of vampires.

Ugh.

What other lies had he told her? Her head spun. She couldn't trust a man she barely knew. That would be foolish. She needed to go back to the office and reassess the reality once she had a look around. Perhaps Ari was wrong, and she could tell him?

Rolling over for the millionth time, Sage wiped her eyes.

She glanced at the clock. Three a.m.

"This is me, protecting my race while I tear my heart apart."

Those were his departing words, and she was unsure what they meant. Or who they were referring to. Sage hoped he meant her, but his cold eyes had sent a chill through her right before he'd disappeared before her eyes.

Disappeared.

Before.

Her.

Eyes.

Did he think it was okay to just do that without warning?

Sage had gasped and buried her face into the cushions and let out a scream. Tele-fucking-portation?

He didn't think to warn her?

"I have no damn idea about anything anymore," Sage said into the empty room. "Give me the answers, God. I'm scared and don't know what to do."

ARI sat in his private office listening to the audio from Sage's tracker. Darren had set up a livestream he could connect to whenever he wanted.

So, basically, a source of torture.

When he'd teleported away, he'd gone down to the street outside her house and listened to her howl. It wasn't loud, but his vampire hearing had picked it up loud and clear. His heart thumped a million miles an hour as he tried to understand the swirl of emotions running through him.

He wanted to go back to Sage and comfort her, but he couldn't. He was a strategic warrior—he knew the importance of patience and letting things unfold.

But Sage wasn't a strategy, nor was she an asset. She was a woman he cared for. A woman he wanted. A woman who could be his mate.

And yet, she *was* all those things.

Only time would tell, and waiting was hell.

Ari headed to his bedroom to get a few hours' rest. He was living human hours right now as they monitored Sage's daily movements. If there was an opportunity to strike a BioZen location, they had to be rested and ready, which meant while his team focused on her audio, the assassins needed to rest.

While Ari rarely went out into the field, he would today. For Sage.

Craig and his team had been training with his guys tonight, while the prince made sure the queen and princess were comfortable. Ari hadn't spoken to them, rather letting his team keep him updated. He was in no mood to be social or polite.

In a few hours, Sage would return to the BioZen office, and he would have his answer.

The next twelve hours were crucial.

Ari sighed. One glance in the mirror and he saw his eyes remained the same as they had forever. No ring. No sign of the mating bond. At this point, it didn't matter. His feelings for her were clear, no matter what happened.

If Sage chose to remain on the team of scientists harming vampires, he could not mate her.

He also couldn't live without her.

Ari cursed, splashing water over his face, then went to lay down on his bed. He opened the app on his phone so he could continue listening to Sage's livestream.

She was now breathing deeply in sleep.

He lay the phone on the pillow and closed his eyes. There was some solace in listening to her breath, but she stirred a need within him. His hand slid down his body and he gripped his cock. Slowly his hand moved over it, wishing Sage was in his bed, and in his arms, so he could be deep inside her.

Protecting her. Owning her.

Sage was his. Ari was becoming more and more sure of it. What a beautiful and disastrous thing.

He woke a few hours later to the sound of her tears. A sliver of hope flashed through him.

CHAPTER THIRTY-FIVE

Sage placed her thumb on the panel to access the foyer to her new offices. The second door activated when it picked up her biometric chip.

Her heart was racing with nerves.

When she'd woken, everything came flooding back. She'd burst into tears, sobbing. If ever there was a day to have a sickie, today was the day.

Yet it wasn't.

Yesterday had been one of the most shocking and emotional days of her life. Vampires were real.

Wow!

Sage had been shocked. She'd also felt incredibly fortunate to be one of the few people on the planet to find out and to be part of a team of scientists selected to learn more about it. This was what she did, animal health, and it was clear now why she'd been awarded the promotion.

It was an honor.

Now, if what Ari had said was true, she had a big decision to make. It changed everything.

Her reason for being a scientist was to progress human knowledge and discover new things. Sometimes that meant sacrifice. She'd been part of a team of students at university working on a project to eliminate live testing on animals in labs, but it was still some time away from being widely available.

While at times it was still part of her job, never did she torture the animals.

Ari had made it sound like BioZen was using this Callan in unethical ways and torturing him. Sage couldn't believe it. The company had sound policies on things like this, and if he had expected her to just pack up her job and leave, he was mistaken.

Ari.

So vampires were real... and she was sleeping with one of them. As in sex. Having sexual intercourse with a being from another species.

Jesus F. Christ.

Even worse, Sage had to acknowledge she had feelings for him. Lust, yes. In spades. But there was more. She'd been fighting it for days and it had only grown stronger.

Tonight she was meant to be going on a date with Carl, and it was the last thing she wanted. Ari had told her to cancel it, but she hadn't. Now she was going to do it for a different reason.

Her life was in turmoil.

Sage carried her box of office things into her new office and placed it on her sparse desk. The only thing on it was the new laptop, which she'd been told had new security protocols for the project.

"Good morning, Sage," Sandy said, leaning against the doorjamb.

"Hi," Sage replied, wringing her hands.

"Once you're unpacked, meet us in meeting room three. We are taking all new recruits on a tour." She pushed away from the door. "Leave your mobile device in your office."

Sage nodded and chewed her bottom lip as Sandy walked off. This is it. If there was a live subject, then she was about to see it. She sat down in her chair.

"Oh, God," she murmured quietly.

What if Ari was right? What if she couldn't do this and had to leave her job?

She couldn't stay, could she? There was no way she could watch a living, breathing being—someone like Ari or Oliver—suffer. There was no price.

That was human trafficking.

But with vampires.

There might not be a law protecting them—because no one knew they existed—but there should be.

Who would she tell?

Sage could hardly call the police and be all like, *so hey, we have a vampire at work, and it looks like he's been kidnapped.* Vamp-napped?

God.

They'd think she was insane.

In any case, even the police wouldn't get access to this area without a very solid warrant. What judge would give them one? What evidence could she produce to convince a judge there was a vampire being kept in the BioZen laboratory?

She felt completely out of her depth.

Perhaps she should text Ari?

For all she knew, he hadn't completely written her off already. Though he'd disappeared last night without another word, leaving her distraught and confused.

She pulled out her phone and stared at their last messages. Her stomach cramped, which it always did when she was stressed.

First, she'd find out the truth.

Sage slipped her phone down the side of her bra. No way she was going in there and not having her phone with her to gather evidence if this was happening.

She walked into the meeting room and planted a smile on her face.

"Good morning."

She recognized the two other team members who had also joined the team.

"Do you all know each other?" Sandy asked, sipping her coffee.

"Kind of." Murray smiled and reached across the table to shake her hand. "Murray Campoza. This is Jenny Richardson."

"Hey," she said, shaking both their hands.

"Isn't this crazy?" Jenny said, sitting back in her chair.

"I know." Sage smiled, pleased for a moment to be able to share this incredible situation. "Mind-boggling."

Dr. Phillips stepped into the room with another scientist. Sage hadn't seen him before, but he looked pale from a lack of sunlight, and rather unfriendly.

"Good morning, everybody. Sorry to rush you, but we need to get the induction started as I am flying out this afternoon," Dr. Phillips said. "This is Brian. He's the lead scientist in the Callan lab. We'll be showing you around this morning. Please follow all his instructions."

Brian stared at them for a long moment. "We'll need you all in PPE gear after you've scrubbed."

There was nothing new about any of that. It was a common procedure to scrub and sterilize beforehand, just as a hospital would. Then they layered up with protective gloves, masks, and hairnets.

They were rushed down a few corridors and through two more highly secure check points which had security guards on them.

"As we showed you in the presentations, this project has been running for approximately six months," Dr. Phillips said. "We've had a number of locations around the world working on analyzing the data we've retrieved."

Sage tried to take in all the areas they walked through and so far, nothing looked terribly exciting. People in white lab coats, gloves, and masks, just as she was.

Then everything changed.

A door swished open, the sound indicating to all of them they were in an air-controlled environment.

Sandy stopped in front of them and turned. "What you are about to see is a real-life vampire."

Sage's stomach lurched.

"There is no reason to be afraid. He is substantially weakened and cannot harm you," Sandy continued.

Jenny and Murray asked a number of questions while Sage drew in slow, steady breaths to stop herself from vomiting.

"Sage," Brian said.

"Hmm?" she replied, looking up.

"Do you have any questions?"

She shook her head. Probably too fast. "No. Mmm mm. Nope," she replied. "Just taking it all in."

Sandy stared at her, but it was hard to determine what she was thinking under her blue mask. Sage held the woman's gaze until she turned. "Brian, lead the way."

"Your job will be to take daily samples from the subject," Dr. Phillips said as they entered a room which looked like a viewing room inside a police station.

Inside the space there were monitors and computers, with all kinds of beeping and noises going on. It was clear they were monitoring and recording data from whatever was beyond the large glass windows.

Sage lifted her eyes.

Lying on the bed in a sparse room was a large man. Except Sage knew it was no man. This was a vampire.

It was Callan. It had to be.

She held back a gasp.

"Can he hear us?" Jenny asked.

"Yes," Brian replied. "He has advanced hearing compared to humans, so he will be able to hear you."

"What if we whisper?" Sage asked. "How much more powerful are their senses?"

"We estimate around twenty-five times the strength of humans, so, yes, if you whisper, Callan will hear you," Dr. Phillips replied.

Callan.

It *was* him.

Ari had been right.

"Remarkable," Murray said. "Is he resting because it's daytime? How close to fiction have you found their species to be?"

Sandy and Dr. Phillips shared a look which sent chills down Sage's spine. Nothing about this felt right. Sage wanted to knock on the window and ask if Callan was okay. She might not be a doctor or expert on vampires, but even she could see from here he didn't look well.

"Coincidentally, fiction writers have been very close, with a few exceptions. They are sensitive to daylight and therefore slumber during the day," Dr. Phillips shared. "Callan has been with us for a while now."

How long?

Had he volunteered as she'd asked yesterday?

Sage didn't want to ask. She knew the truth like she knew her own name.

Another part of her reality shattered before her very eyes.

Before she knew what was happening, words began to fall from her lips. "Did you say he volunteered?" she asked, staring at the vampire while silence fell around her.

That was all the answer she needed.

Sandy began explaining they had a volunteer program run by a top-secret government department, but Sage knew all she had done was not answer her question.

Then she saw Callan's eye twitch.

Oh, my God.

"Well, let's move on, shall we?" Brian said.

Sage let everyone move ahead of her before she quietly whispered, more quietly than she ever had in her life.

"I will get you out. I know vampires."

Callan opened one eye and stared directly at her.

Ari ripped off his headphones and cursed.

"He's there," Oliver said.

"We have to get in there." Craig stood. "Darren, how'd you get on cracking that system?"

Oliver gave Ari a quick glance while Darren carried on tapping.

Ari ignored them all. His heart was thumping. He'd heard Sage's whisper. He had no idea if the others had understood the importance of what she'd done in those eight simple words, but he did.

It was taking every ounce of his strength he had not to teleport to her right now. He wanted to scream and cry and fuck her. And destroy the humans she worked with.

The prince caught his eye and raised a brow. Ari nodded and the two of them stepped out of the room and wandered down the hall.

"You told her?" Brayden asked.

"Yes," Ari said, running his hand through his hair.

The prince wasn't questioning his decision to tell a human about their existence. They both knew Sage already knew about vampires. He was ascertaining Ari's ability to remain in charge of this operation because of his personal feelings.

Ari would have done the same.

Except this wasn't just some job, this was about the protection and future security of their entire race.

"She's your mate, Ari. You know that, right?" Brayden said.

He shook his head.

"I can't be sure. Not until my eyes change."

"Trust me, I've seen this enough recently. Sage is your mate." He let out a short laugh and slapped him on the back.

Ari tensed. "Nephew, I appreciate your joy in this news, but after all these years, this is not something I can assume."

Brayden tucked his hands into his pockets. "I understand. You have waited one hundred lifetimes."

"One hundred and fifty and more, little prince," Ari said, shaking his head. "Fuck, hearing her whisper those words…"

The prince nodded. "You thought she would harm Callan?"

Ari leaned his back against the wall and rested his head. "I didn't know. I met her four days ago. She's a scientist, and it's in her nature to want knowledge."

It could have gone either way. He shoulders physically relaxed as the tension melted away. He hadn't realized how fucking stressed he'd been. But it wasn't over yet. Not by a long shot.

"It was brave of her to do that," Brayden said.

"Sage is in no position to help him," Ari ground out. "I need to get her out of there and find a way to get our teams inside to help Callan."

Ari saw the look on Brayden's face and knew what was coming next. "Let me take over the operation."

"No," Ari said firmly.

Brayden frowned.

"If I thought I wasn't capable, I would step aside, but I will not stand on the sidelines while my potential mate is entwined in this mess," Ari said. "You know how dangerous it could be for her if they get even a hint that she's connected to us."

"Now we have confirmation this is officially royal business. The king could order—"

"That's bullshit," Ari said firmly, standing away from the wall. He stared at Brayden for a long moment, holding back the words he wanted to say. Instead, he said, "We agreed to collaborate on this together. If this was Willow, you would be in there, guns blazing."

That aside, the king had no authority over Ari Moretti. Technically, the king had authority over *every* vampire. Except him. Ari was not of Vincent Moretti's bloodline.

Ari Moretti was his own fucking line.

An original.

If Ari ever voiced those words, he'd be crossing a different line none of them could come back from. He hadn't voiced it in over fifteen hundred years, and he wasn't ready to do so now.

Every single king had known. *He* knew. And no one had voiced it. Not yet.

Brayden cursed.

Ari's phone began to ring. He pulled it out of his jeans pocket and stared at the screen.

Sage.

"I've got to take this," Ari said, and teleported to his quarters.

He swiped the screen and pushed the speaker button.

"*Ciao, mia stellina.*"

"Ari, speak English. I can't... I can't translate that shit right now." Sage spluttered.

His body stiffened at the anguish in her voice and ignored the rude comment. "What's wrong?"

Even though he'd shared much of what they heard yesterday, Sage hadn't figured out she was being listened to. If he could get away with never telling her, he would, but it was unlikely unless he wiped her memory.

Her voice was labored, and he could hear her heart thumping. "Sage, tell me what's going on?"

"I saw... what you told me," she said. "I don't know what to do."

"Where are you?"

"In the ladies' room," she said. "I just threw up. I, he..."

Ari wished he could teleport into the building, but because it was daylight, he was unable to leave the mansion. If he'd been to BioZen and knew of a safe place to teleport into, he could, but there was no safe option right at this moment.

"I need you to stop talking, sweetheart," Ari said firmly but softly. "I want you to do exactly as I say. Okay?"

Silence.

"Are you nodding?" Ari asked.

"Oh. Yes, okay, what do I do?" Sage said, and he afforded himself a little smile.

Ari looked at the clock. It was after three in the afternoon already.

"I want you to tell your boss you aren't feeling well. Say it's a migraine and you need to be in complete darkness, to take some drugs and go to bed."

Sage was muttering *okay okay okay okay*.

"It's going to be all right. Get in an Uber and have them drop you at my house. I'm texting the address now. We will work this out."

"Okay," she replied again. That was a lot of 'okay's'.

"Leave now, Sage," he ordered, knowing she needed some firm guidance.

"Okay."

Ari teleported back to the logistics room when the call ended. Darren lifted his head and nodded to him.

"We heard," Oliver said. "What's the plan, boss?"

Ari ran his hand through his hair. A plan was formulating in his head, but there were only a couple of people under this roof he could share it with.

For now, it was time to bring everyone up to date on the entire situation. Normally a male wouldn't be so public as the mating dance was taking place, but he'd seen enough psycho males to know it was likely he could lose his shit if anything happened to Sage.

It was his job as the director to ensure his team had all the information so they could do their jobs. They all knew this wasn't a normal job because of Callan.

And now, even more importantly, Sage.

It wasn't because she was a vampire's mate. It was because she was *his* mate. And only a few people in the room knew exactly who he was.

"First things first," Ari said, walking to the front of the room and crossing his arms. "Sage is on her way here. She's human and knows about our race but is in a stake of shock. Yes, she's an asset, but I need you all to be aware of something else."

Brayden crossed his arms.

"What have we missed?" Jason asked, glancing around.

Oliver caught Ari's eye, and they shared a look. Ari nodded at him, and the head assassin smiled.

"Sage Roberts is, probably—and I can't stress the probably enough until I have confirmation—my mate," Ari said.

"Shit."

"Fuck."

"Holy shit."

"Fuck me, really?"

Ari let them all get it off their chests. Many of them knew he was old, like really old, but not all of them knew his origin or story. He was just Ari, the director.

"Hopefully, I don't have to spell this out, but under no circumstances should any harm come to her. Am I clear?"

"Got it."

"Yup."

"No fucking way."

Other heads nodded.

"Sage doesn't know anything, so keep your lips zipped," Ari added. "Darren, Oliver, keep working on finding a way for us to get into BioZen. I'm going to greet Sage."

"Pull that map up again," Craig said, spinning a chair and dropping into it as Brayden pulled out his phone.

Ari walked down the hall until he came to his main office.

He had an idea about how they could get Callan out.

They were going to use the power of the Moretti blood.

His blood.

CHAPTER THIRTY-SIX

Vincent stretched his long black-pants-clad legs out in front of him. It was a stark contrast to the cream leather of the private jet he was about to take off in.

His private jet.

Which was taking him to his queen, and the little prince.

It had been hell being separated from them both, and now Kate was situated at Ari Moretti's mansion in Seattle.

Surrounded by assassins.

And Brayden and Craig, so there was that.

She wasn't happy, but his queen had long understood the importance of following the advice of the captain and commander. Even when she hated it.

Now it impacted Lucas, their little heir. Their little miracle.

A smelly miracle most of the time.

He wasn't going to lie. The break from nappy duty had been damn good. And yet, he couldn't wait to get the little vampire back in his arms.

"We're ready to take off shortly, sir," the captain said, doing up his jacket as he stood in the cockpit doorway. "Anything I need to know?"

Vincent turned to Kurt, who was seated across the other side of the plane tapping on a laptop. "No, we're good to go. I'll update you if anything crops up," Kurt said.

The black ops team were scattered around the plane, mostly in the second lounge area. Resting. It had been a big few days in Washington, DC. They didn't own property in the city, so it had been a logistical nightmare preparing the rooms to sleep in during the day.

The good thing was they could survive on plasma and room service, but a bunch of badass-looking guys getting prawn cocktails delivered with blacked-out windows looked dodgy as fuck, so they stuck to the plasma on the first day before the team got supplies that evening.

No one was going to die, but they didn't need to raise any eyebrows.

Well, except the obvious.

Ten powerful vampires walking into a fancy hotel lobby got attention. Even though he'd been wearing an extremely pricey Tom Ford suit. It didn't matter—they had a huge presence.

The others were in their Moretti uniforms and armed to the teeth because he was the king and that was their job. He couldn't have stopped them if he'd wanted to.

And he didn't want to.

Right now, it had never been a more dangerous time to be a vampire, which was a total mind fuck. He'd spent a portion of his time as king ensuring the race remained respectful of human beings and they understood the importance of keeping their existence hidden.

The meetings he'd attended over the past few days had focused on two things: Working to keep the status quo for as long as possible, and preparing for the inevitable moment it wasn't.

Their strategy was coming along well, but it was difficult work. Alongside the obvious management of media and police reaction when the mass exposure happened, the United States president had presented potential FDA regulations to protect his race from experimentation.

Other country leaders were taking these blueprints to replicate for their nations. It was a whole world project, which was important. The only one missing was Italy. After it was discovered Diego Lombardo was working with Stefano Russo, the now deceased leader of the vampire rebellion, and BioZen, he'd been removed from Operation Daylight.

Then Ben had killed him.

Vincent had not stopped him.

He wasn't in the business of punishing humans for crimes, but this was a crime against vampires.

Which was one of the more complex topics the leaders were working on. Vincent had explained vampires adhered to human laws on the planet just as humans did. But they had a few of their own. It was mostly to do with the royal structure.

The difference with vampires, as opposed to a nation with its own laws, was they were spread across the planet. Theoretically, their laws conflicted with humans.

For example, if someone threatened him as king, he had the right to take their head or life. He was also the king, so he could change laws whenever he liked. But it didn't work that way—you still had to win the hearts of your people and he'd worked damn hard on that since the day of his coronation.

Vincent understood the human concerns around this, but he wasn't changing those laws. If someone, and by that he meant another vampire, threatened him or any of the royals, the punishment was death. They needed to realize vampires weren't human.

They were predators.

Like a wolf pack, there were natural laws.

They toned down their nature to live in this world peacefully with humans, but once there was no need to remain hidden, Vincent was unsure how that would change things.

It was quite possible Ari Moretti's organization may need to expand to support the changing needs of their race and the new world in which they found themselves. Not that Vincent could tell his uncle what to do, but it was one opportunity he'd been ruminating on.

Had the conversation with Brayden thrown him?

Yes and no.

He may not know Ari well, but he did know the vampire was loyal, even if he had left them. He had, but he hadn't. He'd always been in the shadows protecting them.

Vincent wasn't stupid.

He was the king. He'd been trained to see everything.

He'd seen the affection in Ari's eyes when he'd been talking to Brayden and then the wash of emotion when he met his new great, great or some ridiculous amount of great's, nephew, Lucas. How could that not pull on the heartstrings of an original Moretti?

So, he didn't perceive Ari to be an immediate threat to his reign, or more importantly, the stability of the vampire race. He hoped like hell he never would.

As king, there were always threats, and it was his job to assess the true risk of them all.

Ari Moretti was currently very low. But not zero.

Right now, BioZen was their greatest concern, and whoever else was behind the financial backing of the project.

The support of the leaders on Operation Daylight to flesh out any powerful people they knew were involved. James Calder, POTUS, had given a stern warning to everyone sitting around the boardroom table. If they found themselves with a financial interest with anyone connected, no matter how many degrees of separation, they needed to cash out immediately.

How much sway the president had over other leaders was questionable, but Vincent would take it.

More effective were his vampires' reactions when he had shared details on the experiments and pain the subjects had suffered. His intimidating security team had gotten a little fangy and growly from the side of the room and the reaction had raised a few nervous brows. Vincent hadn't stopped them, and that hadn't gone unnoticed. In fact, he'd stared at every face in the room, making it clear his position if any of them were involved.

They would die.

Right from the beginning, he'd been clear. He would work with humans if they worked with him. Or the two races would be at war.

And they all knew who would win.

Vincent snapped back to current time and dialed Kate, now the jet was in the air, to let her know he was leaving DC.

Soon he'd have his mate back in his arms.

He was looking forward to seeing The Institute and the world Ari had created after leaving the Moretti family.

It was time for a new beginning for them all.

CHAPTER THIRTY-SEVEN

Sage sat in the back of the Uber, staring out the window as her right leg bounced up and down.

"You sure this is the right address?" The driver asked a second time.

"Yes. Just head in that direction. I'll find it," Sage replied.

"Fancy address," the driver said. "Gates and Bezos live around there. Did you know that?"

Sage nodded numbly. Nothing would surprise her right now. That two of the richest men on the planet were Ari's neighbors was probably a big deal worth noting, but right now, she couldn't care less.

She let out a little crazy snort.

Bill Gates and Jeff Bezos should probably be more concerned they were living next door to a whole lot of big, scary vampires.

After finishing the tour, Sage couldn't get the image of Callan out of her mind. She'd tried to text Ari so many times and, in the end, she'd raced to the ladies, thrown up and then called him.

Who else could she talk to?

She knew she had to help Callan, but how was she going to do that?

Also, she really needed to feel Ari's arms wrapped around her, telling her everything was going to be okay. Even if it wasn't.

Sage knew she couldn't go back to her job after this. Everything was a mess but going into that lab every day knowing that man, or rather vampire, was being tortured and was basically a victim of kidnap, was not okay with her.

Her phone rang.

Shit, it was Piper.

"Hey," she answered, trying for happy.

"Sorry to call you at work, but… wait, what's wrong?" Piper asked.

"What do you mean what's wrong? All I said was *hey*."

Piper *pfft'd* her. "I am your sister. You don't think I know when something is wrong?"

Was she so damn see-through to everyone?

"I'm fine. I have a migraine, so I'm going home to bed." She stuck to the same lie she'd told Sandy. Her boss had given her a long sideways look when she'd gone into her office, but had nodded and told her to get some sleep.

"You don't get migraines," Piper said, her voice thick with suspicion.

"I get migraines," she snapped.

Shit, she just remembered she had the date with Carl tonight and hadn't canceled.

"Is this the place?" the driver asked, reading out the address. They both leaned to look out the window at the enormous solid black gates barely visible because they were set back from the road.

"Sage." Piper called through the phone, which had fallen away from her ear.

"What? Oh, look Piper, I have to go. I'll call you on the weekend." She went to hang up and then stopped. "Love you."

"Wha—"

End call.

Sage climbed out of the vehicle mumbling a thank you to the driver and walked toward the enormous gates. Ari lived *here*.

Sage glanced around her at the thick rows of trees on either side of the gates. There was a security panel to her right, so she headed over to it. Beyond the gates was a long driveway which eventually curved, so she couldn't see beyond it. On each side was a sparse well-manicured lawn.

She pressed a black button and waited.

The gates began to open. There was one single quiet click and then they moved in silence.

Sage pulled her handbag up on her arm and wrapped her coat tighter around her.

Was she supposed to just walk in?

Her phone buzzed.

Walk down to the house and I'll meet you at the front door. I can't come out in the daylight, mia stellina.

Of course, he couldn't. It was still daylight, even though the sun was low in the sky and beginning to fade.

The driveway was long and it took her nearly six minutes to reach the house, so by then she had built up a bit of a sweat and her coat was hanging open. It had also given her a lot of time to look around at the sweeping grounds and the mansion, which had eventually appeared in front of her.

Mansion was not doing the place justice. This structure was nearly a damn castle. A fairly modern-looking one.

For the past week, she'd been sleeping with a man who she thought was human and a gym owner.

Some gym.

Now she knew he was a vampire, owned a dangerous private security company doing God knows what, and lived like a damn king.

Who was Ari Moretti?

She swallowed deeply.

And why did he seem to care for her so much? Another awesome question to ask would be, why the hell was she trusting him?

When Sage had been standing in that room staring at Callan, all she had thought about was Ari. How she wished his large body was behind her in that moment, wrapped around her, making her feel safe. His deep voice would tell her she was safe, and he'd make this right. Instinctually she trusted him.

Her brain told her to run.

Being a scientist had trained her to listen to her brain and trust what she saw, and yet, her instincts were screaming at her to go to Ari. So here she was, walking down this long driveway, with gates at her back she'd never get through on her own, toward an enormous house full of vampires.

Toward Ari.

She focused on that last thought.

The surface under her feet changed to something fancier and her shoes made a tapping sound. She glanced up at the mansion and saw all the windows had black shutters over them.

Gulp.

There was a wide set of stairs with a landing in the middle of them. Before she could take one more step, the double doors opened.

Ari.

She took a second to take in his powerful presence. Today he was dressed in a pair of black sweatpants, which hung low on his hips, and a tight black t-shirt. He was so damn beautiful. Everything about him screamed sex, power, danger and yet he was all she needed.

He was everything she needed.

"Sage," Ari said in that thick, deep voice of his. When he stepped out onto the large doorstep, she began to run up the stairs as if her life depended on it.

"Baby," he cried out, and before she knew what was happening, he had her in his arms and she was inside the house. "I've got you."

She sobbed into his chest and let his big arms and body provide the rock and comfort she needed.

"I'm sorry." She cried.

"Don't." He soothed her. "It's a lot. Trust me, I get it."

She lifted her head to look up into his beautiful face. "We have to get him out."

Ari nodded. "Yes. We do."

SAGE sat curled up on Ari's sofa. He'd moved her briskly through the mansion, promising to give her a tour another time. She was grateful in many ways, but she was still curious and eager to see everything.

"Here," Ari said, handing her a mug of steaming hot chocolate.

"Thank you."

"Sure you don't want whiskey added?"

Sage nodded. The last thing she needed right now was to be intoxicated. She wanted her wits about her, even if she did trust Ari.

He sat down beside her, and she curled into him.

"So."

"So," he repeated, smiling down at her. His lips lowered, and he kissed her gently. "I'm glad you called me."

"Me too." She leaned to put her mug down on the coffee table. "I'm scared, Ari."

He rubbed his hand mindlessly over her hip and nodded. "You should be. I'm not saying that to scare you further, but I am not going to lie or gloss over things. This is a dangerous situation."

Sage appreciated his honesty. While it was nice to be in his arms and feel safe, and she had every reason to believe she was—and one thousand reasons to be scared out of her brain—she'd rather he tell her the truth.

"I can't go back there. I have to resign," Sage said. "I don't know where I'll work. I have some savings, but not a lot. Sorry, I know I'm being selfish, but if I default on my mortgage, it will ruin me financially for a long time."

Ari pulled her onto his lap and brushed her wild hair off her face.

"There is a lot more I need to share with you, *mia stellina*," he said, his eyes shimmering with an affection and strength that filled her with confidence and made her girly bits all warm. "Soon I will. For now, just know that I will take care of any financial hurdles this creates for you."

"I—"

"Please. I know you are an independent, modern woman. Let me take care of you. This is an unprecedented time," Ari said firmly. "We can argue later. For now, wipe all concern from your mind."

That seemed fair, given the circumstances.

"I will pay you back," Sage replied, nodding firmly.

"Okay," he said, and Sage didn't miss the twinkle of humor in his eyes. She let it go and would deal with that when the time came. If he thought she wouldn't, or couldn't, he was mistaken. Sage had no debt except her mortgage and had, on her *Life List*, plans to invest in a diverse portfolio, so she had a secure financial future.

This had truly fucked up everything.

Yet another damn thing on her list not going to plan.

"First, we need to discuss how we get Callan out. Right now, my team and I don't think you're compromised, so I have a plan I'd like to discuss with you. It will require you going back to BioZen."

Ari's jaw tightened as he held her eyes.

"It's dangerous, but we can't get inside, so we need you to do this."

"What do you want me to do?"

Ari let out a long sigh. "Give Callan my blood."

CHAPTER THIRTY-EIGHT

Ari lifted Sage off his knee and walked to open the door. He could have used telekinesis, but the last thing he wanted was for anyone to know he could do it.

Especially the prince.

"Brayden, come in," Ari said, following the prince into the living room.

"Sage, this is Brayden Moretti. My nephew," he said, introducing them.

"Nice to meet you, Sage," Brayden said, giving her one of his handsome smiles Ari had seen many females fall for. "I hope my uncle is being a gentleman."

"Hi," Sage replied, then her eyes widened. "Nephew? Oh, right. Vampires. How old are you both?"

Ari grinned.

All those details were going to add fire to the fuel. Sage was processing enough right now, so he was filtering as much as he could. Especially now he was giving her a challenging and dangerous task. He needed her strong.

He sat down next to her again.

"Let's leave those questions for another day. Although you probably should know that Brayden is our prince. The vampire race has a royal family—it's a bloodline thing— and so you will witness him being referred to as such by others."

Sage's eyes flicked back to Brayden. "Prince."

Brayden smiled, then sat his big ass in an armchair. "Yes, but you can call me Brayden."

Ari was pleased to hear Brayden offer that. Sage would soon become a Moretti herself and the prince knew that. Offering her to drop his royal title was an acknowledgment.

"How many vampires are there in the world?" Sage asked, and Ari could see her mind racing with questions.

"Around ten million. Scattered across the globe," Brayden replied. "We do not procreate at the same speed as humans, so while we live much longer, our children come along much later in life."

Sage chewed her bottom lip.

"It's okay to be interested, Sage. You are a scientist. It's natural. It's also very different from what your colleagues are doing," Ari said, and she nestled into him.

He looked up and Brayden was watching them. He looked happy for Ari, though they both knew what this meant for the entire race, if Sage was his mate. Momentous change.

Perhaps not overnight, but eventually.

She had absolutely no idea exactly how important she was. To him and to all of them.

Brayden and Vincent had to realize he was important to the longevity of vampires. They had always been vulnerable as a royal family. Never had there been so many Moretti vampires as there were today, but that could change.

Ari remembered the time when Frances was king, and they waited for his mate to arrive. It was why he'd been so aggressive in taking Guiliana and changing her.

Right now, though, Ari was forced to risk his *potential* mate to not only help rescue Callan but to destroy the greatest threat to them all.

"I cannot imagine what he's been through. I don't know anything about your bodies…"

Brayden smirked.

"He will feel pain," Ari said, giving Brayden a chastising look.

"Well, we need to get him out."

Ari's heart burst with joy every time he heard her say that. He'd been so ready to step into the sunshine if Sage had chosen to experiment on his kind. That she hadn't, had made him so damn happy he wanted to scream with joy. Yet, until he knew she was his one hundred percent, he was holding back.

"We do." Ari glanced at the prince with narrowed eyes. "Which is why I asked Brayden to join us. I'm about to share a very important secret with you. No one outside the Moretti family knows of this but these are extenuating circumstances."

"Ari—" Brayden started.

Ari held up his hand.

"Nephew. Need I remind you I am an original?" He hoped Sage wouldn't understand what that meant. "My brother and I set these rules."

Brayden leaned forward and his silver eyes burned.

"I don't give a fuck who made the rules. They were put in place for a reason. I forbid you," the prince said.

Sage turned to Ari, and he ran his fingers gently across her skin to calm her. He'd expected this response.

"No one can know what we are doing outside this room, obviously," Ari continued.

"I said no." Brayden stood.

Sage's head flicked between them, her eyes wide.

"Stop scaring her," Ari growled. "Hear me out, Brayden."

Brayden crossed his arms and glared a whole bunch, which he ignored.

"My blood is powerful. As is Brayden's. It runs through the Moretti bloodline," Ari said, as the prince cursed repeatedly.

"I guess we can fucking wipe her mind," Brayden muttered, running a hand over his face.

"What?" Sage asked, tensing.

"Brayden, we can't get in there. We need Callan strong enough to escape."

"So, give him anyone's fucking blood. Not ours. Are you going to wipe her memory?" He pointed to Sage. "Or do I need to do it because she is Not. Leaving. This. Fucking Room."

Ari was losing patience.

"Sage can take a vial in and slip it into his mouth when she's taking samples. You and I both know our blood is substantially stronger, so the small amount will give him the strength he needs," Ari said.

Brayden's lips remained pressed together, but he kept listening.

"I'm not sure I can do it," Sage said. "There are cameras everywhere. They'll see me."

Ari knew he only had half a plan, which was another reason he brought in the prince. He wanted his sharp mind on this, and agreement with the plan. Not that he needed Brayden's agreement, but it would be nice to have it.

Sage was going to be his mate. She would have the Moretti blood running through her veins one day soon. Brayden knew that. Sure, there was no confirmation yet, but if she wasn't they *could* wipe her memory.

"We need to find a way around that." Ari nodded. "How many people are monitoring him? Callan will recharge quickly, but you will need to remain with him to get him through the building, as it's reinforced with tungsten. Our team will be in a van nearby to bring him here safely."

Tungsten was the only metal on the planet that was impenetrable to vampires. Mostly. They could breach it, but that took time—something Callan wouldn't have.

Sage let out a long breath and shook her head.

"I think there were only two. Or three. I'm sorry, I didn't count. Our team was all in the room and there looked to be a counter full of computers. There could even be five."

Ari's brain began calculating the risk.

It was high.

Very high, given who Sage was to him.

He could change her first, but it could take her weeks to recover and be powerful enough—and have control over those powers—to go back in. They'd need to have a good excuse for her being off sick for that long and she may lose the position.

"Fuck. Fine," Brayden spat out. "The idea has legs, but we cannot tell anyone out there and you will need the team support."

Ari nodded.

"I know. I'm not saying it's the perfect plan, but it's a start," Ari said. "They won't believe he'll recover on the first day, so that's where things get tricky."

The amount of blood required for a vampire to recover was way more than a small vial.

Unless it was Moretti blood.

"But…" Sage said, then shook her head.

"But?" Brayden asked.

"You could tell them I'm going to do it every day for, say, a week or two. Then, I don't know, we could say Callan must have been in a better state of health, and the one vial worked," Sage offered. "It appears, from what I read today, that it's exactly what they've been doing. Draining him of life, then reviving him, over and over."

"Fuckers," Brayden said.

Ari shook his head in disgust. They knew it was bad, but focusing on his suffering wasn't helping Callan. They just had to get him out.

"So he's been fed up with human blood and the vampire blood boosts him. Would that work?" Sage added.

He stared at Brayden as they both contemplated the idea.

"Yeah, it could work," Brayden said. "We can't get in, so we get vampire blood in. Sage, it is imperative you never mention it is Moretti blood or its power. Am I clear?"

Sage nodded.

"Yes. I don't understand any of this, but I promise I will keep this highly confidential," she replied, firmly. "I just want to help him."

Ari wanted to pull her into his arms and his bedroom for about ten years.

Brayden stared at the two of them, then sighed.

"We keep this between us. No one else. Rest. Eat. Talk. You both have a lot to discuss," Brayden said. "Nothing happens until daylight tomorrow, so let's brief the team when you are ready, Ari."

Ari nodded.

"Brayden." He stood, and the prince turned. "Speaking of blood. We need to be able to 'path."

The prince nodded. "How have we never done this in all the cent... years?" He grinned and bit down on his wrist.

Ari did the same, and they both held out their arms and took a long lick of each other's blood. He felt the power of the Moretti blood slide through his body and watched Brayden's eyes widen as his did the same.

Connected?

Yes. Ari, what the fuck. Your blood...

We should discuss it another day, nephew.

Brayden nodded, but held his eyes a moment before turning for the door.

Ari turned and found Sage watching him.

"What just happened?" she asked.

"We have the ability to telepath when we share blood with another vampire," he answered. Sage needed to know these things, so he was happy to answer some of the less shocking pieces of information.

Being his mate and learning she was going to become a vampire was definitely lower on the list. At least, he hoped.

"So you just bit your wrist?" she asked, and grabbed his arm where it was already closing up. Her thumb rubbed over the spot, and she watched it return to healthy, clear skin. "Remarkable."

He slid his hand from hers and cupped her face. "No, *mia stellina*, you are."

If only she knew how long he'd waited for her.

Automatically she melted against him, and he took possession of her lips, sliding his arms down her back and cupping her ass.

"I need you. Can I have you, Sage? Are you okay with this?" Ari murmured against her lips. Her fingers were digging into his shoulders, giving him the answer, but he needed her words.

She nodded.

"Say yes, Sage. I need to be sure."

"It feels like I'll die if we don't," Sage gasped, shaking her head. "Yes, please, fuck me, Ari."

He pulled her from the sofa and kissed her completely. Walking backwards toward his bedroom, he pulled her sweater off and she tugged up his t-shirt. When he saw her white lace bra, he took control of the t-shirt situation and ripped his own off.

"Jesus, you are beautiful," Ari said. "Skirt off."

They were standing in the middle of the floor, but he didn't care. He just wanted to be inside her.

Sage unzipped her skirt and kicked it off while his jeans went flying some-fucking-where.

He pressed her against the closest wall and his lips were on hers again.

"So fucking beautiful."

"Ari," Sage cried as his mouth moved down her neck and breasts. He pulled the lace aside and sucked one of her nipples. "Oh, God."

His hand nudged her legs apart and slid under the lace.

"Shit. You are wet." He groaned, sucking her lower lip. "So wet for me, Sage."

"Yes. I need you inside me, Ari."

Fuck.

He wanted to taste her, but both of them needed this connection like their last breath. He could feel her body humming and calling to him.

"Hands up." He spun her around and tugged her panties down. They snapped, and he flung them into nowhere-land with his jeans.

"Oh, shit," Sage cried when his legs spread hers and his fingers slid inside her.

"You are ready for me," he said, guiding his cock to her entrance and gripping her hip with his other hand. "Take me inside you, Sage."

He pressed against her, then inch by inch entered her. He wasn't sure whose cries were whose as they both let out guttural sounds together.

His body slammed against Sage's as he thrust deeply, over and over. His name was on her lips as she groaned her pleasure when he reached to rub her clit.

"Say you are mine, Sage," Ari demanded, panting. "Mine, forever."

"Yes," she cried. "Oh, God yes."

Hearing those words sent Ari's body into a spiral he'd never felt before. His palm slammed on the wall above her, and his body enveloped hers completely. His other hand palmed her stomach as he thrust into her as hard as her humanity would allow.

She arched back her head, and he took her lips. His hand reached up to grip her chin.

"Fuck me, Sage. Clench around my cock and fuck me dry."

The moment she followed his instructions, he clenched his eyes closed, and his cock exploded inside her.

"Ari, shiiiit," Sage said, and he began to rub her clit again to maximize her pleasure.

Moments later, she was jelly in his arms. His forehead landed on the top of her head while he held her up. The coupling was everything he had ever wanted from his mate. And so much more. He took a moment to enjoy the shattered feeling, then she shifted in his arms.

"Shower." He pulled out of her and scooped her up.

CHAPTER THIRTY-NINE

Sage sat in a room surrounded by vampires. She felt marginally safer when she saw the familiar face across from her.

Oliver had greeted her with a hug—until Ari had physically removed him from her.

The prince had given her a wink.

Brayden may have been royalty, but Sage felt like she was the one with royal protection. Ari had washed every inch of her body, slowly with his tongue, in the shower and then provided her with some back-up clothing which hung off her like a giant tent. Then he'd shown her around part of the mansion and introduced her to a few of the vampires.

Vampires. Holy heck.

Now they were in the logistics room. It was nearly eleven o'clock, and she was wired.

"I wanted to get this done tonight so Sage can get to sleep," Ari said. "We're all living human hours right now and it's taking its toll. I appreciate that."

A few murmurs began around her, and Sage glanced at them. All the men in the room were huge, tattooed, and dangerous-looking. Oliver winked at her.

"Oliver, if you want to keep breathing, I suggest you stop that," Ari said, and Sage sucked in a breath as a few of the others sniggered.

"He's joking," Oliver said, though his smirk had disappeared.

"He's fucking not." The really large vampire with green eyes spoke.

Sage turned to Ari and squeezed his leg under the table. His powerful, beautiful face turned to hers and softened. "I think he's just being friendly because I don't know anyone," she said quietly.

Ari took her face and kissed her. Throats cleared around them, and Ari grinned.

"Tomorrow Sage returns to BioZen and she's going to take a vial of our blood to Callan. She's been rostered on to do sample work, so this works to our advantage."

"One vial isn't going to do jack," Oliver said, and Sage glanced at the prince. He didn't react.

"Over time, it will." Ari nodded. "Each day it will build up his strength. If we can get two vials in safely, we will do that."

Sage noticed the green-eyed vampire staring at Ari in a strange way and she waited for him to say something, but he didn't. He glanced at Brayden and then looked away.

Did he know about the blood? Ari had said only the royal family knew.

Wait.

If Brayden was his nephew, then that made Ari a royal member of the vampire race. She turned her head to him.

"What is it?" he asked quietly, but she knew everyone in the room could hear, because yesterday she'd learned about their powerful hearing. Sage shook her head and gave him a little smile.

Ari turned back to the room as he squeezed her hand.

"We need to prepare a van with daylight protection and get into the underground garage. We'll go every day so we're there for Callan whenever he recovers."

"I can get us access into the garage," one of the vampires said, tapping on his computer to bring up a layout of her building.

"Oh, wow. That's BioZen," Sage said, stating the obvious.

"Yup," the vampire said, and began outlining where they had to go and when.

It was so strange seeing her workplace being looked at like a crime scene. Or a potential one. Sage realized just how important it was to play her part. All of them were relying on her.

"I can put it off until around three o'clock but any later and they'll get suspicious," she said.

Ari nodded.

They had drafted a note for her to give to Callan when he woke. Apparently, he would come awake fast when he did, and all she had to do was give him the note and then open the doors so he could get out of the facility.

Easy.

Yeah, right.

"How can I do that without being compromised?" she asked. "There's security everywhere."

"We need to make it look like you're being forced," Oliver said. "You'll have a few moments to tell him what the plan is. We can practice it until you feel comfortable."

Sage frowned.

"He'll be groggy, and who knows what state he'll be in," she replied.

"That's the unknown." Brayden nodded in agreement. "He should be fairly clear-minded, quickly, and I suspect he will be eager to get out. What we need to ensure is that he protects you while he does so."

"I don't like this." Oliver shook his head. "It's too risky. Sage isn't trained for this."

"I agree," Jason said.

"You think I don't fucking know this?" Ari snapped and everyone blanched. "None of us can get in there. No one. Only Sage."

Sage watched as these huge men all shook their heads. Why they cared about her when they didn't know her, she really didn't understand.

"I'll be fine," she said, squeezing her hands together as they shook under the table. She gave them all a brave smile and then turned to Ari, who was running a hand over his face. "Truly, it'll be fine."

The silence around her did not fill her with confidence. But she was doing this. She had to. Something greater was driving her and Sage couldn't find the words to explain it.

Callan had to be freed.

What she didn't know was if there were more vampires kept in other BioZen departments. Tomorrow, while she waited to get into the room where he was kept, she would do as much research as she could.

"I need to get home." Sage glanced down at her outfit. "I need some sleep and fresh clothes."

Ari stood and pulled out her chair, helping her stand. "Come. We'll let my team continue with the plans while we organize what you need."

She gave everyone a wave as they left.

"Bye, Sage," a few of them called out.

"Nice to meet you all." She then smiled at Brayden. "And um, Your Highness."

Brayden winked at her.

"Wish they'd all stop fucking doing that," Ari said as he pushed open the door.

Sage smiled. Being cared for by Ari felt really nice.

ARI stood in the middle of his room, holding Sage's hips.

"So, you're ready? He stared down into her wide eyes.

"It won't hurt?" she asked.

"No." His little scientist had asked a lot more questions than the average person. Not that he'd teleported with many humans over his life. Usually, unless they were one's mate or you were in a pickle, you just didn't expose this much of a vampire's life to a human being. "Like I said, you might feel some nausea, but that's all."

"Let's go," Sage said, and he smiled at her.

"Close your eyes."

"No way. I want to watch."

Ari laughed and teleported them into her bedroom.

"Holy. Fucking. Moley," Sage cried, then wobbled in his arms. Then retched. Ari vamp-sped into her bathroom where she leaned over and dry-retched some more.

Sage pulled on some toilet paper and wiped her mouth.

"So worth it. Oh, my God, that is awesome!" she said, standing. "Imagine the impact on climate change something like this could have."

Ari leaned against the door and crossed his arms. Sure, he was aware of the reduction in carbon emissions if people no longer needed cars to get around, but it wasn't that simple. Seven billion people suddenly appearing anywhere they wanted, plus the lack of control by governments over borders...

"And security," he said cynically.

"Well yeah, but still." Sage waved her hand around in circles.

Ari watched as she rinsed out her mouth and began to pack her things. He'd convinced her to stay at his place a few days, so he knew she was safe. He could stay with her here, but it was easier to be close to his team.

"Sage," a voice called out.

"Shit." Sage froze on the spot. "Oh, hi!"

"We didn't think you were home." Tony, her roommate, popped his head around the corner of the door.

"Yes. We were taking a nap," Sage said, then pointed to Ari. "This is Ari. I think you met the other night."

"Hey man." Tony reached out his hand.

"Hello," Ari said, then held the man's eyes. "*You never saw us; you can't hear us, and you should go back to what you were doing.*"

Tony turned around and walked back into the living room.

"What did you do?" Sage asked, her lips parted.

"Adjusted his memories, so we don't have to deal with them," Ari said. "He'll be fine. He won't remember anything."

And in three, two, one...

"Have you ever done that to me?" Sage asked.

Every single human. Every single time.

"Yes." He answered honestly. "A couple of times. Once when you asked me to bite you while we were having sex. It was a vampire fetish thing from your sexy books. I lost control; my fangs came out."

Sage's eyes flew open.

"I didn't bite you." He held up his hand. "But it was close. It was then I realized who you worked for."

Sage clutched her toilet bag to her chest.

"That's why you didn't message me on Sunday."

He nodded and watched her eyes drift away. Ari took her in his arms and tilted her chin. "I was confused, Sage. I knew you were important to me, but learning you worked for the people taking vampires and torturing them freaked me out."

"But you came back, anyway."

He smiled and nodded. "Yes. Always."

Ari had checked his eyes a few minutes ago. He was checking every hour.

Wishing.

Hoping.

Nearly praying.

Even if they never changed, he wasn't leaving Sage. She was his. His feelings for her were off the charts. Who was to say he would get the ring around his iris? Perhaps that was Gio's trait which he'd passed down the bloodline. Perhaps it would be different for him.

Selfishly, he had decided Sage was his, and he was keeping her, no fucking matter what.

Sage ran her fingers across his lips, and he snapped them into his mouth. She made him playful—something he hadn't been for a very long time. A smile spread across her face, and he released her fingers.

"I didn't like being here without you last night," Sage said, her smile disappearing. "When you left—"

Ari kissed her gently. "I hated leaving you. I needed to know how you felt about live experimentation. It was the worst few hours of my life, Sage. And I've lived a really fucking long time."

"Are you really fifteen hundred and twenty-two years old?"

He nodded.

"Holy hell. This is a lot." Sage shook her head. "Like, you should be a shriveled mess, you know that, right?"

Ari threw back his head and laughed.

"You can take a closer look when we get home." He wrapped her in his arms more tightly. "You need your rest. Once Callan is free, we can talk more about our future."

Sage blinked up at him. "I like you a lot, Ari. Lots and lots and lots."

"The feeling is mutual, *mia stellina*."

He more than liked her.

He would kill for her.

One day soon, she would understand that.

ARI returned to his room a few hours before the sun came up and lay with Sage, dozing and enjoying the feel of her body on his while she slept deeply. There wasn't a thing in this world that could now convince him she wasn't his mate.

He knew.

And he didn't give a fuck about the mate ring on his eyes.

Sage was his mate.

End of fucking story.

Sage was a priority. Over everything. Hour by hour, the feeling grew stronger, and Ari suspected it was the bonding taking place.

Was he happy to let her go back to BioZen today? No. No, he fucking wasn't.

Did they have a choice?

Not so far.

He'd spent hours, while she slept, strategizing with Brayden, Craig, Oliver, Jason, and Alex. None of them had been able to sleep, despite knowing they needed to rest. Unfortunately, none of them could see a different way of getting Callan out, so the plan remained.

The sun was now rising, and Sage began to wriggle.

"*Buongiorno*," Ari said, smiling as he realized he'd waited a hundred lifetimes to say good morning to the woman he loved.

Love.

Yeah, he was in love with Sage.

The fact he wanted to handcuff her to his bed and wrap her in bubble wrap, both for protection and sexy times, gave it away.

"*Arrivederci*." Sage grinned weakly. Ari didn't correct her misuse of the Italian term for goodbye because she was so damn gorgeous for making the effort.

"Your bed is so comfortable. And huge," she said, stretching.

"Alright *principessa*, we can spend all the time we want in my big bed once we finish this mission." He kissed her lips as he pulled her against him. "Right now, you need to get up before my ability to let you out wanes."

She pressed against him and ran her fingers through his hair. "I'm okay with that."

Ari moaned.

Their kisses heated and Sage ended up being the one to break away first. Thirty minutes later, they stood in the doorway of his quarters, and he handed her the vial of his blood.

Moretti blood.

Never in the history of their race had any of them given away the power of their blood—or the knowledge of it—to another. Yet here he was, giving some of it to Sage.

"Guard this with your life. Put it wherever you need to ensure it is safe and cannot be found," he said. "If... fuck... if someone finds it on you, I want you to drink it."

"What? No. Gross," Sage said. "I can't drink blood. It might be normal for you, but I can't. I'd throw up."

Ari gripped her face.

"Sage, you won't. Trust me. It's not like human blood. I need you to trust me. If you're caught with it, you must drink it. Or swallow the entire vial. No one can get their hands on this. Especially not fucking scientists."

She nodded. "Okay, okay. I understand."

Her face paled, but it was important. Ari doubted they could replicate the red liquid in the small vial, but he couldn't risk it.

"Sorry, but you'll have to walk down to the gates again." He walked her to the front door. "An Uber will be waiting for you."

"Its good exercise," Sage replied, leaning into him and he wrapped his arms around her.

"Be safe today. If you think you could get caught, then wait. We can try again another day," Ari replied.

"I'll message you afterwards," Sage said.

"No, I want you to get the fuck out of the building. Jump in a cab and get straight back here," Ari said firmly. "No waiting. Nothing."

"Got it. Man, it's not like we can skip the country and go lie on a beach in the Caribbean for six months like fugitives afterwards, either."

Ari snorted.

"Not unless you want to cremate me before our relationship has begun." He ran his hand over her sexy ass.

"Is this a relationship?" Sage asked. "Is that even a thing between a human and a vampire?"

Shit.

That was a huge conversation and one he knew she wasn't ready to hear.

"You are mine, Sage Roberts. I'm not letting you go." He didn't expand on the details. "Now go, and come back to me so we can do more of those relationship things."

She sighed.

"I know there is more to that, Ari Moretti, but I will let it go." She frowned at him, then kissed him on the lips. "Tonight you are doing some more talking."

"Yes, ma'am." He nodded and winked at her. Hopefully, by tonight, there would be no more need for words.

He led Sage out onto the steps, as far as he could go, and watched her walk down the drive. Eventually, the daylight began to affect him, and he stepped back inside.

Letting her walk away into danger like this went against every instinct in his body.

Sage was his future. His love. His mate.

If anyone laid a hand on her, so help him, he would rip every limb from their body.

CHAPTER FORTY

By three o'clock Sage was beside herself with nerves.

She'd sat through two meetings. One of them Sandy had commented on how tired she looked and asked if she wanted to swap out her duties with Murray.

"Nope, I'll be fine. Just a migraine hangover. I'll bounce back by lunchtime, so will do it later in the day," Sage had said, proud of herself for coming up with the idea to explain her reason for doing it so late.

Now she was on her way.

Sage scanned into Callan's area and nodded to all the staff and security, hoping her nerves simply looked like first week jitters and not like she was about to help a vampire escape.

She let out a snort.

As if anyone would believe this was her life.

The vial was tucked inside her bra. It burned against her skin as if it was a packet of heroin she was smuggling. In fact, Sage was sure this was a lot more serious.

Ari had texted her three times today, and each message had sent a million butterflies dancing around her stomach. Her feelings for him were off the charts.

How was that possible in such a short amount of time? Sure, he was the most spectacular lover a girl could ever dream of. God, the things he did to her body. His tongue, his…

"Hello, Sage," Brian said, interrupting her thoughts.

Crap.

"Hello, Brian." She smiled, nervously. "First day samples," she said, holding up the test kit.

He nodded. "The team will be close by, so no need to be nervous. Do you want me to come in with you?"

No.

Hell, no.

"Oh no, that's okay. I watched Murray do it yesterday, so it's fine," Sage said, "Just another day at the office, but on a vampire, right?"

They had been briefed on the vampire body and how similar to humans it was in regard to their work. Little did they know she had close-up experience with a vampire's body. In fact, two of them, if she included Oliver.

Brian nodded, gave her an empty smile, then left.

She let out a breath and continued. Sage turned the corner and walked to the door which led into Callan's room. Pressing her thumb against the panel, it clicked open. The room was also climate-controlled and was cool. Very cool.

"*Callan, if you can hear me,*" Sage whispered as quietly as she could, while putting the kit on the table next to his bed. "*My name is Sage. I am here to get you out.*"

Callan didn't move.

"*I am going to give you vampire blood, which will revive you. Quickly, I'm told,*" she whispered again.

His eyelashes flickered slightly.

The speakers blared to life. "Dr. Roberts, can you please move slightly to the left?"

Fuck.

Her heart nearly leapt out of her skin. She looked up and nodded. "Sure, sorry."

That was interesting. Clearly, their cameras were being blocked by the angle of her body. She could use that to her advantage.

"*Here.*" She tucked the note into Callan's hand and felt him slightly tighten.

Oh, my God. This might work.

"*Read it. As soon as you open your eyes.*"

Sage wished she could say more but couldn't stall any longer. She opened the kit and began to prepare to take the samples. She lay everything out, then faked a sneeze.

Sage had thought about this moment for hours last night as she lay there working out how she would do this. In the end, she had decided to wear a low-cut top to allow access to the vial inside her bra. As she sneezed, she reached inside and grabbed the powerful blood. Keeping it tucked inside the palm of her hand, she took a couple of swabs from inside Callan's mouth as he lay prone and unmoving.

"*I'm going to give you the blood now. Please get ready. I will pack up as normal and then open the door. When I cough, move.*"

His eyelids flickered once more, and Sage's heart pounded.

"*You need to take me with you to the next exit or you won't get out. Please read the note.*"

If he didn't, she'd just run and get into the stairwell. Darren and his team had shown her multiple exits, many of which she was familiar with.

Sage put all her samples back in her kit and acted as if she were closing it up. Leaning as she stood, she flipped her thumb against the vial and it opened, then she quickly pressed it against his lips. Callan's lips parted, and she poured it in.

Then she moved fast. *Click, clack.* She snuck the empty vial into the pack and closed it. Silently, she stood and walked to the door. Her thumb pressed against the panel, and it opened.

She coughed.

Even though they'd planned it, when Callan's body swooped up off the bed, Sage startled. He scooped her up and growled in her ear. "Which way?"

She pointed in a direction, and he moved them incredibly fast toward another door. Alarms sounded around them, and red lights began to flash. Screams and cries surrounded them, and a whirring noise began.

"Fuck," Callan yelled, his voice dry and gravelly.

Sage pressed her thumb against the panel, and it opened. Callan moved them through the door, out into the offices near hers. He glanced around and they saw security flying toward them.

"I will protect you as much as I can, but I cannot go back in there." He growled. "Which way?"

Sage nodded, understanding completely. No sentient being deserved to be experimented on. "Down there."

Again, Callan sped them toward another exit knocking past four security guards with complete ease and power.

Then found themselves in the stairwell.

"It's daylight right now. You need to get to the basement to a black van. Go down to the ground floor. At the door, push the red button and it will let you out."

He stared at her a quick moment, touched her cheek, and then disappeared.

Sage slumped to the floor just as the door burst open behind her and she was pulled to her feet by two security guards. Douglas Phillips came running toward them, looking furious.

"What have you done, you stupid fucking girl?" he yelled and slapped her across the face.

"No, I—"

She felt a sting in her neck and the world went black.

CHAPTER FORTY-ONE

Ari adjusted the comms in his ear and glanced at the vampires sitting across from him in the back of the van. Where the fuck were they? Callan should be down here by now.

Oliver, Brayden, and Craig were in the van with him.

The 'A' team, because this wasn't an operation Ari was willing to trust with anyone but the best.

"Fuck," Craig said, and ran a hand over his face. "He's flashed out. You know that, right?"

Shit.

"Of course he fucking has. He's shit scared." Ari growled, slamming his hand down against the side of the van. "Fuck."

With his blood in Callan's system, he would have enormous power, but only for a short time. Hours at best.

Unfortunately, because he hadn't swapped with the vampire, Ari was unable to communicate with Callan. They also couldn't track one another like one fiction author had written about—a skill he'd love to have despite it being a little creepy and intrusive.

Much like being able to read another's mind.

Thing was, if you knew how, you could stop another from being able to enter your mind, but it had taken years to master that skill, and few could do it.

"They have Sage," Darren said through the comms. "She's still in the building."

"Get hold of Ben and Tom and ask them to put out a missing vampire alert to our teams across North America," Brayden said to Craig. "It's not a quick fix, but if he's gone into hiding, we may be able to find him in time."

"We need his intel," Ari growled. "God only knows what state he is in, but he's free so that's good."

Sage was not.

Ari had to get her out and his entire focus was now on her.

"We do need his intel. Until we know more these assholes can continue their work," Brayden said. "He'll be in touch with someone and while we can't put a blast out on VampNet or it will scare everyone, we can use our network on the ground."

"There could be others," Oliver said, voicing what they were all thinking, and Brayden nodded.

"For some reason, Callan was important to them," Brayden said. "So it's a win, you guys, let's take it."

At any other time, Ari would appreciate the little pep talk, but not today. Not while his *potential* mate was trapped inside by these fucking soulless monsters.

And they thought vampires were the dangerous ones.

Well, today Ari was, and he wasn't fucking around.

Brayden narrowed his eyes at him and cursed.

Ari frowned back. "What? If you're looking for a round of applause for your speech, today is not that day," Ari snapped.

"No asshole. Look." Brayden flipped his phone around and pressed the camera.

Ari gripped the phone and lifted it to his face.

Holy fuck.

He froze. Never in his life did he think he'd see this. Two black fine rings around his irises.

It was official. He was mated.

Sage *was* his mate.

"Congratulations, man." Oliver thumped him on the thigh. It seemed appropriate the vampire he'd shared her with first was with him at this moment.

Ari handed the phone back to the prince and their eyes held. "Congratulations, Ari," Brayden said.

"Welcome to the club," Craig said, reaching out his hand for one of those fist pump things.

Sage was his mate.

He'd known. Deep in his heart, Ari had known from the beginning. Never in his wildest dreams had he imagined it could feel this wonderful and terrifying. There was a wild feeling within him to protect her and possess her to the very core.

Which was bad luck for their enemy.

Ari had no idea where Sage was or what they were doing to her. All they could hear was silence. Did that mean they had deactivated the tracker? Or hurt her?

Fury rose to the surface like an atom bomb ready to explode.

Ari pulled out his phone, scrolled and found a number. He pressed dial.

"You ordering a pizza?" Oliver asked. "Hell of a time, but I'll have extra cheese."

Ari ignored him and waited for the call to be answered.

"Welcome to BioZen, how may I help you?" A standard friendly reception voice answered.

Craig cursed silently.

Brayden lowered his brows, but Ari looked away.

This was his mate and his responsibility. They were playing by his rules now.

"Put me through to Douglas Phillips immediately," Ari said firmly, not using the man's title. He deserved no respect and wasn't about to get it from Ari.

"Ah, who may I say is calling please?" the woman asked. "Do you have an appointment with him?"

"Put me through," he repeated darkly.

The call went through to another woman. "Dr. Phillips's office. How may I help you?"

Fuck's sake.

"If Douglas is not on the end of this phone in three minutes, I will start taking lives," Ari growled into the phone.

"Ah, who is this?"

"Two minutes, forty-five seconds."

"Uhbh, arh, sir—"

"Two minutes, thirty seconds," Ari said.

The phone dropped onto the desk, and he heard the woman race out of the room, bumping into her desk and door, muttering *ouch, fuck, shit,* and calling for the scientist.

"Ari, what the fuck?" Oliver asked.

There was a redirect, a ringtone and then someone answered. It was longer than three minutes in the end, but Ari wasn't worried about that and turned out it wasn't Douglas Phillips who answered the phone.

"Who am I speaking to?" the voice asked, and Ari recognized it from their surveillance. Beside him Oliver tensed, and Ari gave him a look which said to stay very fucking quiet.

Craig let out a silent *mother fucker* and Brayden leaned forward.

"My name is Ari Moretti, and you have something of mine," Ari said in his darkest and most deadly voice. "If Sage Roberts is not returned in the next fifteen minutes, I will rain fire across this planet. Do not fuck with me,

Xander Tomassi. I know every single member of your family, where they live and who they care about."

The man laughed.

They didn't know much about the man himself, but Ari hadn't expected him to cower and follow instructions. What he did know was if Xander was capable of the things they were doing to vampires, he wasn't a compassionate or healthy-minded individual.

"Start with my wife, will you?" Xander said, laughing.

"The clock is ticking." Ari growled.

"You can't harm me, Moretti," Xander said. "If you could, I wouldn't be sitting here right now."

Oliver threw back his head, bashing it against the van, frustrated as fuck.

"I don't think you realize who you're fucking with, Tomassi. And you never will," Ari growled. "Your team has crossed a line today by taking Sage. I don't care who I have to kill. One by one, I will rip the heads off every single member of your team and then I will come for you. I will destroy your security and anyone who gets in my way. I am faster, stronger, and more deadly than any being on this planet. You will not stop me. No one can stop me."

Silence.

The funny thing was, Ari had never felt so calm. All his life he'd had to hide and contain his enormous power.

Now, he had nothing to lose.

Brayden's eyes were burning into him, but Ari was not interested in following their race laws. BioZen had Sage, and he was getting her back, no matter the cost. He answered to no one.

Ari needed Xander Tomassi to understand the odds had shifted. There were no rules now. No rules except his.

"I will burn this building to the ground and every BioZen property until everything you have created is destroyed." Ari was planning to destroy it anyway, but going rogue was easier. "Protecting the existence of my race is no longer my priority. Release her and you will live."

"Shit, Ari," Brayden muttered, rubbing his forehead.

More silence.

"You have messed with the wrong vampire, you stupid fucking human. Tell your team to let her go and we can all go back to playing this little game within the rules of our society. Fifteen minutes or consider your life over."

Ari pressed the red button.

"Jesus," Craig said. "I like your style."

FIFTEEN minutes was a really long time. Even for someone as old as him. It felt equivalent to five million years.

Longer.

He couldn't even pace because he was stuck inside the goddamn van with Brayden, who was still glaring at him. At least he was smart enough to keep his mouth shut.

They had moved the van out to the front of the building and the sun was low in the sky. It was four o'clock in the afternoon and there were still three more minutes on the clock.

Three fucking minutes.

"You should all go," Ari said, only just hanging on by a thread. "There is no reason for any of you to be involved further. If they don't return Sage, I will come back to the mansion for my weapons and then I'm on my own."

"Nope," Oliver said.

Craig crossed his arms.

Brayden continued to glare at him, but stayed put.

Suddenly the doors to the BioZen building opened and three security men carried a very dopey-looking Sage out. She could barely stand.

"Fuck." Ari pulled open the door.

"Jesus," Brayden said, jumping away from the daylight. "Are you fucking crazy?"

Yup. Was that not obvious?

"Dude," Craig said. "Just wait. It's not cloudy enough out there today."

Ari looked to the sky and back to Sage, who couldn't focus her eyes. She'd been drugged. Now he was feeling extra murderous. His fangs extended as the men continued to drag her down the footpath while people around them watched.

"Sage?" A man ran up to them. "What's going on? Is she all right?"

The security guys asked him to leave, but the tall man ignored them and kept walking around them in circles.

Ari narrowed his eyes. He didn't know who the man was, but he seemed to care for her.

"Hey stop. You're hurting her. Sage?" said the man attempted to stop one of the security guards by grabbing his arm.

"You want her, Carl? Take her," one of them said, and when he let her go, Sage crumbled to the ground.

Ari realized this must be the man she had been planning to date. She'd mentioned his name was Carl.

Carl reached for her, and Ari nearly lost his shit.

"Calm. She's safe with him," Brayden said, gripping his arm.

"Sage." Ari called out from the van and Sage's eyes lifted to his.

"Ari." Sage croaked out a reply and then looked up at the man. "Pleavhelpme getovatoschim."

"What's going on?" Ari heard him ask. "What's wrong with you? And where were you last night? I waited out here for over half an hour."

Ari's fists clenched. I have bad news for you, buddy.

"Pwevecarl," Sage begged.

"Who are they?" Carl asked, looking over at them all crowded in the van. Ari admitted it probably looked dodgy as fuck. He likely wondered why they weren't exiting the vehicle to help.

Ari took another look at the sky.

"Fuck man, I am trying to keep you alive for your mate," Brayden said, his grip on Ari's arm pure Moretti strength.

Sage began to take wobbly steps toward them, and Carl reluctantly assisted her. His eyes held hers, even as they opened and closed in her drugged state, until she was just a few feet away. Then he ripped his arm from Brayden's and sped to her.

He pulled her into his arms, and vamp-sped back into the van.

"Sage!" he cried, almost crushing her.

"Ariohmugodhelp." Sage mumbled against him. "Ishdrugs."

"Don't talk. We'll get you the help you need," Ari said, knowing exactly what he was going to do. No one would ever hurt Sage again.

Never.

He glanced out at Carl, who was a few feet from the van, staring in horror.

"Deal with him," Ari said to Oliver.

"Let me," Craig said, whipping out into the dull daylight and grabbing the guy. He jumped back in and perched on the step while he rearranged Carl's memories.

Sage began to whimper against Ari's chest, and he pulled her onto his lap. "What did they give you?" he asked, holding her face to look into her eyes. "Do you know?"

Her head wobbled about. "Pwoffolxanx."

Okay, none of them knew what the fuck she was saying. Ari looked up just as Oliver pulled out his phone. "Googling it," he said.

"Propofol. Or Xanax," Oli said a few seconds later.

"Will it harm you?" he asked. She was a scientist, after all, and figured she'd know that no matter what stage she was in.

She tried to move her head about. "Proffablynotbutjustsleep."

Craig looked up and Carl wandered off as if nothing had happened in his life. At least that was one loose end tidied up.

"She's right. She'll probably sleep for a few hours but unless they gave her a shit ton, she'll be okay." Craig shifted to look down at her. "Can't say I'm not disappointed we aren't burning down the city, though."

Brayden slid the door shut and banged on the wall. "Let's get the fuck out of here."

Home.

Ari was taking his mate home.

CHAPTER FORTY-TWO

"**A**nswer." Xander snapped as the video conferencing app began calling. He was pacing back and forth on the mat in his office as the large digital screen on his wall lit up with three faces.

He turned and lifted his whiskey to his lips.

"Good evening, Mr. Tomassi. I hope you have good reason for this urgent call." Joe Nutler, Secretary of Homeland Defense, said in a low growl.

"Mr. Secretary," Xander replied.

"Mr. Secretary. Xander." Cash Waltmore, Director of BioZen, said. "I hear we had some excitement in Seattle today. I presume that's what this is about."

Xander wasn't in the mood for official niceties, so he got straight to the point. "Yes. I have bad news. Our test subject from Project Callan has escaped. He had assistance from the Moretti vampires."

"Do we still need him?" Cash asked. "And what risk does he pose? He's been out of it most of the time he's been with us. Am I right?"

Idiots.

It was foolish to underestimate these powerful beings.

Callan may not have been able to escape or overpower them, but Xander had reason to believe he was more cognizant than he'd made out much of the time.

He took a long sip of his whisky and swirled it in the crystal tumbler. He knew he was a confident, cocky asshole, but today had given him pause. All right, yes, it had shaken him.

None of the vampires had directly tried to contact him before, and the one thing he'd had control over was their passionate and fearful desire to remain anonymous.

Ari Moretti made it clear he played by different rules.

Without Diego to speak to he'd had to cast his net wider to find out who the vampire was. Until then, Xander was staying in Baltimore. Right now, he had reason to believe they didn't know where he was. The fact he was breathing was a good clue.

"Cut to the chase, Tomassi. I have a briefing with the president in twenty minutes," Joe demanded. "Do we have a reason for concern? Will this delay the next phase?"

"No." He then added. "Perhaps."

Whoever this Ari Moretti was, Xander knew the vampire wasn't bluffing when he'd said he would rain hell over the planet, or at least Seattle, until he got her back. Stefano Russo had given them enough information about the mating of vampires to know they would kill or die for their mates. It was why he'd ordered Douglas to let Sage go.

Xander may not love his wife, but he knew the tone in a man's voice when he was protecting those he loved most. He'd heard it in his own while he screamed, night after night, helpless as he watched his father beat his mother.

He may have only been a boy, but the essence of his screams was the promise of death. And he had killed his father.

Just not straight away.

And not with his bare hands.

But death was death.

And he had heard an undeniable promise of death in Ari Moretti's voice.

"I had a phone call from one of them today," Xander said, and updated them on the situation.

"Animals," Joe growled. "We need to take control of this situation. Having them loose across the planet like this is a danger to us all. We're vulnerable and I don't like it."

Xander didn't care what they did once they purchased the BioZen protocol. He'd long suspected the US government, and others, would create a bio army with what he was developing.

That wasn't his responsibility.

"We need to find out who Ari Moretti is. Russo never mentioned him, even though he shares the same surname as their royal family," Xander said. "He seems like the most dangerous one. I say we eliminate him and work our way through these senior vampires."

The three men nodded.

"I'll get my team to investigate him. Now listen, I know we've held off doing this, but I think it's time I brief the president," Joe stated. "With threats like that, I'm obligated."

Fuck.

Xander remained silent. He may head up the project, but at the end of the day, Cash Waltmore was one of the directors of BioZen and it was his call.

"Mr. Secretary, we understand your position, but do you really think James Calder would be happy with what we've been doing here? He's an ethical man, not a man of science," Cash said. "Let's hold off a while longer."

Xander threw back the last of his drink and dropped it on the coffee table. "I agree. The last thing we want is for POTUS to freeze the program. Other countries around the world are progressing. Do you really want the United States to be left behind?" He knew full well he was pushing the man's buttons.

"Watch yourself, Tomassi," Joe replied. "This is a good partnership, but don't try to manipulate me. I won't put up with that bullshit."

Whatever. He'd been threatened by someone far more powerful than the secretary of Homeland Defense today.

"I'm sure the billions of dollars we could all lose if Calder stops us might be more of interest to you then," Xander replied, not willing to be intimidated by the Secretary. "Give us a couple more months. If anything further happens, I will let you know immediately."

Joe gave him a dark look through the screen, then nodded and signed off.

Xander waited for his video to disconnect and then turned his attention to the president of BioZen.

"We need to proceed carefully. How much risk does this new Moretti pose?" Cash asked him.

Xander shook his head.

"I have no doubt he would have been a deadly risk to all of us if we hadn't returned Sage to him. Vincent and his brother Brayden are well known in global elite circles as influential billionaires. I've never heard Ari's name mentioned. He's an unknown and I don't like it."

"They're all dangerous," Cash said.

"More so when they have nothing to lose," Xander said. "But they do. They love their women, so now we just have to work out how to use that to our advantage."

Still, he had one ace card up his sleeve, and that was his next call.

CHAPTER FORTY-THREE

Sage sat with a blanket around her on Ari's sofa and sipped on a glass of apple juice. She'd asked for a freshly squeezed glass, knowing it would help her with mental clarity after the drugs which had been pumped through her system.

Ari hadn't left her side since they arrived home. He'd lain on the bed next to her until she'd finally begun to feel better. Then one of his team had shown up to remove the chip from her neck. Apparently, there had been two.

"Would you like to eat?" Ari asked her. "It's your dinner time. Anything you want, I'll get it for you."

She shook her head.

"What happens now?" she asked. "I can't go home, can I?"

Ari shook his head.

Sage stared out the window at the night sky, wondering what this meant for her life. She'd lost her job and had been drugged by her employer. How on earth did she move forward from that?

"I'm trying to take this slow and ease you into it, Sage, but I think my patience has finally dried up."

Ease her into what? "Into eating dinner?"

"No, sweetheart. Not eating." Ari smiled, then it faded as he cupped her cheek. "There is so much to tell you, but nothing more important than how I feel about you."

Heat flushed across her skin.

"Some animals mate for life. As a scientist, you probably know this. Wolves, penguins, some eagles," Ari said.

Sage shrugged. Sure, she knew this. As someone specializing in animal health, it was something they had learned about in college. "Yes, of course."

"So do we, Sage. Vampires mate for life," Ari said.

Sage felt her stomach turn into a pit of nothingness. "Oh."

Did Ari have a mate? Or had he had one many years ago and now he couldn't ever love her? God, was it even possible for a vampire to be with a human?

"Oh," she repeated. "So this, between us, this can't happen? I get it. I mean, you probably should have said something earlier, though Ari."

Anger, hurt, shame, all fought for dominance as she felt the pain of losing him flood through her. Sage had lost one man in her life, and now she was losing another.

She looked at Ari. No, losing Colin, her high school love, didn't even come close to how she felt about this vampire.

When had she begun to care so deeply for Ari? From day one, she'd not wanted to be parted from him. Now what? She needed his protection and had no idea how to navigate this new world. Would she need to stay under his roof and never be with him?

That was heartbreaking.

"Stop. No. Sage." He turned her. "Sage, sweetheart, *you* are my mate."

What?

She couldn't speak so she just stared at him.

She was his mate?

Ari's mate?

He… did he? Did he want her?

"I have waited over fifteen hundred years to meet you, *luce dei miei occhi.*" Ari smiled and his eyes filled with more emotion than she'd ever seen in her life.

She'd be Googling…

"It means light of my eyes. I only see you in my world, *mia stellina.*" He read her mind.

"Ari…" Sage began, but had no words. None as beautiful as those.

"It is different for humans. I do not expect you to love me," he said. "Yet. But I hope—"

"I think I've been in love with you from the moment I saw you. I just didn't know it." Tears fell down her face.

Oh God, she did love him. So damn much.

"You are worth every damn second I've waited for you." Ari caressed her face and lowered his lips to hers. Their kiss was slow, and as she leaned into him, it deepened until they both clung to each other as if their life was about to end.

Suddenly, she pulled back. "And there are no other women?"

Ari narrowed his eyes. "Please clarify your question. There have been many women in my life. And men. But you are my only mate. It will always and only be you, Sage."

"It is pretty clear you're not a virgin, Ari."

He smirked, but she tilted her head, and his smirk dissolved. "What is it, mate of mine?"

"You haven't said the L word, just that I am your mate."

"That I *lust* you?" Ari pushed her down onto the sofa.

Sage shook her head.

"That I *long* for you?"

She smiled, realizing he was messing with her.

"That I want to *lavish* you with everything and anything you desire?"

"Well, that sounds quite nice." She sighed as Ari kissed his way down her neck and then found her lips again.

"Or that I *love* you with all that I am."

"Yes, that," she said, breathless, staring into his beautiful face. Her legs wrapped around him as his kisses of love turned more lustful. "Make love to me."

ARI rid them of their clothes and lay over his very naked and beautiful mate. He'd been battling with his decision for hours. Telling Sage he loved her tonight was his priority. She *was* his priority, and he was confident she understood that.

Regardless, he would spend the rest of his eternity showing her and enjoy every moment.

He'd waited forever for her.

She hadn't resisted him, and her declaration of love had filled every cell in his body with such utter pleasure he wanted to be inside her.

This was the right time to do it. It would also change everything.

Sage had yet to connect the dots, but he knew in the back of her mind she would eventually work it out. It was why he hadn't introduced her to Willow or Brianna yet.

Ari kissed the inside of her thighs as he spread her legs and licked lightly over her clit.

Groan.

He loved the noises she made.

"Ari." She reached for him and threaded her fingers through his hair. He moved up her body, laying kisses in spots he knew made her shiver in pleasure.

His cock nudged at her opening. They were bonded now. His vampire was not going to stay hidden. His fangs were itching to release. Sage's hand ran over his chest, and he wanted to howl at the moon with desire and love for this female.

She was his.

Ari pressed inside her.

"Mine." He growled.

"Oh, yes! Ari," Sage cried and arched, revealing her beautiful creamy neck. Ari began to thrust fast and hard, watching the stars align.

"God, Sage," he cried, knowing the time was now. "Sage, look at me. I fucking love you. I need you to remember that."

"I love you, too."

Now.

As their orgasms exploded together, Ari's fangs released, and he stared one last time at his mate in her human form.

Then he sunk into her neck and bit.

CHAPTER FORTY-FOUR

Oliver marched through the castle halls. He could have teleported, but marching was much more gratifying right in this moment.

Stomp, stomp, stomp.

What the fucking hell was she doing back here?

He pushed through the front door, teleported to the bend in the driveway and then continued his marching until he reached the gates.

There she was. Leaning against her car like she was the goddamn queen of the world. The only thing missing was a long cigarette. It would suit her well.

"What are you doing here, Piper?" Oliver growled, taking in her short skirt and bright pink cropped jacket. What a ridiculous outfit in this cold weather.

"What are you doing here?" she replied.

Oliver snorted. "I live here."

"Obviously, but I asked to see Ari." Piper sighed as if he was fucking stupid.

"He's busy," Oliver replied, folding his arms. "Now, answer the question. What are you doing here? *Again.*"

Piper stepped away from the car and walked toward the gates, gripping them as she glared at him.

God, her eyes were gorgeous.

Bitches could be beautiful—he wasn't blind.

"Where is my sister?"

Sage was inside the mansion, but Oliver wasn't going to share that piece of information with Piper. Partly because he knew it would irritate her, but also because he knew Ari was telling Sage she was his mate this evening.

It was a big damn deal, especially if he decided to change her into a vampire.

And if Oliver knew Ari, after what had taken place today, he wouldn't be waiting a moment longer. The vampire had waited an eternity for his mate, and no one deserved this more than Ari.

It was the right thing to do, especially given who he was. It was a new moment for the vampire world, though very few knew or may ever know. Sage needed to be protected. She was an important person in their history now.

Oliver had no desire to mate.

Most vampires looked forward to meeting the one male or female to make them complete, but he was quite happy with his carefree life. He'd just been promoted to head assassin and had all the pussy he could ask for.

Why would he want to settle down with one girl?

Nope. It wasn't for him. He hoped it took a damn long time.

"How the hell should I know?" Oliver shrugged, responding to her question. Piper narrowed her eyes at him, and it was as if she could see right through him.

God, she pissed him off.

"Sage hasn't been home for two nights and she's not answering her phone," Piper said. "Is she in there or not?"

One thing Oliver didn't like doing was lying. Not directly. And that was a direct damn question.

Fucking journalist.

"Yes."

"So you just lied to me," she accused.

"No."

"Yes, you did, you said *how should I—*"

"I asked a question. I didn't lie. You translated it into an answer." Oliver interrupted her.

"Why are you such an asshole?" Piper crossed her arms.

Oliver smirked and held out his arms. "It was a skill I was born with, sweetheart. Now goodnight."

He turned and began walking back down the drive. Oliver heard Piper huff behind him, and he started grinning.

That would teach—

The horn of her car began bleating. Over and over and over and over.

"The fuck?" Oliver spun around.

What's going on? Alex telepathed him.

Fucking women is what's going on. Open the goddamn gates.

Holding himself back from using vamp speed, Oliver marched across the road and ripped open the car door.

"Oh, hey. Fancy seeing you here," Piper said, smiling all innocently.

He noticed her skirt was barely covering anything now she was seated. Was she trying to get herself raped?

"Get out of the car," Oliver said, reaching for her.

Piper pulled her arm away.

"I said, get out of—"

"Will you take me to my sister?" Piper demanded.

Oliver groaned.

"You aren't going to leave, are you?" he asked. He could wipe her memory and send her home, but she was now the sister of Ari's mate, and he would need to speak to him about how he wanted this *issue* dealt with.

"No."

"Then follow me," Oliver said.

Shit.

This was the last thing they needed with the royal family in residence. Still, it was likely they'd wipe her memory so until then he'd hide her in his room.

Fucking great.

CHAPTER FORTY-FIVE

Ari stood by the end of the bed and watched Sage sleep. For the rest of his life, he'd never unsee the look of complete betrayal in her eyes when he'd lifted his head after biting her.

The taste of her was more divine than anything he'd ever tasted, and she'd had to watch him lick his fangs and lips in utter ecstasy while her life fell away.

Literally.

He'd wiped his mouth and told her he loved her while he continued the transformation process, taking her blood and feeding her blood.

Rich and powerful Moretti blood.

Sage had been through a trauma tonight and he could have waited, but he could smell the drugs in her system and knew his blood would heal her. It was also far too dangerous now to leave her a vulnerable human.

Ari reached for his phone, knowing that staring at his mate wouldn't help anything now.

Houston, we have a problem. Piper is back. In my room. Pop by when you lift your head.

The fuck? Piper was in the mansion? In Oliver's room? The fucking king and queen were in residence. What was he thinking?

Ari parked his judgment. Knowing Piper only for five minutes was enough to know Oliver had likely been put in a situation by the sassy brat he was unsure how to navigate. And she was Sage's sister.

His mate.

They all needed to remember that now while dealing with Piper.

Damn it.

The last thing he needed was to upset his now vampire mate.

Be there in a minute.

Brayden.

Yup, what's up? Is Sage all right?

Yes, she's in transition. I need you and Willow to sit with her. I have something to take care of.

We'll be there in a few minutes.

There were very few people Ari would trust to sit with Sage while she was in this vulnerable stage, but Brayden was family. Sage was also now a Moretti, and he had no doubt the prince would protect her with his life.

It was the way of the Moretti family.

He opened the door when he heard the knock.

"Hey." Willow smiled and gave him a quick hug. "Congratulations."

"Thank you," he said. "She won't wake up, but I don't want to leave her unattended."

Brayden slapped him on the shoulder. "Go. I know the anguish well. We will watch her."

"Oh please, I gave you permission," Willow said, and Ari grinned, leaving the couple to their debate.

He teleported down to Oliver's room and knocked even as he could hear the bickering through the door. Oliver ripped it open and stared at him like a madman.

"Thank fuck." Oliver pulled him inside.

Piper came at him, and he held up his hand to stop her coming closer. He was on edge right now with his mate in transition. He shot Oliver a look, and the vampire nodded, understanding.

"Piper, get your ass back here," Oliver snapped, and for some reason Piper did as he said.

"Where is Sage? I want to see her!" Piper demanded.

"No," Ari said firmly. "She is asleep."

"Why isn't she answering my calls?" She spoke loudly. "She hasn't been home for two days. I rang her work, and they said she doesn't work there anymore. What is going on?"

That was interesting. BioZen had responded quickly in deciding Sage was no longer an employee. Understandable given the circumstances, but still.

"She has a migraine," he replied. "BioZen must have been mistaken. Go home and I will get her to call you."

Ari had no idea how long it would take for Sage to wake up, or more importantly, forgive him. It could take months before she could be trusted to contact her family.

"We're going to have to wipe her," Ari said instead, looking at Oliver.

"I figured. With the royals here, it's just too fucking tricky. I'm sorry. I wanted to check with you, but you were… you know, busy."

"Ex-fucking-scuse me! What the hell are you two talking about?" Piper said, moving closer again. Ari took a few steps away and she narrowed her eyes at him. "What is going on here?"

He slid his hands into his pockets.

"You have stepped into a dangerous place, Piper. Do not come here again. It is admirable you care so passionately about your sister, but for your own safety, you need to leave."

Piper's sass dissolved.

"Wait. Where is Sage? Is she okay?" Her voice was shaky as her eyes darted between him and Oliver. Ari could see real fear, for the first time, on her face.

"Yes. Sage is safe and very loved," Ari replied, his voice lowering and genuine. "You won't remember any of this, but know in your heart your sister is cherished."

Piper stared at him.

"What have you done to her? Please tell me," she pleaded, emotion filling her eyes.

Ari contemplated telling her for a moment. He respected the fire within this human and the love she clearly had for Sage. They had that in common.

But he would never risk Sage's life. Not for anything.

He looked over at Oliver.

"Take care of it." He walked out as Piper screamed his name.

CHAPTER FORTY-SIX

Sage rolled over on her beach towel and sighed as the warmth of the sun heated her skin. Beside her lay Ari, looking like the Adonis god he was. His natural olive skin was now tanned dark. She loved him so damn much.

They were on their honeymoon in... in... where were they?

A beach somewhere. It was hot. So damn hot.

There was sand... wasn't there sand?

She was hot.

So hot.

Fire.

There was fire in her veins.

"Sage." Ari yelled out to her and she turned. He was no longer on the beach with her.

"Ari," Sage called, sitting up and scrambling to get to her feet. "Ari!"

"Sage, baby. I'm here," he said, but she couldn't see him. She'd lost him.

She couldn't lose him.She loved him.

Tears poured from her eyes.

"Ari!" she cried.

"Sage. Open your eyes," Ari demanded fiercely, and she felt him lower her back on the... not sand. It was a bed. Slowly, she opened her eyes and blinked to clear them. It was bright. Her hand flew up to cover her eyes and she bashed herself in the head.

Jesus.

She croaked out an *ouch.*

"Easy tiger. There is a lot to adjust to," Ari said and, as her eyes cleared, she saw he looked drawn and tired.

"Are you okay?" she asked, her voice still dry.

"Me?" He let out a little laugh. "Yes, gorgeous. I am fine now you are awake. Here, drink this."

She half sat and took a few sips of water and lay back down. The room was weird. All the colors were bright and stark, as if she were looking through one of those unrealistic Instagram filters.

"How do you feel?" Ari asked, gently brushing the hair from her face.

"Was it the drugs? What did they do?" she asked, and Ari just stared at her.

Nope.

Nope.

Nope.

Sage was determined to ignore the memory knocking on her mind. She couldn't look at it. She knew if she did, she'd hate him.

She didn't want to hate him.

She loved Ari.

How? How could he do this to her?

Tears fell one by one until she was sobbing.

Ari lifted her into his arms, and she let him. In fact, she clung to him.

"That's how I did it, *mia stellina.* Because I cannot live without you, just as you cannot be without me," Ari said. "In time, I will earn your forgiveness. For now, it is enough that I know you love me, and you are alive and safe." He kissed her head and lay her back down.

Sage closed her eyes and rolled away from him, crying.

ARI busied himself for two weeks while Sage refused to talk to him. He contacted her bank and paid her mortgage. His money was her money now.

He hadn't sold the house because he knew she loved it, and she could decide what to do with it when she was ready.

He ensured Tony moved out and sent cleaners around to tidy it.

More complicated, he'd visited her mother and manipulated her mind, so she thought Ari and Sage were on holiday together. A romantic holiday which thrilled her mother, who only wanted to see her daughter happily married.

Oliver had taken care of Piper and they hadn't heard anything more from her in the past two weeks.

Willow and Brianna had taken turns to go and sit with Sage, telling her about their experiences turning vampire from human.

Sage wouldn't speak to anyone, but he knew she listened.

During the daylight hours, when the blinds were shut, he climbed into bed and wrapped around her. She would nestle into him and cry, but recently the tears had stopped. One night he had kissed her, and she had responded, then pulled away.

Ari walked into their bedroom and found Sage sitting in bed dressed in one of his t-shirts. He stared at her, wondering if it meant anything, but she glanced away.

He showered, brushed his teeth, and then climbed into bed. Turning off the lamp, he reached for her just as he always did, and she came to him. His lips found hers and this time, she didn't pull away.

His need for her was growing, but he'd never force her. He wanted Sage to give herself to him. That was the only way it would work for him.

"Are you being pleasured by other women?" Sage asked, surprising the hell out of him. It was the first time he'd heard her voice in weeks.

He pulled back and gripped her face. "No," Ari replied, his voice thick. "Never. You are it for me. Forever, Sage." His heart thumped against his chest. "Can you ever forgive me? Please *mia stellina.*"

"Kiss me again," Sage replied, and Ari gently took her mouth.

Sage responded hungrily, their tongues dancing as he ran his hands down her body. Her thigh lifted over his and he found her bare and wet.

"God." He murmured against her mouth. "Tell me you forgive me, Sage."

"I…"

"Let me inside you. Forgive me," Ari begged.

"I need you," Sage breathed, her eyes opening and looking at him for the first time in weeks. "I can't be without you anymore. Take me."

"Say the words, *mia stellina,* and we are one forever."

"Yes, yes, I forgive you," she cried. "Forever, I am yours."

Ari pressed inside her pussy and thrust. Her arms wrapped around his neck, and he lifted her hips to get every inch of himself in her. God, it was incredible to feel her wrapped around his cock once again.

"Mine." Ari growled as he spilled his seed into her.

One day he hoped his seed would produce the first of a new line of vampires, but for now, Ari was beyond joyful to have Sage's forgiveness and love.

"And you are mine." Sage said, as tears ran down her face.

THEY lay in the dark, wrapped around each other after making love for hours.

"I can never say I'm sorry and mean it in the way you want, but I *am* sorry for what I've taken from you," Ari said, kissing her gently. "I was once human."

"You were?" Sage said, surprised.

"Yes." Ari nodded, feeling like the stars were finally aligning. He'd waited all his life to have this conversation with someone he loved and trusted. "I was human, and there was no such thing as vampires. My brother and I were the first."

Sage sat up and leaned over him, her fingers pressed into his chest. "How is that possible?"

So he told her.

He told her his entire life story. After all, she was now a Moretti with his blood running through her veins. His powerful original blood.

"So you're the only original left alive?" Sage asked. "What does that mean?"

"I am." He smiled. "I'm not interested in being a king, but I am not hiding anymore. We will be known as the House of Moretti and create a family of our own."

"Wow. That's a big deal, Ari," Sage said, letting out a long breath of air.

"It is, but we will do it together. How we fit into the royal family will be up to all of us. There are many discussions to be had in years to come, mate of mine."

"I want to have a wedding," Sage suddenly announced. "I don't get a beach honeymoon, so I want a wedding. I need to do something on my damn *Life List*."

Ah, the *Life List*. Piper had told him about it, so he knew it was important to Sage. Ari kissed her on the lips with force. "Then a wedding we shall have, my love."

He closed his eyes and pulled her down onto his chest, smiling as Sage listed all the things they would have at their wedding.

He'd give her the world, the moon, and the stars if he could.

She was his everything.

His *stellina.*

His little star.

Turn the page to read the first chapter of The Vampire Lover – the next installment in the Moretti Blood Brothers series.

FREE GIFT:
Download The Vampires Origin to read the short story about the beginning of Ari and Gio Moretti's life.

THE VAMPIRE LOVER

CHAPTER ONE

Oliver sat in the driver's seat of Piper's car with one hand on the steering wheel, as they drove through the dark streets, and one hand ready to grab her.

Or protect his balls.

It could go either way with her.

"So, kidnapping and now theft?" Piper snarled at him, her arms crossed and her long dark hair falling around her shoulders. "Your rap sheet is getting longer, asshole."

Oliver shook his head.

"For a journalist, you're pretty stupid," Oliver snapped, darting a quick look at her and trying to ignore how plump her breasts were. Piper Roberts was far from stupid, but she *was* fucking pretty.

Correction. She was fucking gorgeous.

If she wasn't Sage's sister, and a goddamn pain in the ass, he'd take her home and fuck her until she lost her voice.

But Piper was a pain in the ass, and all-round annoying human. First, she had followed him back to the mansion after seeing him leave Sage's house a few days ago, and tonight she'd turned up there again demanding to see her sister.

Who was now a vampire.

So, yeah, that meeting wasn't going to happen.

Actually, Sage was in transition, and they had no idea when she would wake. Oliver had been instructed by Ari, the Director of The Institute, and Sage's mate, to return Piper home and wipe her memories.

So, just another day at the office.

"I'm stupid for letting you take my car," Piper said, shaking her head at him or herself—he wasn't sure.

Oliver rolled his eyes. "For God's sake, let me spell this out to you. I haven't *taken* your car. You are *in* it."

"Without my permission." Piper stamped out.

Like she could stop him.

He was a powerful vampire and assassin at The Institute. Recently, he'd been promoted to head assassin after his friend and colleague, Ben, had mated and moved to Italy. Ben was now back in Seattle with them, along with the Moretti royals.

Oliver was looking forward to catching up with him for a few drinks, but this time they wouldn't be ending the night with one, two, or five females and a handful of sex toys. When a vampire mated, he was mated for life to that one vampire. If the mate was a human, the vampire turned them. Simple as that.

Of all the vampires he'd expected to mate, Ben had not been on his list. The guy was lethal, charming and sex-driven. Which, okay, fine, described Oli as well. That's why they were such good friends.

Giving and taking pleasure with beautiful women was his favorite pastime. Well, that and killing baddies with a shiny AT308 rifle.

"I didn't kidnap you. Alex and I took you back to your place after you *followed* us, and then we restrained you." He realized how dodgy that sounded.

"Usually when that happens to me, it's for much more pleasant reasons," Piper said, and Oliver felt his cock respond.

No. Fucking, no, no, no.

"I'm sure they gag you, too. I would," Oliver said under his breath.

"You won't. Ever. Because you aren't touching me again," Piper said, and ripped open the door when he parked outside her house.

Again?

It had been Alex who had restrained her last time, although, sure, he'd taken her arm and pulled her inside.

Okay fine, yes, he remembered every millisecond of it because Piper's soft warm skin had burned into the palm of his hand, sending electrical sparks through his body.

But he wasn't thinking about that.

No.

Not thinking about it.

Oliver shook his head and got out of the car, following her to the front door where she punched in a code to open the door.

"Keys!" she demanded when it opened, holding out her hand.

"Inside," Oliver said, lifting his chin.

"I don't fucking think so." Piper crossed her arms.

Oliver picked her up and threw her over his shoulder, kicking the door closed with his foot and stomping up the stairs.

Meanwhile Piper shrieked in his ear like a banshee.

"Put me down." She yelled as he deposited her on the sofa in the least gentle way he could.

Well, he could be way less gentle with her, and his cock was very interested in the idea.

Never happening.

"Let's get down to business," Oliver said, squatting in front of her and placing his hands on her knees.

"Oh my God, are you going to rape me?" Piper said, retreating on the sofa.

The fuck?

"No!" He growled. "I don't rape women. Do I look like I need to rape women?"

Piper shrugged.

Shrugged!

Oliver stood up and glared down at her.

"Well, you don't exactly look like an accountant with all those tattoos and leather!" she exclaimed, then shrugged. "You could be a rapist."

Oliver ran a hand through his hair.

This wasn't cool.

He bent down in front of her again. "Piper, I am not going to harm you," he said more gently. "We don't do that."

She narrowed her eyes at him. "Who is *we?* I just want someone to tell me where Sage is and if she is okay."

The emotion from earlier was back in her eyes and her fight was subsiding. She was tired. Not surprising, given it was nearly eleven at night. She had yelled and screamed for hours at him while they waited for Ari to join them earlier. That she was still sassing him was admirable.

In fact, he much preferred being aggravated with her, then he could pretend she was just a pain in his ass, and not a woman he'd been thinking about for days since they'd met.

Because there was no way he was mating.

Ever.

Not fucking ever!

"I promise you; she is fine," Oliver said, taking her chin in his hand as their eyes connected. "Now, Piper, you little sexy pain in the ass, I want you to focus on my words."

"What are you doing?" she asked in a whisper, already half under his vampire hypnosis.

He took in her startling blue eyes as his hand rested on the bare skin of her thigh. God, she was too fucking beautiful.

"I'm making you forget," Oliver said.

Mostly.

To continue reading Oliver and Piper's steamy romance in The Vampire Lover click the book name!

BOOKS BY JULIETTE N. BANKS

The Moretti Blood Brothers
The Vampire's Origin
The Vampire King (1) FREE
The Vampire Prince (2)
The Vampire Protector (3)
The Vampire Spy (4)
The Vampire's Christmas (5)
The Vampire Assassin (6)
The Vampire Awoken (7)
The Vampire Lover (8)

Realm of the Immortals
The Archangels Battle
The Archangel's Heart
The Archangel's Star

The Dufort Dynasty Trilogy

Sinful Duty
Forbidden Touch
Total Possession

LET'S CONNECT

Official Juliette N. Banks website:
www.juliettebanks.com

INSTAGRAM:
https://www.instagram.com/juliettebanksauthor

FACEBOOK:
https://www.facebook.com/juliettenbanks

https://www.facebook.com/groups/authorjuliettebanksreaders

Printed in Great Britain
by Amazon

84476642R00202